Hidden Within the Bling

Hidden Within the Bling

Kathleen Balota

Hidden Within the Bling

Table of Contents

Acknowledgments

What is anything worth without the love and support of your family. I would like to thank my husband, Dennis, for the constant encouragement to write another book, as well as supporting the time commitment when I write, attend writers' meetings, conferences, etc. His love of playing guitar at home is one of the reasons that I pursued a creative outlet that I could also do in our home. I would also like to thank my mother, Irene Andritsch, who asked me to write this particular book, as she and her friends wanted to know what happened romantically to the heroine of my last book, "The Ethical Business Woman". There are many situations where I used something that my mother would have said in my writing. My brother, Mike Andritsch, and my nephews (Mike, Jim, Scott, Troy and Todd Andritsch) and their families, are also a big source of writing adrenaline. They have always been so supportive of everything I do, and it's comforting to know that they are my cheering section. I also want to thank my in-laws, Mary and Joe Balota, who ask me every time I talk to them when my next book is coming out. It's finally here!

I owe a big thank you to my friend, Connie Petryszak. Not only has she been a constant supporter of my writing, but she has become my proofreader (which isn't a small task). Connie has accompanied me to writing events, book signings, etc. She's been a true friend as well as a great couples companion, as she and her husband, Mike, and Dennis and I have been on several trips together. Thank you, girlfriend.

Lastly, I would like to acknowledge two of my talented Southwest Florida Romance Writer chapter members, Sonja Gunter, and Jackie Floyd. Sonja spent many hours with me while editing a story I wrote in our chapter anthology. Romance writing has different criteria expectations than my past writing experience, and Sonja was determined to teach me. Jackie Floyd also spent time with us as they critiqued and improved my story. Thank you, ladies. I know that the intention of the chapter is to help each other become better writers, and you two walk the talk.

Prelude

"Your feelings and emotions are your strongest indicator if your life is moving in a purposeful direction or not, so listen closely to how you feel."

—Rebecca Rosen, from "Awake the Spirit Within"

Noel Noirty thought about her current situation until it curiously occurred to her that she had asked these same questions throughout her life. What is my purpose? Do people like me? Am I loved?

She recalled her earliest thoughts as a little girl, wondering if her schoolmates liked her. She remembered her inadequacies as a teenager wondering if she was pretty enough to be asked to the school dance.

Surely, as an adult those questions would be answered. But today, all of those questions loomed in her thoughts. She wondered if these feelings were part of the journey of life, and vowed to confront them once again.

CHAPTER 1

A Relationship in Peril

The bedroom suite was extraordinary and ornate. French bedroom furniture adorned the room while soft cream satin draperies billowed inward from the opened arched windows. Silk tapestry rugs were carefully placed over the white Italian marble floor with intricately carved mahogany wardrobes perched against the wall. The room was a work of art, worthy of being featured in any decorating magazine. But today its beauty was interrupted. The bedding was pushed to one side, tissues lay crumpled on the silken bedspread and pictures from an old photo book were scattered around the room.

Noel Noirty sat at her makeup table with tears flowing down her face and dripping onto her brocade robe. Her eyes were red and her face splotchy from hours of crying, while her delicate hands were shaking so badly that her four carat emerald cut diamond had wrapped around to the inside of her palm. Staring into her mirror, she began a sobbing dialog,

"I can hear them all talking now. First they will ask, 'Did you hear about Noel and Dave?' Then they will share all the juicy gossip. They'll make up things to fill in any blanks."

She hesitated a few seconds to wipe away her tears before adding, "But soon their words will be, 'Poor Noel. What is she going to do?'

I might as well put a notice in the paper."

Thirty-something ex-socialite, Noel Noirty, was dumped by her husband of fourteen years, Dave Noirty, for a younger woman. Noel, with no education or skills, has no future, and hopefully will leave the Naples area soon. Dave Noirty, besides having his dashing good looks, owns a prosperous yacht business. He and his new mistress will have an amazing life together.

She lifted her head and studied herself in the mirror. Her long, brown hair tumbled loosely on her shoulders. She remembered better times, when Dave would run his ruddy fingers through her curls until he would pull her face towards him for a kiss. She folded her arms and gently rubbed her hands on her shoulders while pretending to be in his embrace, trying to remember his strong arms caressing the small of her back and the smell of musk from his aftershave as he nuzzled her neck. Her arms dropped onto her lap and her eyes glazed over as she remembered her current situation.

Trying to fend off her sadness, she posed her body defiantly and stared into the mirror. She noticed subtle signs of age on her body. Her five-foot-six-inch height held her diminutive frame well. She still had long, slender legs and a small waist. Her breasts had become fuller and hung a bit lower than when she was in her twenties, but she knew her husband liked her fuller bosom. The only sign of aging was a few wrinkles on her bodice and neck.

Maybe I need to get some Botox?

She walked to one of the wardrobes and picked up a small silver picture frame. It was a small wedding picture of her and her husband. She drew the frame to her mouth and gave the picture a light kiss before placing it back. Suddenly, a dazed look appeared on her face as her features contorted.

"If only I was able to have children," Noel whispered. "That must be what drove him away from me. I'm in my mid-thirties and his girlfriend is young and probably fertile. Soon, he'll be marrying her and having babies."

She sat on the chaise lounge and decided to focus on her positive traits, but she soon realized that her prominence in Naples was due to her husband and his business, not her contributions. They were A-listers for charities or other cultural events, and she was regarded by the community as a beautiful and resourceful woman, capable of getting anything done through her network of friends and business acquaintances. She was often pictured in the local newspaper as chairing different events, or listed as a major contributor to different charities, but her entry into this community was due to her husband's business and wealth.

She felt her body tense up and her stomach churn as she tried to think of anything she had achieved to put her own mark on the community. It was futile. Her involvement could have been handled by many other competent community members.

I brought nothing into our marriage. No wealth, no intelligence, no children. I need to talk to someone. I need to unload some of this pain. Who can I talk to that won't tell anyone?

She quickly dismissed her gossipy society friends, when one name jumped into her mind. Francine.

CHAPTER 2

A Friend to the Rescue

Francine Pacque had just passed by the Tampa, Florida exit, while driving south on Highway 75 towards Naples. She fidgeted in her seat, clearly agitated.

"Why are you being so unreasonable, Brian? You know that I'm trying to build my business here. My name is my brand, Francine Pacque, LLC. I can't just hire people to take my place and come back to Chicago."

"I get how it works, Francine. But enough is enough. You have been back in Chicago only a couple times in the past year. It's no way to keep a relationship."

"I don't want to sound defensive, but remember that I would have lost my townhouse and my Audi if I hadn't taken this opportunity. We knew I would be traveling a lot. I'm getting closer to being able to give some employees more of the reigns, but not quite yet."

"Then when, Francine? I'm serious. If you don't make a commitment to come home to stay soon, then I'm moving on."

Francine grimaced and stepped harder on the pedal, almost swerving into another car. She took a quick breath and breathed deeply.

"Let's talk about this when I'm home in a couple of weeks. OK? I'm dying to see you too," she said frantically.

"I'll talk to you later, Francine. Goodbye."

She heard a click and stared at the phone quizzically, not quite believing the conversation was over.

I can't lose Brian. He's the best thing that has ever happened to me, but for now, I better concentrate on my driving.

Her cell phone rang and her heartbeat sped up, hoping it was Brian calling her to apologize. She glanced at the phone and saw it was Noel Noirty. She quickly answered the call.

"Hello. This is Francine."

"Hello, my friend. This is Noel Noirty. I was wondering if you were in the area today, or are you working elsewhere."

"I'm on my way back to Naples from Ocala." She could hear a small gasp and asked, "Is everything ok?"

Noel's voice cracked as she answered, "No, I have a big problem. I was hoping that we could meet, and please, don't mention it to anyone."

She furrowed her brow, intrigued, as she tried to recall anything that may be upsetting to Noel, and if so, who would she discuss it with. Her business kept her traveling eighty percent of the time through various states. She wasn't in the same society circle of friends as Noel.

"Of course we can meet. Do you want me to come over to your house or meet you somewhere?"

"Oh, no. Don't come here. I don't know where we can meet that someone won't recognize me."

Francine squared her back in her carseat and wrinkled her nose. *I can't imagine what has shaken up Noel.*

"Do you want to come to my apartment? It's not the famous Rum Row neighborhood that you are used to, but I doubt if you know anyone living there besides myself," she offered.

"Perfect. I may want to spend the night. Would that be ok?"

"Oh, gee, Noel. This must be something bad. Bring your pajamas. I'll pull over and text my address to you right away."

"I'll see you in two hours. I'll stop by Dave's office first, but I bet he won't be there," Noel added.

Francine heard the phone click off for the second time in a few minutes. She took another deep breath.

I guess drama is the daily fare for me today. I wonder what that was all about? At least Noel doesn't sound angry at me for the big lie I pulled on her and her friends last year. But, after I stayed in all those low-rent hotels and ate all that fast food, pretending to be "Cinderella" for one evening sounded like a good idea. I hope she doesn't bring it up, and I learned my lesson. They almost ran me out of town.

She reflected on the way she cherished her friendship with her beautiful society friend, and knew Noel was very devoted to her as well. They were the perfect pair to confide in each other with problems or dreams.

"Maybe I can confide to Noel about my problem with Brian. I cannot lose him, that's all there is to say about it. I won't give up my business either," she said aloud as she exited the highway at Corkscrew Road and headed towards her small one bedroom apartment in Naples.

She hoped to turn up the air conditioning at the apartment and unpack a few of her items from her suitcase before Noel arrived. But she arrived too late. Noel was already parked and pacing in front of her pearl white Lexus. They greeted each other with a quick hug, before wheeling their respective suitcases into the building. When they finally stood face to face in Francine's apartment, she saw Noel's splotchy face with dried mascara coating her cheeks.

"Noel, you poor thing. I'm sorry it took me so long to get home, but traffic was heavy. I hope you weren't waiting too long."

Noel's chest heaved up and down as several fresh tears ran down her face.

"My life is ruined. I don't know what to do, Francine. I didn't know where else to go. Thank you for letting me come here."

"Sit down, Noel, and relax. I'm just going to put my things in my room," she said as she tugged her suitcase handle and pulled it towards her bedroom.

Her head was still spinning from the conversation with Brian, but she decided to put her problem aside and attend to her friend's needs. She deposited her suitcase, put on a fresh casual shirt, and walked past Noel into the kitchen, where she put a bottle of wine in the refrigerator to cool. Returning to the living room, she sat on the sofa across from the chair that Noel was curled into, and asked her friend to tell what was the matter. Noel nodded, and wiped her nose while curling up in the oversized chair.

"Francine, please don't tell anyone about this right now. Even Angela. I know you work closely with her, and you two are friends," Noel pleaded while tears rolled down her face. "I think Dave is having an affair. I suspected that something was wrong several months ago. He seemed more withdrawn, more secretive. At first I thought it was something about the business, so I left him alone to work it out. You know, there's always things that happen, like a sale falls through, or something goes wrong with a yacht order. Sometimes there is a lot of money at stake, and Dave has to cover the investment until things work out."

She replied, "I can't imagine the financial stress if something goes wrong in the yacht business. Heck, in my business, we can be out thousands of dollars, but in Dave's luxury yacht business, it could be in the millions."

Noel nodded her head in agreement before speaking, "The business is doing fine. I know enough about the business to look at his computer files, and I didn't see anything negative. In fact, the business is doing great. I also snuck a peek at his emails, and I didn't see anything there either. But, then things got worse."

Noel continued between sobs, "He started leaving the house and saying he had to go to work. But since he was acting so strange, I started to wonder if that was where he was going. I didn't want to call the marina because his workers could be covering for him. So I drove over there each time he said he was going there. His car was never there."

Noel hesitated and slowly shook her head as in disbelief, before saying, "This happened three or four times. I didn't say anything to him about it, because…well, because I was afraid of what he may answer."

Francine listened attentively. She nodded occasionally to show her friend that she understood her concern, and interjected some possible explanations, "Maybe he was working, but not at the marina. Maybe he was helping out one of his friends where they have their boat dock, or developing a new client, interviewing, whatever. Maybe you're overreacting."

"I wish that was true, but there's more," Noel stated before taking another sip of water and blotting her eyes.

"I decided that I needed to follow him, so one day as he was leaving, I grabbed my purse and keys and followed him in my car. I stayed far back, but his red Ferrari convertible is hard to miss, so I tracked him to a restaurant off the highway in Fort Myers. The parking lot was quite full, but there was an adjacent parking lot with some open spaces. I parked there and waited for him to reappear. When he did, I saw her," Noel said with pouted lips. "She was so pretty, and young," Noel added.

Francine didn't know how to respond, so sat there quietly and lowered her gaze while trying to comprehend what Noel was explaining. She quickly thought about her boyfriend, Brian, hoping that he wouldn't give up on her and find a new girlfriend.

"I saw them embrace. He hugged her right in the parking lot, in front of everyone," Noel blurted.

"Did he kiss her?"

"I think so. But it was pretty hard to see from the other lot. They stood there for quite a while and continued to talk. She reached out and touched his hand before she went to her own car. I don't know what to do, Francine. Dave is my life. I thought we were happy. I thought he was happy with me. Now I don't know what to do."

Noel paused and blew her nose into a tissue while her mascara continued to run down her face.

"You know, I don't really have any skills. I didn't go on to college. I'm not artistic. I'm just an old, washed up 'has been' model whose husband is going to leave her for a younger woman. Maybe you don't know this, but this type of thing happens all the time in our circle. The men get that middle age urge to keep young, and they either have affairs while their wives look the other way, or the men divorce their wives and marry the other woman. Oh God! Maybe he's going to marry her and have babies!" Noel babbled as her eyes widened with despair.

"Babies! Noel, maybe you are jumping the gun a bit," she gasped.

She knew that Noel could be right about successful older men getting involved with younger women. She saw that while living in Chicago when she walked down the Magnificent Mile. Often there were older men, too well dressed to not be successful, walking with much younger women. Sometimes they were pushing baby strollers. She realized that Noel could be onto something.

Her thoughts returned to her own boyfriend. Brian had his heart broken by his ex-wife, who cheated on him and remarried. He was reluctant for quite a while to have another relationship due to his fear of being hurt again. She felt confident that Brian would not be one of "those men" who left her later in life. Then she remembered their own situation,

We're not even married yet…not even engaged. Who's jumping the gun now?

She refocused her thoughts toward her friend, as Noel continued, "Dave and I always wanted a family. We tried to have kids shortly after we married and kept trying for ten years. We went to fertility clinics and we went through exhaustive testing. Finally we gave up. I always hoped that it would still happen just naturally. I'm only thirty-five, you know. Dave's a little older than me. He's forty-four," Noel confided. "We're not too old for me to get pregnant, but I just don't seem to be able to do it."

Francine answered, "You and I are the same age, and I hope to have children someday too. Of course, I want a husband first. Hopefully that will be Brian."

Noel nodded, but she was too absorbed in her own problem to comment about Francine.

"I brought up adoption several years ago, but Dave said 'no'. He wasn't against it, he just thought that if we were meant to have kids, I would get pregnant. I remember him saying that if it didn't happen, he would be happy being a family of two. He said that I was all the family he needed."

Noel continued through her sobs, "I'm so afraid of losing him. I don't know what to do, Francine. What should I do?"

Francine gave her friend a light pat on her shoulders. The information was so new to her, and she wanted to take a moment before responding to her friend.

"Let me digest everything you just told me and think for a while. There's a nice garden area in this apartment complex. Let's walk outside and get some fresh air. When we come back, we can decide what we want for dinner and I'll cook something. Then we'll open a bottle of wine and talk about 'what's next'. I have a couple of things on my mind already."

The women walked silently to the garden area and were astonished at the beautiful flowering Hibiscus around the property. Noel momentarily forgot about her problems, and soon they were laughing at some dogs playing in the complex's dog park. It was a good diversion.

The women returned to the apartment where Francine broiled a couple of ribeye steaks and made some wild rice. She slid the small dinner onto her bare dinette table and suddenly realized how bare her apartment looked. Francine had only purchased a few necessities for her Naple's abode, a bed and dresser, a couch and a tv stand, and a two person dinette. She peered at her surroundings as her face reddened in embarrassment.

"You must think this place is horrible. I'm here in Naples so infrequently, that I never decorated with pictures, rugs, or anything."

"That's not true. I know your main home is in Chicago. This is just a convenient crash pad for when you are in this neighborhood. It's a nice place," Noel answered as she gazed around the room, suddenly noticing its bareness.

They dined at the small table sharing only small talk, but they soon settled into the soft couch cushions with two glasses of wine. Noel started up the conversation.

"Thanks for a great dinner. I needed something substantial to eat. I haven't been eating well since all this began."

"I can understand that. When something is bothering you, it is either hard to eat or you can't stop eating. Since you look thinner than when I saw you last month, I know you're the "non-eater" type," Francine replied. She hesitated a few seconds before continuing, " I want to ask a couple of things, and then I may have a couple of suggestions."

"Shoot!"

"I know you said that Dave was acting distant but does that mean that he and you haven't been intimate?" she asked, knowing the tell-tale sign of infidelity is that there is a sudden stop of sex.

Noel shifted her legs and lowered her gaze. "No, we haven't had sex in quite a while. I guess that's a bad sign, isn't it?"

"Well, it's not good," Francine admitted. "Have you tried initiating sex?"

"I have, and he either says he's tired or he doesn't respond at all."

"Do you and Dave still go out and do your normal activities like going to your club, attending parties, or going out to dinner?"

"Yes, we still do those things. I'm afraid to look around to see if that woman is lurking somewhere. You know, maybe he would invite her too, just to steal a glance," Noel answered.

"Enough with the self-pity, Noel. You're a beautiful woman in her mid-thirties. Everyone in your group of friends admires you. I always thought you were a force to be reckoned with. So let's make one of our game plans to change your attitude about yourself. You have to portray yourself as a victor, not a victim," she sternly replied, realizing that she learned that strategy from a past sales training session.

She noticed that Noel's eyes gazed downward as she reflected on the words. This gave Francine time to reflect on them as well. She recollected several of her sales and business conference sessions that trained her on personal life skills as well as business life. One of the best remembered was a session on portraying self-confidence. She knew herself to not be a natural take-charge, self-assured business woman, but her job in major manufacturing sales in Chicago made that trait a necessity. She learned how to present herself confidently, making people more willing to listen more intently to her.

Today's conversation with Brian made her feel insecure about her personal life. She decided to hold her head up high, put her shoulders back, and initiate the conversation as a confident person would do.

"Noel, you have to find out what is really happening. We may have to do some surveillance."

"I would die if someone sees us. I don't want anyone to know about this yet. Francine, please, don't tell anyone about this right now, until I can handle it better," Noel pleaded.

"That's why we have to plan this carefully. We have to blend in so that no one notices us watching them. We are going to have to study how investigators and spies get away with it. We have to be hidden within the crowd."

"Do I look like I blend into a crowd? I'm more like a beacon in the middle of the crowd," Noel joked.

She laughed as she thought of her flamboyant friend blending into a crowd. She had never seen Noel without flawless makeup and hair while wearing expensive, designer high-heeled shoes. As she gazed at Noel sitting across from her, she admired how Noel's brown tresses were tipped in several shades of blonde highlights. She expected that Noel wore extensions to make her hair thicker in appearance. Her hands and feet were polished with glossy acrylics in neon colors to match her Floridan colored clothing. Not to mention Noel's extensive and expensive jewelry collection. She turned heads wherever she went in a good way. She could be the poster woman of luxury living in Naples…beautiful, tan, flawless.

"Yes, my friend. You'll need a complete overhaul," Francine laughed as she imitated the way Noel walked with long, graceful strides and swaying hips. "No spy ever had the "Noel walk", much less the hair, jewelry, and clothes."

"I must be hideous. That's probably why Dave went looking for someone else."

"Stop that kind of talk, Noel. You don't even know for sure what's going on with Dave."

"Well, one thing I know for sure is that I do not want the rest of the girls to know that something is going on between Dave and I. That means don't tell Angela, Babs, Mitzi, Pepper, or Shauna. I'm serious about that, Francine."

"I won't say anything to them. You have my promise, Noel."

Francine knew that little went on in the Naples community that escaped any of those women. She wondered if the girls didn't already know the answer to what was going on with Noel's husband.

But she owed loyalty to Noel, and she knew she needed to do some surveillance homework before any discussions of "next steps" could take place.

"Noel, I never heard how you and Dave met? Did you meet him here, in Naples?"

"It's a long, but nice story. We may need to refill our glasses."

She topped off each of their glasses and resettled into her deep cushion, ready to hear Noel's story. She watched her friend as she gathered up her thoughts, clearly enjoying her memories before she started to speak.

"I was only twenty-one when I landed a modeling job at a major boat show in Atlanta. My job was to stand seductively next to expensive yachts being featured, as a promotional spokesman talked about each yacht's features. All I had to do was smile and point to features of the yacht, kind of like Vanna White."

The girls giggled and swayed their arms, reminiscent to the famous TV assistant, before Noel continued, "The underlying job description, though, was to entice the many balding, paunchy male spectators into thinking that their lifestyle with this yacht would include having a beautiful, young woman at their side. It wasn't all that far-fetched of an idea."

"Were you living in Atlanta at the time?" Francine asked.

"Yes, I was born near Douglasville, about an hour west of Atlanta, and raised to be a proper southern belle. But my parents were not wealthy. My father had a hard time keeping jobs and my mother worked for a while as a waitress, but they provided a loving home me. I was their only child."

"I didn't have clothes or money, but I was lucky to have my mother's looks. People used to say that my beauty was undeniable, but I never felt that way myself. Anyway, I did pretty well in school, but didn't have money or the desire to go on to college. I thought the best way for me to get a better life was to take up modeling."

"So, I ventured out to Atlanta, thinking I could be some big-time model, which they laughed at, saying that at five foot six inches, I wasn't 'high fashion modeling' material. I was so disappointed until they said that I was perfect for small advertising and promotional work, such as the boat show, so they signed me."

"That's great to hear, and very interesting. I thought you were born in this area and happened to meet Dave. So, how did you two end up together?" Francine asked.

"On the day I met my future husband, I had to wear a seductive black gown while posing next to a small yacht. I performed the necessary "smile" and pointed to the outside yacht features. But I also had to quickly walk up a small staircase onto the yacht deck, dash into the privacy of the cabin, drop my dress, and reappear in a bikini on the deck top. This was accomplished while the promoter continued talking about the yacht's features."

"Oh, my lord. How corny," Francine stated.

"Yes, but this was what we had to do in those days. All of the models had to do some provocative things. I was the lucky one, though, because Dave was in the audience."

"Dave was thirty years old at that time. He was born into a wealthy family and squandered his wealth throughout his early post-college years. Dave was quite a catch for any young woman and he knew it. I understand that the eight years between finishing college and meeting me had been a continuous blur of women, liquor, traveling, and fun. Finally, his parents had enough of his antics and they threatened to turn off his funds. His father gave him an ultimatum to turn his life around and begin a career, or he would be permanently cut off financially from his family."

"Dave knew that his free lifestyle had run the gamut, and he had to hold a responsible job at some point. He had expected his parents to put an end to his foolish lifestyle, but he didn't have a clue as to his field of work. When he discussed this with his father, his father gave him some sound advice,

'Find something you love, and make a business of it. You have the brains, money, and family connections to start your own business. Don't work for someone else. Make it your own.'"

From what Dave told me, he spent several months of half-heartedly thinking about his future, but one day it occurred to him that he loved boats, traveling, water, and warm climate living. So he went to his father and asked his opinion of getting into the boat business. His father was overjoyed. He was an avid boater himself, and he gave his son his blessing to use family funds to open a boat dealership at a small marina. His father and he worked together to find the right category and brand of boats to feature. They finally realized that there was a gap in the luxury yacht sales and service business in the Naples, Florida area. So they leased a marina and opened an office. The business started small in comparison to his current business a little more than a decade later, but it was a good, solid business, and he was a natural at running it well."

"So get to the good part, Noel. How did he notice you?"

"Well, Dave attended the Atlanta Boat Show shortly after opening his business. The Boat Show was a great opportunity to see how boat promoters did their craft and he could make connections with boat builders and boat service providers. He heard one of the promotors begin his 'spiel', so he walked over to a small group listening to the promoter. Soon, he spotted me. He told me that he saw a beautiful woman with porcelain skin and long, brown hair walk by, lifting her arm to point to the stern of the boat. Dave said he was mesmerized by this young woman. He said that he knew I was quite a bit younger than him, but he was attracted to my 'sweetness'."

"I bet that wasn't all he was attracted to."

The girls laughed a bit before Noel continued her story.

"Dave said that I didn't appear to be a 'showgirl', as were some of the other boat models, but just a beautiful, sweet and humble model doing her best to convey the boat's features. He said he couldn't help but notice that I had a great figure in the clingy, black silk gown. He liked soft curves, not 'porno'."

"I understand that he didn't see me disappear into the yacht cabin and he was listening to the promoter when I reappeared in my bikini on deck. I was watching him by that time. He was so handsome. I was hoping to get his attention, and I saw him almost fall back a step when he noticed me half-naked. I could tell he was acting unnatural, almost nervous, as he watched me."

"He probably was getting aroused," Francine said with a giggle.

"Probably," Noel said shyly, knowing that was exactly what had happened.

"He told me that he could not stop watching me in that little black bikini with my alabaster skin. Of course I knew, that my curves, previously hidden by my gown, were now in clear view. I was hoping that he would talk to me later, and that is what happened. He said he was smitten and he vowed that he would not be leaving Atlanta until he had me on his arm."

"You must have been a vision, Noel, standing there in your little bikini. I can imagine that he was instantly attracted. But did you notice him in the crowd?"

Noel grinned and nodded, "Let me explain that the boat show had three types of men who attended the function; younger men showing off with their friends, men and their wives just spending an enjoyable day together, and actual, potential boat buyers. When I saw Dave in the crowd, I quickly scanned around looking for signs of his friends, girlfriend, or a wife. I even wondered if he was another sales representative, but his casual attire didn't make that seem plausible."

"After realizing that he was alone, I took notice of his athletic shoulders and toned body under his tee shirt, along with his curly dark brown hair and the scruff of his beard. But what I really liked were his curious smile and kind eyes."

"It sounds like you were smitten too, Noel."

Noel nodded her head and Francine noticed her friend's eyes clouding as she managed a slight smile.

"I can tell you that I was not a novice to men. I had been intimate with several men, but I knew early into each of those fleeting relationships that I would not get seriously involved with any of them. They were good looking and nice to me, but I knew that I wanted a different type of life than most of my school friends."

"You must realize, Francine, that I desperately wanted a family, but I wasn't interested in having babies and living a lower class lifestyle. I hoped that my appearance could get me noticed in higher class circles, and attract a decent young man that could provide me a better life. Does that make me a bad person, Francine?"

"No, it doesn't. My mother used to say that it was just as easy to fall in love with a rich guy as a poor guy. You just happen to be successful," she answered.

"I guess I was, but now it may all have fallen apart," Noel said before tears started streaming down her face.

Knowing that she needed to lighten up the atmosphere, she asked Noel another question, "So what happened next? How did he ask you out?"

"Dave walked over to me after the boat presentation and introduced himself as starting a boat business. He handed me his business card with his name, business, and marina information. Before I could even respond, Dave told me how impressed he was with my presence in such a big crowd. He said he had come to the boat show to make some contacts, so he was unable to spend more time with me now, but asked if he could see me later."

"I was a little taken aback at his forwardness, but then again, I was looking for that type of man. So, I said that I would be more comfortable meeting him tomorrow, before my shift at the boat show. We agreed to meet at a restaurant across the street from the convention hall."

"I remember asking him if this was a business meeting or a date."

"Wow, Noel. What did Dave answer?"

"He made a coy, crooked smile and said, 'Oh, make no mistake. This is a date. A big date.' Then, he flashed a big smile towards me before turning and disappearing in the crowd." Noel continued, "I was as equally smitten with him as he with me. But being a bit skeptical, I watched him as he approached another boat dealer's display. The promoter of that dealership appeared to know Dave, and I was thrilled to watch the interaction between the two men. Later in the day, I wandered over to the boat promoter and asked him if he knew Dave."

"What did he say?"

Noel proudly answered, "He said that he knew Dave and his father. He said Dave's father had been a customer of his for years, and that his family was the salt of the earth. I remember him saying something like, 'consider yourself lucky that he asked you out, although I would say he's lucky too, after meeting you. Dave's had many a woman try to get his attention'."

Noel shrugged and added, "That was all the assurance I needed to feel comfortable with a luncheon date. The rest is history. Three months later, we were married. Those were the most glorious months."

Noel hesitated before adding, "Well, most all the months have been good."

Francine moved closer to her friend and gave her a solid hug.

"We'll get through this, Noel. If things go badly, I'll be there to pick you up. But I may need your help too, because I have a problem myself.

CHAPTER 3

A Husband's Secret

D ave Noirty was not a man to fluster easily, but as soon as he returned to the marina, he closed his office door and quickly opened his desk drawer to retrieve a small lockbox. He opened the box and removed a small framed picture of a beautiful young woman with striking long dark tresses. He carefully ran his finger across the frame and smiled at the face staring back at him. Soon, the interoffice phone rang, but he did not hear it, being so enthralled with the picture. A loud knock on his door finally relieved his trance.

"Yes, what is it?" he asked while carefully putting the frame back into the box.

"I just wanted you to know that Noel stopped in here a little bit ago," his assistant replied.

"Thanks, I'll see her at home soon."

"She said to tell you that she was going to see one of her friends, someone named 'Francine'. She said she may stay at her house tonight, but you could call her if you needed her."

He felt relieved that Noel had not called him directly or had not stopped in at the marina. He didn't want to talk to her right now. His head was swooning with his current distraction, and Noel might recognize that something was wrong. He couldn't deal with Noel's interruption right now.

Noel. What am I going to do about her? I'm not ready to tell her about Brianna. She'll go crazy.

He stole a glance at his wife's picture sitting on his desk.

"Noel, I'm so sorry."

He reopened his desk drawer and removed the lockbox. Opening the lock, he picked up the picture of the younger woman again and traced the outline of her face with his forefinger. He laid down the picture and took out a pad of paper and began writing some information on the pad, frequently looking at the picture between his writing. He was eager to make a list of items that must be done within the next few weeks before he could pursue the next step of his future.

Carefully returning the picture to its hidden location, he secured it in his desk. He was satisfied with his next course of action. His next step was to go to the bank and change some of his finances, but he knew he had to keep his guard up so that Noel wouldn't find out. He decided it was best to use his business account for the transaction. He fired up his computer and made an account entry that he could use for the hidden account, calling the entry "Yacht Business Development Fund".

CHAPTER 4

The Society Girls

Shauna Delgado and Babs Simmons were sitting in the lounge of their country club after finishing a round of golf. Shauna was reluctant at first to bring up a sensitive topic to her friend, but the friends had long decided that it was best to tell each other up front if something strange was going on.

"So, do you know what's going on with Dave and Noel?" Shauna casually asked while stirring her martini.

Babs jerked upright in her seat at the names being mentioned and shook her head negatively.

Shauna continued, "I heard that Dave may be seeing someone. He has been spotted a couple of times with the same woman."

"No way! Dave and Noel are the couple we all want to be. I never thought she would be one of the 'first wives'. Who did you hear that from?"

"I heard from Antoine, my hairdresser. He knows pretty well everyone in town, including Dave Noirty. He said he was meeting some of his friends at the Ritz Carlton and he saw Dave and a young woman together. Antoine said they looked very cozy."

"What? Let's not jump to conclusions. Maybe it was a relative or a client? Antoine might be stirring up a little rumor like he has done before," Babs suggested.

"That's what I thought too, but Antoine said something was 'off'. Dave acted real nervous. He kept looking around, and when he spotted Antoine, he quickly grabbed the woman's arm and whirled her in another direction. I heard that the woman was stunning…and young."

"Hmmm, I haven't run into Noel lately, which is a little odd. Usually she's here at the club, or at some meeting or luncheon. Maybe we should give her a call? What do you think?"

"I think that is a good idea. Let's ask Noel to go to lunch, and maybe she will bring it up. I know we have a 'tell all' pact with each other, but, let's not act suspicious this time. She'd be devastated if she knew that we suspected something," Shauna replied.

"I agree wholeheartedly. When I found out about my own husband's affair, I was so thankful that I was alone at the time. My whole world shattered in an instant. I was a complete wreck. Let's see if Noel brings up anything, and if not, let's tell her at a private place, not in a restaurant."

Shauna agreed and gently touched her friend's arm. She remembered how Babs went through a painful time several years ago when her husband had a brief affair with his secretary. The affair ended and the secretary moved to a job in another city, but Babs' pain was never relieved. She had become depressed and convinced that her husband could and would start another affair with someone else at some future time. Their circle of friends tried to support her as best they could, but they all knew that her husband was quite a "horn dog", so promiscuity would probably return easily to him.

"I'm sorry to question a sore subject, Babs, but it seems like you and John are doing well since…since that time. Everything has been good, hasn't it?"

Bab's replied, "Yes, but the wound is easily opened. John meets so many people in his line of work as a financier. There are many beautiful single, divorced, or widowed women who come to him to invest their money. I am always worried that one of them will flirt and it'll lead to something more."

Shauna nodded and tilted her head down, knowing that she also worried about her own husband.

"I understand, Babs. My Tony owns so many businesses, and there have been many times when I suspected him of getting too friendly with some of his employees or business acquaintances. It's one of the negatives of being married to a successful man."

"You too? I never suspected that you had those fears, but I know that Mitzi worries about her husband, Paul. In fact, she told me that Paul had an affair once with another broker in his firm."

Shauna's eyes widened and she took another sip of her martini. After a long taste, she said, "I forgot about that. I think Mitzi made him break all ties with that broker, but he continued to see her for quite a while." She hesitated before adding, "I think we all have fears of losing our husbands to other women. It's probably natural. But let's get back to Dave and Noel Noirty. I think we owe it to Noel to let her know about Dave, if she doesn't bring up herself."

The two women agreed to contact Noel and make a lunch date. They also agreed not to tell any of their other friends until they knew for sure what was going on with the Noirty's.

CHAPTER 5

Daily Life at the Noirty's

Noel looked over the grocery list that her cook prepared.

"This will be fine, Maria. I could pick up these things myself, rather than you going to the store," Noel suggested.

"No, Mrs. Noirty. I prefer to go, because I purchase certain items from special stores. That way, you and Mr. Noirty get the best cuts of meats, fish and vegetables."

Noel nodded approvingly. She was desperate to have a diversion from staying in the house and thinking about her looming problem, but she didn't want to disrupt her cook from doing her natural duties. She walked into the foyer where her cleaning lady was dusting some of the art displayed and continued walking until she found some privacy in the formal living room. She sat on one of the matching Grace armchairs by Marioni, and gently stroked its soft suede fabric. She closed her eyes and swayed back and forth in the chair as she continued her thoughts.

There's nothing for me to do here. I'm going crazy. Maybe I could do some games on my phone until the cook and maid leave? I need to keep a low profile from my friends, and I want to be ready to follow Dave if I have a chance.

She thought about their daily life together and how it recently changed. Their usual routine was that Dave came home from his work at the marina, and they would have a cocktail and discuss the day's events. They would eat their dinners together, and afterwards, settle to the outside living area to enjoy some fresh air under the beautiful evening sky, or take a dip in their private infinity pool. They usually had guests or clients over to the house to dine once or twice a week. But recently, Dave would come home and eat dinner, and then say he had to do some work. He would go into his den and close the door. Neither of them suggested having any guests over.

What I hate the most is when he says he has to work and he leaves the house. Where is he going, and who is he seeing?

Noel rose from her designer chair and wandered through the beautiful home, a home that she and her husband made into their special sanctuary. It gave her some solace as she sat alone beside the pool.

Neither of us have suggested inviting our usual friends over for dinner or cocktails. It's so strange how things changed so quickly. Of course, neither of us have brought up the "other woman". I don't think he even realizes that I know something is wrong.

She continued to sit by the pool and watch an occasional boat on the canal as it moved towards the Gulf of Mexico or to one of the restaurants that dotted the shoreline.

What is going to happen with our home if we get divorced? I don't think I could maintain it. We are wealthy, but it's Dave's business that pays for these niceties that we share, such as the smaller pleasure craft boat docked at our pier, and unlimited use of the yachts that the marina owns. The majority of our wealth is due to his business.

She roughly contemplated their net worth, and if she could afford to keep such a grand house. Her features tightened and she realized that her hands were shaking.

"Noel, get a grip on yourself," she whispered.

She couldn't control her thoughts as she started to compute the dollar amount she would need to buy Dave out of his share of the home.

It would take everything I would get through the divorce to buy out this house. I can't stand to think that Dave may be here with some other woman, so maybe we would have to sell it.

She felt tears running down her face.

I don't care if I have to sell the house. I can rent something less expensive. It's not about the money, I love Dave. I can't understand what happened between us. Dave, please don't leave me.

Her phone rang and she saw Shauna Delgado's name appear on the display. She pursed her lips as she contemplated answering the call.

"I'm just not up for chitchatting and lunch," she said aloud to herself as she silenced her phone and put it back in her pocket.

CHAPTER 6

Blending Into a Crowd

Francine sat at her computer and typed "blending into a crowd". She gasped at the variety of websites. Some pertained to individuals not wanting to draw attention, animals blending in to their surroundings for survival, and even fascinating stories on artists, such as Liu Bolin, known as the invisible man. She was fascinated to learn that SWAT teams were moving away from the typical black clothes in favor of more a camouflage uniform with police insignias. Suddenly she frowned, as she realized that evil doers probably read some of these same internet articles to avoid detection.

…Wear loose fitting clothes

…do not wear bright colors

…wear little or no jewelry

…avoid direct conversations

…wear your hair conservatively or pulled back off your face

…light or medium brown hair is preferable

…wear sensible, low heeled shoes with no embellishments

…wear sunglasses

…keep your head slightly downward

…avoid cameras

…facial expression should be a slight or no smile

…light or no makeup

…walk with purpose

…keep in a crowd if possible

The suggestions were plentiful. She thought about Noel's appearance and laughed. Every single suggestion was opposite Noel's regular dress. She thought about herself, and realized that she herself wasn't so inconspicuous.

I wonder how come I always felt so invisible in Chicago? Looking at this, I should have been noticed everywhere I went.

As she thought about it, she questioned her Chicago look. Her thoughts drifted to some of her lonelier times in Chicago when she did not have a significant boyfriend. Francine reflected on the time when she was trying to meet a nice man. She spent about a year and a half alone, and being in her thirties at the time, found herself depressed while her co-workers were getting married and having babies.

She considered her look.

What made me feel "invisible" to eligible men? I had a business conservative style when I worked in sales at Magnacraft. Sure, I didn't wear anything flashy at her post-work get-togethers, but what could I have done to get noticed and still look like a nice girl?

After reading the "blending in" websites and considering the alternative, to be seen, she realized that all she needed to do was to wear a pop of something more bright and visual, like wearing high jeweled shoes, wearing a red color, or letting her hair fall onto her shoulders, etc. She filed that information into her brain to share with some of her single, Chicago friends who were still trying to find a mate.

At least I don't have to worry anymore.

Francine smiled and felt a tingle down her arms as she thought of her boyfriend, Brian Sherman. She met Brian after she was let go from her job and attended employment counseling at an agency. Brian, a contract civil engineer, also used the agency to find employment between work assignments.

They had an immediate attraction, and after one late afternoon of grueling private employment counseling, Francine was surprised to see Brian waiting for her at her desk. She remembered how he inquired about her counseling session and then nervously asked if she wanted to get something to eat.

Their romance kindled slowly, because Brian had been badly hurt by his ex-wife. He desperately wanted another relationship but he was reluctant to commit to a relationship because he had been a "first husband" victim. His wife had left him while he was running a civil engineering job in a different part of Illinois. His wife and their young child moved with another man living in their complex. When Brian returned home, he found a note laying on the table stating where his wife and their son, Jonathan, had moved. It also read that his wife loved someone else and wanted a divorce.

Francine looked out the window and watched a young couple walk hand in hand. It stirred emotions within her that she suppressed when she was working abroad. Her heart ached to see Brian, but she knew that she needed to keep building her brand in the southern United States. It would be weeks before she would be back in Chicago.

She suddenly felt lonesome, and started to talk to herself, "I'm Francine Pacque, LLC, representing Standard Products Distribution Corporation. My territory range is from mid-Louisiana, through Mississippi, part of Georgia, and most of Florida. I love my business and I'm good at it. Why do I have to compromise? It took a tremendous effort to build my business, and even more time to cultivate and train local help. By the end of my first year, I was able to hire several full-time employees to handle the day to day business in those areas. But the responsibility was still mine. I made commitments to my customers that I would personally be in their facilities at least every six weeks."

She reflected on the paradox between the love and success of her business and finding love with possibly a long term relationship with Brian. This wasn't the first time she thought about her issue. She didn't know how to resolve the conflict.

Her loneliness for Brian overtook her, and she dialed his work phone. She bit her lip nervously, awaiting him to answer.

"Civil Engineering Department, Brian Sherman speaking,"

"Hi, Brian. Its me."

"Francine, It's great to hear your voice. I have a meeting starting in a few minutes, so I can't talk for long, but I'm so happy you called," he said.

"I just wanted to say that I miss you," she said, gently biting her lip while waiting for his reply.

"I miss you too. In fact, that brings up a good point. When are you going to be back in town? This is ridiculous that you are gone so much," he said in a low voice.

Francine's defenses rose, as she felt her face flush and her heartbeat become faster. She quickly thought, *What am I going to do? I know this is going to come to a head with Brian when I return home. He's been questioning me continually why I can't be home more often.*

She carefully replied, "Can we talk about that later? I have business here in Naples, and my friend, Noel, has a personal issue that I want to help her resolve. Also, remember that I paid for Lilly's ticket to come to Naples next week for the big gala that one of my customers is having. I should be returning in about a month."

"A month! Are you kidding?"

She remained silent, knowing that her schedule allowed only two weeks in Chicago every two months.

After the awkward silence, Brian said, "I have to hang up now. I have all the crew chiefs in town for updates on all the highway work being done in the city. At least I don't have to be on the road visiting all the construction sites, but I'm still responsible to check on the safety and progress of the contracted crews."

"You have a very important job, Brian. I'm so proud of you. I know its a difficult job, but at least you are home most nights and see your son, Jonathan," Francine replied.

"Yah, it sucked when I had to travel more. Now at least I'm home most nights and able to share custody of Jonathan. Living in close proximity to my ex-wife's home does have some advantages so that Jonathan's life can be as normal as possible. That's why it bothers me so much that you are gone so frequently and for so long. I want Johnnie to know you better."

They said their goodbyes and promised to talk again soon. Francine remained seated at her table. She knew hat Brian was happy with his new job and his life since they began dating, but she also knew that he deeply desired to have a normal, long-term relationship with her. He had been hinting to her that he wanted to make their relationship permanent, and she suspected that he was waiting for the right moment to ask her to become his wife. A faint smile appeared on her lips and she raised her left hand, looking at her bare ring finger.

"I better get back to checking the websites on camouflaging

oneself. The sooner I can help Noel track her husband's whereabouts, the sooner I can return to Chicago," she said while firing up her computer screen. An hour later, she was ready to talk to Noel about practicing to be invisible in the crowd. She dialed Noel's phone number.

"I found out how you can spy on Dave to see what is really going on with him," Francine said to Noel.

She discussed her internet findings on being hidden within the crowd.

"Perfect," Noel replied. "I need to do this myself. I need to see him and her with my own eyes, but I sure don't want him to know that I'm watching."

"I agree, Noel, but we better practice before you spy on him for real."

CHAPTER 7

Preparing for a Different Life

Dave Noirty was nervous as he entered the bank that he and his wife used for their personal affairs as well as his business accounts. He was immediately greeted by one of the personal bankers who attended to high dollar clients. After some pleasantries were exchanged, the two men sat down in the banker's office. He presented some paperwork to the man, who initially looked confused. The banker asked him several questions and then left the office to retrieve some paperwork.

Dave tried to appear casual as he took in the office's surroundings, but his stomach was knotted and he felt that every movement was exaggerated.

I'm doing the right thing. I have to get myself into a stable, financial and emotional position before I talk to Noel.

The banker returned and set several bank cards in front of him. One was a personal safety box lease which he opened in his company's name and only his name as the only signature. The second bank card was for a new bank account, which read only "Dave Noirty". He deposited a sizable check, written out originally to his business, into that account. The beneficiary's name was listed as Brianna Flagler. The relationship to owner was listed as "personal friend".

He realized that the banker was used to these transactions, as many of the prominent, wealthy men in the area had special accounts made out for expenses for their mistress. The banker was unusually quiet, as was he, rather than their usual spirited conversations about boats, yachts, and family. When the transaction was complete, Dave asked for the privacy of one of the safety deposit rooms where he put several documents in the deposit box.

He left the bank and drove to the Ritz Carlton-Naples hotel. He nodded to the concierge, whom he had known for many years, and continued directly to one of the rooms. He knocked on the door and announced that it was him to the person on the other side of the door. Brianna opened the door and quickly closed it behind him.

CHAPTER 8

The Surveillance Test

Noel had decided that she'd rather know the truth about her husband's affair than hearing from someone else. She decided that she wanted to personally watch over her husband rather than hire a private detective. There was no need to involve an outsider. She had asked Francine to help, and Francine provided a list of how to blend into a crowd. But she still thought she may need some help with her disguise. After several conversations with Francine about how to appear inconspicuous, they decided to practice their budding surveillance skills before trying it out with Dave Noirty.

Today was their "test run", as they decided to meet at a crowded section of a popular shopping mall called Miromar Outlet Mall, in a neighboring city. Miromar was a large, outdoor mall with many upscale shopping venues including Saks, Calvin Klein, Desigual, Eddie Bauer, and more. It was a tourist attraction to thousands of visitors each day, as well as a favorite shopping area for local residents.

The two women agreed to individually dress in their "spywear", and walk through the mall trying to identify each other. They agreed on a specific wing of the outlet mall and a time. If one of them identified the other, they were to take a picture and text it to the other. After an hour, if both women did not identify each other, they were to meet at the bar in one of the many restaurants within the mall, a place called Ford's Garage.

Francine had studied all the literature she could find on how to disguise, and opted for a simple large gauze outfit that she knew her friend had not seen before. She sat on her bed and pulled on a pair of extra large pantyhose, dreading the thought of wearing hose in Florida's heat. But she had carefully wrapped support tape around her hips and waist so as to make her size significantly larger than usual. She also had wrapped separate lengths of support tape around each thigh. Francine looked thirty pounds heavier than normal after she stuffed a DD-cup bra with tissues and pulled up her panty hose to secure the tape. She then put on her beige gauze lounging pants and tops. She did not recognize herself in the outfit.

She had purchased a brown hair root concealer and carefully sprayed her highlighted hair so it would appear one brown shade, and she pulled her hair back off her face in a simple, short ponytail. She put on a pair of cheap costume pearl earrings and a large pair of black sunglasses. She slipped on a pair of simple flip-flops that were available at every inexpensive beach shop. Instead of her Michael Kors purse, she took her gray make-up bag with necessary identification and keys inside of it.

Francine looked in the mirror and thought she looked like a million other tourists in the area. She took a picture of herself for later use and headed out the door. Not wanting her car to be identified, she parked in another wing of the outlet mall and walked to their target area thinking how uncomfortable the extra weight felt on her.

When she got to the main section of the mall, she went into one of the first stores she saw and bought an inexpensive item for the purpose of getting the store's bag. She then strolled through the mall, holding her purchase in the hand facing the other shoppers. She casually strolled the mall, appearing to look in each of the store's display window, while secretly scanning the crowd for Noel in her disguise.

Francine spotted Noel almost immediately. She had to turn into one of the stores as to not laugh in public while she watched her friend trudge along the row of shops.

"If there was anyone in the mall who knew Noel Noirty, it is safe to say that they wouldn't recognize her as Noel, but everyone is noticing her," she said softly to herself.

She took in Noel's appearance from the privacy of the shop window. It appeared that Noel was wearing a pair of men's fishing pants hiked up over her waist with one of her husband's golf shirts tucked into her high-waisted pants.

She looks like Barney Fife from the old Andy Griffith Show.

She returned her gaze towards Noel and studied her hair. Noel must have purchased a white wig cut in a straight bob to wear to a Roaring Twenties costume party some years ago. She was wearing that wig along with a pair of white golfing shoes.

"At least she isn't wearing her open-toed Prada shoes."

Continuing to watch Noel, she noticed that Noel forgot entirely about downgrading her purse, and held her distinctive Louis Vuitton purse as she walked.

Oh man, Noel looked like someone dressed in drag', ready to go golfing. No wonder everyone is looking at her.

Francine reached into her purse and turned on the camera function of her phone. She took a picture of Noel and hurried out of the store before texting "Gotcha" under the picture. She sent the picture and text to her friend and waited for her reaction.

Casually sitting on one of the mall benches, Francine observed Noel when she opened her text. Noel frowned and quickly scanned the passerbys. Not finding Francine, she walked across the mall to where the picture was taken, but no one was there. She frantically searched the crowd in each direction, even quickly moving to the middle of the mall to search in both directions. She didn't take notice of the overweight woman sitting on the bench. She was too busy moving her head from side to side searching the pedestrians.

As Noel turned and walked in the direction of Francine, Francine pretended to be interested in her purchase within the shopping bag. Noel walked directly past her. After she passed by, Francine took another picture of Noel with several people turned around looking at the woman in "drag".

"Nope, there's nothing subtle about Noel," Francine muttered to herself.

At the prescribed time, Noel went to the bar at Ford's Garage and ordered a martini. She looked perturbed as she searched the customers, waiting for her friend's arrival. Soon, a small container of olives were set in front of her. She thanked the bartender as she told him that she hadn't asked for any olives.

"Compliments of the woman sitting at the end of the bar," the bartender replied.

Noel looked down the bar still with no recognition, until a small hand waved towards her. Soon, Noel's eyes widened in recognition of her friend.

Francine moved to an open seat next to Noel and said, "I hope no one thinks I'm dating you."

"I guess I'm going to have to be a little more understated," Noel said as she looked her friend up and down.

"That may be impossible. I may have to do the surveillance, my friend."

Soon, both women started to laugh, and they continued to laugh for the next hour while they enjoyed their drinks. They made a pact to continue practicing their undercover skills so Noel could spy on her husband, Dave, in the near future.

"We have more to discuss than my philandering husband. We have your friend, Lilly, coming to town this week and our gala next week Saturday," Noel said to Francine with a wink.

"We certainly do. I cannot wait for Lilly to meet you and the other girls, and I am so excited to see Dominic's gallery for the event. Remember, I helped him with the design of his warehouse and supplied him with all the glass cabinets to hold his inventory."

"Yes, I remember," Noel said. "You will be surprised to see how beautiful the gallery and the warehouse is, one year after it opened. Dominic has the best art and antiquities in the area. This event had been advertised for months and people have been calling like mad to get tickets. The crowd will include icons of industry, celebrities, politicians, and anyone who called Naples "home" for the winter season."

Francine remembered when she was awarded a generous contract to supply display cabinets for his art and antiques, as well as the contract to oversee the entire design of his gallery. She designed a magnificent area with rows of glass doored cabinets, displaying art pieces and antiques. Each row displayed a specific color so that shoppers could quickly look for accent pieces for their homes. The rows faced each other with beige, cushioned benches running the length of each row so that shoppers could sit and enjoy the art. Large pieces were displayed at the end of each row in a grouping with pastel couches placed at various angles to enjoy the large art pieces.

"That project was very special to me. It was the largest contract I had during my first year of business. I understand that you are helping Dominic plan the event. Angela Fratilo told me that Dominic picked you as his co-chairperson because you know the best caterers, bartenders, valets, and musicians," Francine stated.

"Thank you. I guess I am good at planning parties, but for me, the best part was the distraction from my crumbling marriage," Noel added. "So what about Lilly? Is she still your roommate in Chicago?"

"Yes, Lilly and I share my townhouse near the Magnificent Mile. Do you remember that she recently graduated with her Master's Degree from Northwestern University in Illinois. So, Lilly is flying down here next Saturday, and I told her that I would bring her to the outside Naples art fair at the Waterside Shops to meet the girls'. Is that still going to work for you, Noel?" Francine asked.

Noel nodded affirmatively.

"I told Angela, Shauna, and Babs that I would go with them to the fair, and that you would be meeting us there with Lilly," Noel added

"That sounds good. Lilly is a little shy, but I think the art show will be enough distraction for her that she won't be too intimidated by all of you."

"Intimidated? Really?"

Francine laughed and answered, "Intimidated not in a bad way, but remember that Lilly is a young foreigner who isn't used to the glitz of Naples and all of you ladies."

"I understand. Actually, I probably was a lot like her when I first arrived to the area with Dave," Noel answered.

Noel became mesmerized in her private thoughts and the conversation ceased.

CHAPTER 9

Lilly and the Accident

The plane's wheels gently touched down at Southwest Florida International Airport. Lilly quickly picked up her purse and took out her cell phone to notify Francine that she had arrived. Looking into her tote styled purse, Lilly shuffled through her belongings until she found a zippered compartment. She proudly removed several items including a thickly beaded bracelet and a long green necklace. She smiled as she fingered the beaded bracelet that she bought at a drugstore in Chicago. It matched the green in her necklace. She wanted to look like a fancy girl when she met Francine's society friends today.

After another fifteen minutes waiting for her suitcase, she texted Francine that she was ready to be picked up. Excitedly, she exited the airport baggage area and waited for the familiar white Audi to drive up to the curb. An arm extended from the driver's window of an oncoming car and started waving. It was Francine. Lilly leaped off the curb and headed towards the Audi.

The women embraced when Lilly reached the car. Francine quickly opened the trunk for Lilly's suitcase. The women jumped into the car, and it sped away towards their first stop, a Naples' Art Fair.

"I'm so excited," Lilly exclaimed. "This is the first vacation trip I have ever been on in the United States."

"Really? Even when you were an undergraduate in Seattle?"

"Including Seattle. I never told you that my parents were supportive of me studying in the U.S., but they wouldn't let me live by myself. My mother came with me for two years. We never travelled. I was expected to study. The only place we went was back to Japan to visit my father."

"So your mother was here for two years. What about the following years?"

"Mother and Father eventually located other Japanese families in the area. I was able to stay with one of those families for the following year. They were very nice but had strict instructions to notify my parents if I didn't concentrate on my studies. I went to school or studied all the time and I graduated in three years" Lilly explained.

"With honors, I understand."

"Yes, with honors. I was very lucky to have great teachers who instructed me well," Lilly added.

"Lilly, you never cease to amaze me. I didn't know you finished undergrad in three years, and with your usual 'Lilly' grace, you gave credit to your instructors."

"Thank you, Francine. But my favorite time since I arrived in the US was being your roommate… until today. This vacation is now my favorite time," Lilly confessed.

Francine smiled and gently squeezed Lilly's hand.

"Lilly, without you becoming my roommate, I wouldn't have had the funds to hit the road and develop my business down here. I would have been stuck in some low paying job to pay my bills. You are my angel. No one could ask for a better roommate or friend."

"Thank you, Francine," Lilly strained to say as her throat constricted with emotion.

The women drove about thirty minutes south before they exited the highway on Corkscrew Road. Francine turned right and headed west passing beautiful hedges and flowers that lined various housing developments. It was a beautiful ride and she reminisced about the first time she drove through Naples a little over one year ago. She turned her head and realized that Lilly had the same expression of awe as she looked at the beautiful surroundings.

"So, let me tell you a little about the Naples' Art Fair and the women we are going to meet today," she stated. "First of all, Naples has some of the best art and antiques in Florida. This particular art fair features artists from around the country who were vetted by a panel of local experts and deemed appropriate for the fair. The fair is in a parking lot at one of the major shopping centers in the area. There will be serious art customers as well as many tourists attending the event. Some will be sightseers just looking for something to do, but others will be serious art collectors who have big bucks to buy items."

"Yes, I looked on Google to understand the art fair better. But I'm especially interested in meeting your friends, especially Noel and Angela," Lilly admitted.

"Oh yes, and they are very excited to meet you too. Remember that Angela Fratilo, besides being a good friend to me, is one of my customers. She is also responsible for introducing me to many of my other customers in this area. But most importantly, she is the niece of Dominic Pepino, the man who owns the gallery for the fancy event we are attending next week Saturday," she explained.

"And Noel is the society lady that you had so much fun with last year, right?" Lilly asked.

"Yes, Noel Noirty is a fabulous woman who happens to be very wealthy. Yes, I did have lots of fun with her and some of her other friends last year. But remember, I also portrayed myself as a society woman to gain her friendship. It turned out to be quite a disaster when I was exposed as an imposter, and I am so happy that we all remained friends when they learned the truth. I'm still so ashamed of myself, and I'm still so grateful that I kept my job," she admitted.

"Angela and Noel are so excited to meet you. We have lots of activities that we will do this week. You are going to have a great time, my sweet friend."

Traffic increased as the Audi approached a busy street. Lilly admired the cars going down the street and started saying their names, "There is a Porsche…look at that Cadillac…Wow, what is that car?"

Her friend laughed as she acknowledged that Lilly quickly realized that Naples is a special, beautiful place. They finally arrived at the Waterside Shops and turned into the parking area. In a few minutes they were parked and ready for their first adventure. Lilly changed from her tennis shoes to a fancy pair of sandals. She wanted to look presentable for her meeting with Angela and Noel.

"Lilly, I've never seen you dressed up so beautifully. Your beige shorts and top are offset beautifully by your jewelry."

"Thank you, Francine. I want to look good for everyone. You also look beautiful today," Lilly answered and smiled.

Lilly gently pressed her hand against her necklace and checked out her bracelet on her wrist.

"I wanted to wear some jewelry so I would look more like a working woman than a student," Lilly said quietly.

As they walked along the outskirts of the crowd, she could see admiring glances toward Lilly. Her black straight hair against her alabaster skin didn't look like the norm for Florida. But she looked more sophisticated and more like a member of the society group than most people attending the function.

"Oh, Francine! Look at those flowers! They are so beautiful," Lilly said and she turned towards the foliage around the perimeter of the Waterside Shops. "Can I look at them for a minute before we go look at the art?"

"Sure. Why don't you look at the flowers while I locate Angela and Noel," she replied as she pulled out her cellphone and dialed Angela's number.

Soon she disappeared into the crowd as Lilly walked around the flowers.

There was a small stairway up to the shops and Lilly walked three stairs to look at the flowers blooming around the side of the shopping mall. She walked into the shade of the overhang and peered down into the planter. Suddenly, she felt a sharp blow to her head and she stumbled down the stairway. The pain in her head was excruciating and she felt dizzy as she lay in a tangled heap until she felt nothing at all.

In a few minutes, Francine, Angela, and Noel emerged from the crowd and walked towards the shops. They all had huge smiles expecting to see Lilly standing there.

"Hmmm, I wonder where she is?" Francine questioned.

She scanned the crowd from which they just exited and looked up at the shops.

"Maybe she stepped into one of the shops," Noel added. "Let's go up the stairs and see if we can find her through the store windows."

"That sounds good. And, if she did go into the crowd, she may see us on the landing," Angela said as she bounded up the small staircase.

Angela and Francine started looking into the shops on the front of the complex, as Noel started to look at the shops on the side of the mall.

"Oh my God!" Noel shouted. "Call an ambulance!"

CHAPTER 10

A Crack in the Bling

Francine ran to the side of the building with Angela behind her. There, laying in a heap at the bottom of a set of steps on the side of the complex, was Lilly. She appeared unconscious and a small amount of blood trickled down the side of her face. The women quickly went down the steps and were relieved that she was breathing. Beads from her jewelry were laying around the sidewalk from when she fell.

"I have the ambulance coming," Angela said. "They have a crew stationed nearby due to the Art Fair."

With the blare of the siren approaching, she bent down to whisper calming words to her unconscious friend. Within two minutes, an ambulance appeared and Angela ran over to direct them. The EMT quickly proceeded to the spot of the accident and started taking Lilly's vitals. They gently straightened her legs and put her arms straight down the side of her body. A stretcher was brought along side Lilly and the men gently lifted her onto the stretcher in one movement as to not jar any of her bones.

"Do you know who this woman is?" one of the EMTs asked.

"Yes, she is a friend of mine. Her name is Lilly Lee. She just arrived today from Chicago," she answered.

"Did any of you see what happened to her?"

Francine explained that Lilly wanted to look at the flowers while she located their friends. Noel and Angela answered "no", and explained how they had just walked over from the exhibits to meet her, and found her laying on the ground.

"Tom, look at this," said a young policeman who had followed the ambulance, to one of the EMTs.

"See this blood on the planter? She must have forgotten that there were stairs as she walked and looked at the plants. She probably stumbled on the steps and hit her head on this spot."

"Oh, yeah. I see what you mean. We need to tell the doctors when we get to the hospital," Tom answered.

"Do you want to ride with us to the hospital, ma'am?" Tom said to Francine.

"Yes, of course I do."

"OK. Why don't you pick up her belongings while we get her into the ambulance."

The women started to pick up beads as Francine tried to locate Lilly's purse.

"I don't see her purse. Angela! Noel! Someone must have taken her purse!"

A policeman was assisting the EMTs. He quickly turned to the women picking up the beads and shouted, "Stop! Don't do any more! If this woman's purse is missing, then this isn't an accident. This is a crime scene. Tom, let me get a couple of pictures of the injured woman, and you can leave for the hospital. Miss, I think your name is Francine, I'm going to have to make a report. You can go to the hospital with your friend, but I will need to meet up with you there."

Francine nodded, her face wet from tears. Angela and Noel were teared up as well, and they held Francine upright to make sure she was steady before walking.

"Francine, we will stay here and pick up any belongings we can find. We will meet you at the hospital," Noel stated

CHAPTER 11

The Hospital

Lilly's eyes opened slightly during the ride to the hospital. She frantically tugged at the oxygen mask on her face as her eyes scanned left to right. Francine lunged towards her quickly.

"Lilly, It's all right. Don't pull at the oxygen mask. You had an accident and bumped your head. We are in an ambulance right now headed to the hospital," she said in as calm of a voice she could muster.

Lilly's eyes looked towards her and nodded. She took her hand and continued talking slowly and calmly to her friend as the ambulance hurried towards the hospital. She was elated that Lilly had regained consciousness as she choked up from relief.

The ambulance pulled to a stop at the emergency entrance of the hospital and the EMTs quickly removed the stretcher from the vehicle, pushing it inside the hospital. The EMTs announced "traumatic head injury" to a nurse who quickly pointed to an empty station. Francine was impressed to see how quickly medical attention was given to her friend as she nervously stood in the emergency waiting room.

Soon a medical assistant found her and motioned to a nearby admission station. Francine was able to give the assistant some information on Lilly as far as name, address, and nearest relative's name. But without Lilly's wallet, she didn't know her insurance carrier, or even Lilly's parent's address or phone number in Japan. Francine felt helpless as to how to help her friend, but the assistant reassured her that the balance of information would be obtained from the patient.

About thirty minutes later, the policeman who assisted the women at the scene of the accident appeared in the waiting room.

"How is she doing?" he asked.

"She's conscious. So, that is a good thing."

The officer nodded and continued, "Miss Pacque, My name is Officer Jason Breakly. I need to ask you a few more questions regarding today's activities."

She nodded and followed the officer to a more private area within the waiting room. Officer Breakly wanted to hear everything from the time that she first saw Lilly at the airport until she was found unconscious. Francine answered as best she could, even verifying the time that Lilly contacted her to pick her up at the airport. After the officer was satisfied with his questions, he lifted a satchel from the floor and opened it up. It contained Lilly's purse.

"The purse was found about fifty feet from where Ms. Lee was found. It was thrown into some bushes in the parking lot. The good news is that her wallet and cell phone were still in the bag. I looked in her wallet and found her ID and charge card. I also found her temporary Student Visa. It looks like the only thing taken was her money. I don't know how much money she was carrying, but there was none in her wallet."

"That's a relief, At least her IDs were there and her charge card. Did you see any type of insurance card?"

"Yeah, I think so. Let me look again."

He opened the wallet and pulled out an insurance card.

"Can I have the card so I can give the hospital her insurance information?"

"Sure. I'm going to see if I can talk to Ms. Lee and get a statement. I'll give you her purse for safekeeping."

The officer briefly spoke to one of the nurses before being escorted to Lilly's location while she quickly went back to the assistant to fill in the missing information on Lilly's admittance form. She was just finishing with the assistant when Noel and Angela appeared.

"We came as quick as we could. We picked up all the beads and put them into a bag," Noel said.

The women sat in the waiting room while Lilly underwent some CT scans on her head to make sure she didn't have a concussion. While they waited, Officer Breakly returned and asked the women a few more questions. After he verified that none of the women saw anyone close to Lilly before the accident, he said, "I'll be looking at any video surveillance tapes I can find. Hopefully there will be one on the side of the building."

"Do you think someone tried to hurt her or just tried to rob her?" Noel asked.

The officer hesitated before answering, "It's a little too early to tell, and if we can find a video, then we will know. My first instinct is to say that it was some kid that saw a young woman standing by herself, and the kid pushed her while he yanked her purse loose."

"That does sound plausible," Noel commented. "Then she lost her balance and hit her head on the planter."

"It's really too early to tell. I need to hear from the victim first," Officer Breakly replied.

The women looked at each other with concern. No more was said until a doctor came into the waiting room and asked for Francine and the officer to come with him to a small private room in the ER. While he was walking, the doctor explained that Lilly did regain consciousness and did not have a concussion. He explained that it would be better to keep Lilly overnight, and he would reexamine her in the morning before discharging her.

"She is lucky to not sustain a head concussion or any broken bones from falling down the stairs. But having two head wounds could give her a powerful headache and dizziness. I would feel much more comfortable if she stay here overnight."

"Did you say two head wounds?", Officer Breakly asked.

"Well, yes. She had a head trauma injury on the back of her head and a contusion on her cheek."

"We are pretty sure the cheek injury was a result of hitting her head on a planter when she fell, but I don't know how she would have gotten a head trauma," she added.

"I do," Officer Breakly answered. "Someone hit her on the head. Doctor, I found a coconut at the scene. There wasn't a palm tree nearby. Would you think that her type of injury could have been caused by a coconut?"

The doctor reflected on the wound and answered, "Actually, if she was hit by something, it would have to be with an object that was very hard, but not too hard as to not crack open the skin. A coconut could be such an object."

"I would like to speak to the victim alone before she has visitors," Officer Breakly announced.

She nodded, understanding the officer's concern. She remained in the hallway while the doctor and the officer entered Lilly's hospital room.

Several minutes later, Officer Breakly emerged from the room and motioned for Francine. He explained that Lilly couldn't recall anyone in the area prior to her accident. He gave Francine his business card and verified where Francine and Lilly would be staying during the week. Francine watched him as he walked down the hallway making notes. She entered Lilly's room and found her friend with iced towels on her head and an IV in her arm.

"Lilly! Oh my friend, I'm so sorry that this happened to you," she whispered to Lilly.

"I know you are. I'm sorry too," whispered a weakened Lilly, in her sedated state.

"Do you want me to call your parents for you?"

"No, no! Please, Francine, don't call them," Lilly pleaded.

"But they should know that you are in the hospital, and eventually the insurance bill will get forwarded to them."

"Let me tell them in my own way. I'm twenty-one so I'm an adult. If they knew, they would be on the next plane flying here. I'm still planning on having fun with you this week," Lilly said with a weak smile.

"I'm thrilled if you think you'll be in good enough shape to still have some fun," she said dubiously.

"Count on it. But I think I need to sleep now. They gave me a lot of medication and I'm getting drowsy."

"Very well. I'll leave. The girls are here too. I'll tell them that you need to sleep and we will see you tomorrow."

"No, don't tell them that."

"Why?"

"Because they are standing right behind you," Lilly said with a smile.

She turned and saw Noel and Angela in the doorway. Nothing would keep the girls from coming in to meet Lilly, regardless of the circumstances. Soon they moved in front of Francine and started introducing themselves to the patient. After lots of hugs and kisses on the cheek, they finally agreed to leave the room while Lilly continually waved them goodbye.

After they left, Lilly's expression on her face hardened. Noel had placed the beads from her broken jewelry in a plastic bag and put them on the bed table before the women left the room. Lilly carefully lifted the bag and examined its contents.

"Oh no, oh no, oh no," Lilly muttered.

A tear fell down her cheek with the realization that her heirloom antique jade necklace was not among the beads in the bag, especially the large hand-carved jade stone that made up her pendant necklace.

My grandmother's necklace is not here. What am I going to tell my mother? She'll never forgive me for wearing it before my wedding day. And now it's gone forever.

Lilly buried her throbbing head in her pillow and cried until she fell asleep.

CHAPTER 12

Back to Semi-Normal

"**B**rian, something terrible happened," Francine said into her cell phone to her boyfriend, Brian Sherman.

"What, honey?," Brian asked, expecting it to be some little detail that didn't go right for his over-achieving girlfriend.

"Lilly got mugged and is in the hospital."

Brian jarred to attention quickly, "What? Our Lilly?"

She related all the details, her heart still beating wildly. Brian could clearly realize that his girlfriend was very upset and he didn't know how to help.

"Francine, where are you now?"

"I'm just leaving the hospital. Noel and Angela are going to take me back to the parking lot where I left my car."

Brian felt his chest contracting from anger that someone would hurt a young, defenseless woman. But that feeling didn't compare to the rage that he wasn't there to help his love, Francine, through this difficult time.

"Can I talk to either Noel or Angela?"

"Sure, but why?"

"Just hand them the phone, Francine."

She handed the phone to Noel, who was standing closest to her. She tried to overhear the conversation to no avail. In a couple of minutes, Noel handed the phone back to Francine, winking and saying,

"Your Brian is a 'keeper'."

She nodded in agreement, but furled her brow wondering what had just transpired as she took back control of her phone call.

"Brian, what was all that about?"

"You shouldn't be alone tonight, so I asked Noel if you could stay by her house overnight. When you're calmer in the morning, you can pick up your car."

"Oh, OK, if that's all right with Noel," she said while turning back towards her friend who was nodding affirmatively.

"You need to pull yourself together for Lilly's sake. Noel mentioned that all of you need to go to the police station tomorrow to make written statements with the officer in charge. You need to be rested and have a clear mind. Lilly will be discharged tomorrow, so that's good news. You need to be calm for her, Francine."

He continued, "I wish I would be there for you. If you want me to come, I'll find a flight and be there tomorrow."

Her tense body instantly relaxed. She felt that her heart could burst with love for Brian. They had been dating for over a year. Their relationship grew from a chance acquaintance at a job placement firm when they both were out of work, to torrid love in the following year. The only issue was that Francine's job kept her on the road eighty percent of the time. When she did return to her company's headquarters in Chicago quarterly, she was only there for a few weeks.

Those weeks were so precious to her and to Brian.

"Thank you, Brian, but I know you have your son this weekend and Jonathan is excited to go to the aquarium with his dad. I'll pull it together for everyone's sake.

They spoke for a few more minutes before hanging up and she walked over to Angela and Noel.

"Well, I guess one of you has a house guest."

Noel nodded and took Francine's arm while holding up her other arm, indicating that she was taking her home. The three women drove off and talked about tomorrow's agenda for making formal statements at the police station, picking up Lilly at the hospital, getting her to the vacation condo that Francine had rented for the week, and possibly meeting for dinner, if Lilly felt up to it.

CHAPTER 13

The Police Station

At exactly ten a.m., Francine, Noel, and Angela walked into the Naples police station. They were cordially escorted into a small conference room and told that Officer Breakly would be with them shortly. All three women were nervous because they had never been in a police station before today.

"I wonder if this is an interrogation room?" asked Angela.

"No, it couldn't be. Doesn't an interrogation room have a two-sided mirror on the wall and a high intensity light to shine in your face?" Noel asked.

"You two watch way too much TV," laughed Francine.

Soon, Officer Breakly appeared in the doorway and greeted the nervous women. He was holding a well-worn coffee mug with one hand and the other hand held a large folder. Lilly Lee's name was on the folder when he tossed it onto the table.

"Good morning, ladies. I hope you had a good night after your stressful day yesterday. I asked you here to make sure that I wrote the details down properly. I have already been to the hospital and spoken to Lilly Lee. She doesn't remember anything specifically except feeling a sharp pain on her skull before the fall."

During the next hour, the women reviewed his notes and they were satisfied that the officer had the details correct for as much as they knew. They were not able to add any more details than what they had already told him yesterday.

"So what is next? Did you look at all the video footage yet?" Francine asked.

"Yes, I have reviewed the surveillance tapes from the shopping mall but I haven't seen anything useful yet. Today I will go through each tape in more detail and also review some other surveillance footage from the perimeter areas. I expect to see some teenager, or several teenagers, that just 'don't fit' into the profile for a mall or art fair shopper. If I find someone, it'll probably be someone we already know because they will have a prior record," Officer Breakly explained.

"So do we get updates?" Noel asked.

"Well, no, ma'am, you would not. I would be contacting Lilly Lee directly when we find anything out."

"Lilly will only be in Naples for a week. Do you think you'll find the assailant by then?" Francine asked.

The officer looked at each of the women individually before answering, "Actually, either we will find the offender very quickly or probably not at all. Don't get your hopes up."

He got up from his chair and picked up his folder and mug. Nodding to the women, he quickly strutted out the door. Suddenly he stopped and turned around towards the group.

"Oh yeah, I wanted to ask you if any of you know Jacque Bonafare?"

"No, I don't recognize that name. Do you guys know it?" Noel said looking at Francine and Angela who were both shaking their heads negatively.

"Why? Is he a suspect?"

"No. Actually, he's an artist who was showing his art at the fair."

Noel stood there, arms crossed, waiting for more information. The officer appeared amused that she was standing her ground, obviously waiting for more information.

"I guess you want to know why I brought up his name."

Noel raised her eyebrows still waiting for an answer.

Deciding that it was better to be up front with the women, the office re-entered the room and sat on a chair.

"Mr. Bonafare contacted us this morning and said that he is missing several pieces of expensive silverwork that he was displaying at the fair. His booth displayed high dollar silver jewelry in windowed cases, but he also had sculpture work displayed on shelves. Several small sculptures are missing."

"I don't know him, but I am aware of the silverwork booth. He had beautiful art on display and there were a lot of people looking at his items," Noel responded.

"Yeah, someone looked at them a little too much. But, we occasionally have had people tell us something is missing when it really wasn't missing. They are looking to collect on their insurance."

The officer stood up and left the interrogation room, ushering the three women to the exit door. He said his goodbyes to the three women and expressed his condolences for their friend and for asking them to come to the police station that morning.

As the women walked to their car, Noel grabbed Angela's arm and said,

"Something is going on here. First, Lilly was mugged, supposedly by a kid. Now, we hear that there was art stolen. Either we have some clever kids that can blend into the crowd, or we have a thief."

"Let's not jump to conclusions, but it is something we should be aware of," Angela remarked. "Let the police do their job and let's concentrate on getting back to normal. Remember that we have a gala this Saturday to attend, and a guest, Lilly, that we want to make sure has a good time."

Noel shook her head in agreement, but the wheels in her head were turning. She had no intentions to let her beloved Naples get dangerous. Francine, Noel, and Angela looked at each other blankly. They expected resolution and more energy to find the assailant than what the police had suggested.

"This is completely unacceptable. I've lived in Naples for almost fifteen years and you never hear about muggings unless you are at some bar off the beaten track and late into the night. Heck, we pride ourselves that Naples is so safe. I don't want to think about a mugger while I'm jogging, or shopping, or whatever."

"I couldn't agree more," Angela replied. "I've also been here a long time. Actually, I've been here my entire life. We can't take things so lightly. I remember someone saying recently that car thefts were up."

"That's not good!"

"I know, but it's not a police emergency," Angela continued. "I guess it really isn't. But Lilly was hurt. That to me is more of a violent crime, and I would expect the police to be investigating every lead."

The women finished their frustrated discussion and left the station to drive Francine back to her car at the Waterside Shops. They were unusually silent during the drive. When they arrived, Francine hugged them and thanked them for being such good friends. She was ready to go to the hospital to pick up Lilly.

CHAPTER 14

One Secret Revealed

Francine got to the hospital just as Lilly was being released. Lilly was smiling ear to ear when Francine walked into the room.

"I'm ready to go!" Lilly gushed waving her arms wildly while the nurse finished up the paperwork.

She had to laugh seeing her friend so giddy. Soon, Lilly was sitting in a wheelchair and a hospital volunteer was pushing her to the exit door. Within a few minutes, the twosome was driving down the road.

She was so relieved that she had rented a small Naples condo for a week within a golfing community rather than staying in her small one bedroom apartment with Lilly. The condo wasn't as grand as her friend's, Noel's home, or as the grand house she managed to stay at last year while in Naples. But it was still in a gorgeous, lush community. She knew that Lilly would be thrilled when she saw it. The community boasted an eighteen hole golf course, a huge community pool, a clubhouse with a restaurant, bar, and fitness center, and several tennis courts. Staying in a condo would be much more comfortable for her friend, and Lilly would have a better idea of what living in Naples really is like.

"Here it is, Lilly, on the right. This is where we are staying."

Lilly's expression had not changed since Francine picked her up at the hospital. She was smiling broadly and uttered "oohs" and "aahs" as they passed every community. Now her attention was focused on the flowering bushes that lined the wall of the gated community. Francine slowed her car to turn into the entrance drive. As she swung the car around the corner, Lilly gasped as the tall, stately Royal Palm trees that lined the street. When they arrived at the gate, an attendant stopped their vehicle until Francine showed him her pass. The arm of the gate swung up and allowed the Audi to enter into the community.

"I think you will really like it here, Lilly. I checked in the day before you arrived to make sure the condo was clean and acceptable. It is really lovely."

"I love it here already," Lilly responded while her eyes opened wide with excitement. "It's perfect."

She proceeded driving down the main street as they passed beautiful homes, ponds, and lush foliage. She purposely drove towards the clubhouse as she wanted Lilly to see it from the front. The building was huge and had a large overhang with stately pillars. Comfortable lounge chairs and rockers were placed on the porch for restful enjoyment while enjoying a cocktail.

"If you are up to it, we can eat here tonight with Noel and Angela. If not, we can stay at the condo and I'll order a pizza."

"Let's eat here, Francine. I want to experience it all. I want to see the people who live here too."

As they passed the clubhouse, the golf course came into view as well as some low-rise buildings. She explained that they were staying in one of the condos, on the second floor, so Lilly could sit out on the lanai and look at the beautiful landscaping all she wanted, or just keep her windows open to get some nice Florida breezes while she slept.

The women eventually reached their rented condo and she pulled Lilly's suitcase out of the trunk.

"What on earth do you have in here? Rocks?"

Lilly laughed and said that she almost took her whole closet with her. She explained that she didn't know what they would be doing during the week, and she wasn't quite sure how warm it would be, so she brought many things, including a coat.

They entered the condo and Lilly took in her surroundings. She walked into the main living room and saw soft white leather couches and contrasting red chairs. Floridian landscape pictures adorned the room in richly colored frames. An updated kitchen with beautiful black granite countertops lined the back of the space. But Lilly's attention was straight ahead. She quickly walked past the furniture and opened a wall of sliding doors onto a large screened lanai.

Sitting on one of the chairs on the lanai, Lilly said, "I'm never leaving here. Can I find a job in Naples?"

"I'm not sure if this area is ripe for behavioral scientists. But maybe, if you are serious about wanting to live here, you would find a suitable job."

Lilly unpacked her bag in the master bedroom and she was thrilled to see a king-sized bed, plush side chair, tray ceilings, a huge closet, and her own bathroom. She hung her clothes in the closet and tried to smooth out the wrinkles. Although she packed so may clothes in her suitcase, she looked at her meager belongings and knew that she needed to buy some new clothes when she got a job.

Her happiness was short-lived when she relived yesterday's trauma. Lilly got up and silently closed the door. She sat down again in her chair and tried to remember everything she could. She remembered looking at a planter by the stairs and carefully examining one of the flowers.

"Was there someone else there? There had to be." Lilly weakly exclaimed.

She remembered movement in her peripheral vision, but not enough to know who it was. She was certain that the shadow was one person but couldn't remember more.

What am I going to tell my parents? They will have to know soon because it would be cruel not to let them know that I was injured. Good thing that I didn't sustain a concussion. But there will be bills to pay, and without a job, mother and father will have to help me out.

Lilly knew that her parents would be excited to hear about her trip, so she would talk to them about Naples rather than the accident. The accident information could wait until she got back to Chicago.

Her thoughts drifted to her grandmother's necklace that was stolen. Her grandmother received that necklace from her own grandmother as a wedding present. The necklace dated back into the 1800's. The jade pendant was ornately carved and set in a gold mounting. The pendant hung from a string of jade beads. Lilly didn't know the exact value of the necklace, but she knew that a similar one was sold by Sotheby's Auction House for thousands of dollars. The personal value was priceless to her mother.

I never should have taken the necklace with me. What was I thinking? Who cares if I didn't have expensive jewelry to wear. Everyone knows I just graduated. I'm not a rich girl.

There was a knock on the door and Francine's voice asked if Lilly still wanted to go to dinner at the clubhouse. Lilly asked her to come into the room.

"Are you feeling tired? We can blow off our dinner at the club," she said while pulling up a footstool to sit close to her friend.

"I think I should stay here and sleep so I feel better tomorrow, but you could still meet your friends. Before you go, though, I have a problem that I need to share with you. It's a secret and you cannot tell anyone about it," Lilly said in a stern voice.

She nodded that she would keep her secret and Lilly began her story about her necklace. She shared the family history of the heirloom and said there would be great shame if the necklace was lost. She withheld the value of the necklace because she knew that Francine would want to report it stolen to the police.

"I will try to purchase a similar one when I'm working and have more money. I don't know if I'll find the same one, but I might be able to find one that resembles it. Then on my wedding day I will wear the new necklace," she said lowering her eyes.

"Lilly, I'm so sorry. The right thing to do would be to let the police know. It may show up in a pawn shop in the area and you could get it back. You need to tell them, my friend, so they can put it in their report."

Lilly paused to reflect on Francine's words. She nodded her head and agreed to let Officer Breakly put it in his report. Francine agreed to call the officer while Lilly collected her thoughts. She was contemplating how to explain the reason that Lilly did not tell him immediately, when Lilly interrupted.

"I don't want Noel or any of your friends to know about my necklace. You have to promise me that you will not tell them. I don't want them to feel any worse about what happened to me. Remember, this is my vacation."

"I'll promise, for now, but we may have to revisit this issue because there were two thefts. One was with you, and the other was with another artist at the show. We were told about the artist's theft at the police station. I don't think it will be a secret long in this tight-knit community."

"I understand," Lilly said reluctantly.

CHAPTER 15

Another Secret Develops

Back in Chicago, Brian Sherman was feeling alone and nervous as he thought about this latest incident with Lilly. He had always feared for his girlfriend, Francine's, well-being, because she traveled to various remote territories by car. He didn't like the idea of is girlfriend being on her own in case of a car emergency, or that she was living alone in small towns along her route. But, he had always felt secure when Francine was in Naples. Naples is a safe, affluent, beachside city. He also knew that Francine had some people to depend on in Naples if she ran into a problem.

He searched his wallet for a paper Francine gave him with some emergency contact phone numbers. He spotted a listing for "Noel Noirty - Naples, Florida" among the list. He immediately telephoned Noel.

The two of them spoke a few minutes before Brian asked Noel about Lilly's muggings. He believed the version that Francine had told him, but he wanted to make sure that she told him everything, and that she was not in any danger. Noel explained the facts just as Francine had previously related them, and explained that she and Francine had been to the police station to help identify suspects.

Noel smiled as she considered Brian's concern for his girlfriend. She briefly mentioned that Francine was helping her do some surveillance, omitting their involvement in tracking her husband's dalliances. She knew that Brian wouldn't like the sound of that. Francine will have to tell him herself.

"I wish she would leave this all to the police to solve," Brian admitted. "I don't want to see her get hurt or involved in any trouble."

"Brian, I'm so happy that you called me. I'm so pleased that you are concerned for Francine. She is special to all of us, you know. I'm hoping to meet you soon. Are you planning to come down south to see her sometime?"

"I can't leave the Chicago area for a while," Brian admitted. "I don't know if you know that I have a six year old son and that have joint custody of him. Besides my work with the city and tending to him, my time is very limited. But, I wish that I could come down to the Naples area. Francine is in love with the area and I would love to see it for myself."

"I did know about your son and your new job, so I understand. I only know how difficult it is when you are not with someone you love, and Francine is alone most of the time."

Brian was slightly taken aback with the word "love". It was something that he was uncomfortable saying, although he knew he was very in love with Francine.

"It's not easy for me either, Noel."

Always the event arranger, she couldn't hold herself back when she added, "Maybe you and she should consider the next step. Maybe live together so that you could be together when she is back in Chicago."

"Did Francine mention this to you?" Brian asked.

"Actually, I brought it up to her as a natural next step. Francine broke out in a wide smile and said that she hoped to 'some day'."

"She said that?"

Brian carefully thought of the interaction between Francine and his son. It was a very good relationship although it was always brief.

"I have to consider how Jonathan would fit into this all. I am actually hoping to make Francine and my relationship more formal at some point, before she would move in. I think it would be easier for my son to understand."

Brian quickly thought about what he just admitted to Noel. He insinuated an engagement or marriage. The thought of it scared him and excited him at the same time. He hoped that talking to Noel might be a good entryway to understand if Francine felt the same.

"Noel, please don't say anything to Francine. I want it to be a surprise, and from me, not you," Brian stated.

"I understand completely, and I will not tell her anything," she answered, trying to hide her excitement.

"What do you think she would answer?"

"As you said, that should come from her, not me. But, between you and me, I think you would like the answer."

It was on that day that Brian and Noel made a secrecy pact to keep each other informed on any "developments", and agreed to be clandestine friends on any surprise.

CHAPTER 16

Another Plan Hatched

Francine called her Naples friends and told them that tonight's dinner was cancelled so Lilly could get more rest. The girls decided to get together on another night. Soon afterward, Noel decided to telephone Francine.

"Do you think you could break away from Lilly and come over to my house for a little while?"

"Lilly should be asleep for some time. I guess I could come over," Francine answered, a little concerned as to the reason.

Francine wrote a note for Lilly just in case she woke up and found herself alone. She then jumped into her car and drove quickly to Noel's home.

Francine could feel the tension when she arrived. The usual festive atmosphere with seasonal decorations and lighting in every room was replaced by a silent, dim look. Francine walked into the kitchen with Noel and asked if Dave was home.

"Yes, He's here, somewhere. We had a quiet and uneventful dinner, and as we were finished, Dave announced that he had to go back to the office for a little while."

Noel shrugged her shoulders and retreated into her entertainment room's bar, grabbing an expensive wine.

"I think it is time that we follow him," Francine replied.

"I want to, but I'm afraid of what I'll find. Maybe not knowing is better."

"Nonsense. Even if it is the worst news, you can prepare yourself better."

Noel nodded half-heartedly.

"I'm not sure if I can do it yet without being seen. Anyway, my mind is racing in many directions. I have my on-going problem with my husband, and now this happens to Lilly. How could someone do that to a sweet, young girl? She must be terrified. This is such a bad impression of southwest Florida. Remember when the policeman told us about the local artist that had something stolen? He has another art show on Tuesday in downtown Naples. Many of the same artists will be there. I wonder if the artists are afraid of theft since last week's episode?"

"Another art show this week? Hey, I have an idea. What if we try some surveillance at that show? Some practice. Let's plan to do a little undercover surveillance at the smaller art show, and see if any of your friends recognize you. What do you think?" Francine asked.

She thought about it for a short while and indicated that she was up for the challenge. The women came up with a plan to ask Shauna and Babs to walk around the art fair with Lilly while they did a little shopping for a surprise present for her. They knew that the girls would be agreeable. Then they would duck into one of the downtown hotels, and change into their undercover clothes, spend an hour doing some surveillance, and meet their friends for a great lunch an hour later.

"Whew! I hope we can pull this all off. The only hiccup is, we will have to come up with a present for Lilly," Francine added.

"Have you ever been to 'Noel's Closet'? I have plenty of things with tags still on them. Lets have a little shopping spree when we finish our wine."

"Don't bring aGucci purse this time when we do our surveillance, Noel," Francine lectured.

The women laughed as they remembered the first disguise Noel wore at the Miromar Mall. They walked into her bedroom to look in her closet.

"Is this a closet, or a boutique store? I've never seen such a big closet or so many clothes, shoes, and jewelry," Francine gasped as she looked around the room.

"I hate to break it to you, but this is only one of my closets. I have another one just for my gowns and furs."

"Why would you need fur in Florida?"

She shrugged and purposefully walked towards one section of the built-in wardrobe. She pulled out several sundresses, all with price tags secured.

"I wanted to support one of the local designers by buying these dresses, but they are a little plain for my liking. Do you think Lilly may like either of them?"

"These are absolutely beautiful, Noel. Of course she would like one of them."

"Great, then choose one of them for her, and the other is for you, if you would like."

Francine stared at her generous benefactor. Each sundress cost over $200. She thanked her with a hug and they put the dress indented for Lilly into a pink bag so it would look as if it was purchased during the upcoming art fair.

CHAPTER 17

Bling in Full Force

The sun was brilliant and the sky clear when the women arrived at the fair. Noel quickly escorted Lilly away from the crowd to explain the area, "'Season' in Naples is something to be experienced. Although the city has a casual, vacation vibe to it, most of the residents and vacationers are wealthy."

Lilly nodded as she noticed large diamonds adorning most of the women's hands walking past her.

"Fifth Avenue is the downtown center of our little city, and it has dozens of sidewalk cafes and restaurants mixed in with designer shops. Today's art fair is a small venue set up directly behind the Fifth Avenue shops," Noel explained

Babs and Shauna were waiting at the corner. After greetings and hugs were shared, Lilly left with Babs and Shauna and walked into the group of shoppers at the fair, being totally enthralled with the booths of art.

Noel and Francine hurried back to their car, retrieved their respective suitcases, and hurried into one of the local hotels.

"I reserved a room for us to change into our disguise. I thought it would be easier than using the public restroom," Noel explained.

Francine had dressed in the same disguise as she had worn before, realizing that were was no need to change in from the simple, gauze outfit. The girth she added to change her size, however, was another matter on this very hot day.

"I'm already dripping! My makeup is going to run," Francine stated.

"It won't matter if your makeup is ruined. Everyone will think you are a slightly rotund tourist that sweats a lot."

Francine playfully slapped her friend's arm.

She jolted away to avoid the slap noticing that she had successfully toned down her outfit from her last surveillance trip. This time she wore a simple gray jumpsuit, but still had her severe white wig.

Francine took off the wig and combed Noel's hair into a simple ponytail fastened by a scrunchee.

"A scrunchee! No one wears them anymore."

"Exactly," replied Francine.

Francine looked over the flawless makeup that Noel had on and wiped it off with several tissues. She told her that she could put on makeup again before they met their friends for lunch so she would look more like a tourist who exercised rather than a makeup model.

She agreed. Francine took a pair of simple Skechers tennis shoes out of her bag and handed them to her friend. Thankfully, the shoes fit. She looked like any of a thousand tourists.

"One more thing, Noel, you have to take off your rings, and put on your large sunglasses."

They were ready. They were discussing walking around together in their disguises at the art fair, when they realized that they didn't really know what to observe. So they took a few minutes discussing things that they could accomplish. Their list included watching for any suspicious people by Jacques Bertrand, the artist that had some items stolen several days earlier. If they saw anyone, they would photograph them and produce the pictures to the police if anything was stolen.

Noel and Francine made their way to the corner of the art fair and took a brochure of the exhibits. They located where Jacques' booth was and made their way in that direction, stopping at various booths along the way as a distraction.

"Francine, I just passed several people I know. They didn't seem to recognize me," she said excitedly.

The women spotted Lilly, Shauna, and Babs, and decided not to press their luck and go too close to them. Thankfully, the three women were already past Jacques' booth. They carefully looked at the items and made small talk as they looked at the art for sale. The silverwork was beautifully sculpted and pieces were displayed in various sizes.

Francine noticed that Jacques stayed at the back of the booth, but he had a female partner that stayed at the booth entrance. She noted that he was not going to take any chances that his art would be stolen at this fair.

After they spent about ten minutes inside the booth, the women decided to leave so that they didn't look too suspicious themselves. They didn't know what to do or where to stand after they left, until they spotted some small tables and chairs stationed by a musician stage.

"I can't believe that a small venue like this would have a musician," Francine exclaimed.

Noel explained that a musician would keep the spectators in the art area longer. It also would give the husbands a place to sit while their wives were shopping. Francine was amazed at her friend's business acumen.

They found a small table and bought a couple of waters. Their vantage of the art fair from their table was very good, allowing them to sit there for a long time without appearing suspicious. As they rested, the musician crooned to soft rock tunes on his guitar. He was a very good musician and singer and a crowd started to gather to enjoy his show. The crowd clapped after each song completed and she noticed that several people were swaying to the music during the songs. After the musician's set ended, he announced that he would be taking a ten minute break. He got off his stool and rested his guitar on its stand while he drank some water.

"I enjoyed your music. Do you play around here often? I can remember seeing you before."

"I haven't played in public much, but my dad suggested that I start playing at some local places so I can get some experience. He's one of the organizers for this art show," the musician answered.

"Really? Maybe I know him then. What is his name?"

"My dad is Joe Franklin. I'm his son, Dennis."

"You are Joe and Pepper's son? Oh, my God. I know them well,"

Francine kicked her friend under the table as Noel had forgotten that she was disguised. Noel's eye's widened as she realized her mistake. Francine quickly looked around to see if Joe Franklin was within earshot and she quickly thought up two fake names.

"It's nice to meet you, Dennis. I'm Connie and this is my friend, Donna," Francine quickly interjected.

Noel looked at Francine for her reaction. Francine was as cool as a cucumber but made a mental note to remind Noel that one of the rules of blending into a crowd was to "avoid direct conversations".

Thankfully, the young musician was more interested in taking a short break and getting back to his music than answering the strange woman's questions.

Dennis nodded before standing up, "I better get back to work. It was nice meeting you both."

He headed for the stage and started tuning his guitar.

"I forgot about not getting familiar with anyone. Good thinking, Francine, to change our names."

"Let's keep those two names for future use, if we need to," Francine replied while scanning the crowd. "And remember to avoid direct conversation with others when you are doing surveillance. It is easier for people to recognize you or remember you when you have a conversation."

Francine continued, "The good news is that I think we are 'good to go' for watching your husband, Noel. No one seems to have noticed you. Do you think you are ready?"

She shrugged her shoulders and said that she thought it was time to know what really was going on with Dave. She sadly reported that Dave told her he had a business dinner tomorrow night with someone she didn't know existed. Noel said it was another scam and she was going to follow him to see this other woman.

"Gee, Noel. I can't leave Lilly alone another evening. I'm not going to be able to go with you," Francine reported.

"I think I can handle it myself. I'll stay in my car, or maybe I'll rent a car so he won't recognize it. But I want to know where he is going, and who he will be with."

The two women continued scanning the crowd to see if anyone looked suspicious. They saw some interesting characters, but no one that stood out. After about an hour, they returned to the hotel room and changed back into their regular clothes. They reapplied their make-up and used various hair styling tools to get their hairdos back to natural. Noel held the pink bag with the sundress that was to be given to Lilly.

They were checking out at the hotel lobby when they heard a commotion on the street. Sirens and squad cars were surrounding the area. Francine and Noel peeked out the door to see five or six policemen running towards the art fair in back of the Fifth Avenue hotel. After a quick glance at each other, the women dashed out the door in the direction of the fair.

"Oh my God," exclaimed Francine, "We have to find Lilly quickly. I'd die if something else happened to her."

As they ran, Noel grabbed Francine's arm and poInted to an area outside of the exhibits. Lilly, Babs, and Shauna were standing there watching the policemen who were talking to some of the art booth dealers. Immediately calmed down, Francine and Noel headed over to their girl friends.

"What's going on? Do you know?" she asked.

"We understand that someone got some art stolen from one of the jewelry booths. A number of precious stone rings," Shauna answered.

She quickly glanced at Francine with a look of despair. They had been observing the fair, but focusing on only one exhibitor.

"The art dealer was helping a customer, and when he turned around, his noticed that his display case looked different. When he looked at it more carefully, he noticed several high dollar rings were missing. No one seems to know what happened. They are interviewing some of the people who were standing at that booth now. We also heard that there were no cameras at this fair, since this plot of ground is just green space."

Francine spotted Officer Breakly taking an exhibitor's statement. He had a deep frown in his brow as he interviewed the person and scanned the crowd.

"This is terrible! Another theft in our little town. I wish there was something we could do to help," Babs mumbled.

Francine and Noel glanced at each other but held their tongues.

CHAPTER 18

Dave Gets His Information

D ave was unusually quiet at the marina. He participated in several meetings and made his rounds through the various salesmen at his dealership, but quickly returned to his office and closed the door.

The envelope he was waiting for was laying on his desk. It was a thick brown envelope with only a Post Office number as a return address. He had always had strict rules to his clerical staff to not open anything addressed to him personally. In his business, there was always some confidentiality required with the clientele that he serviced. Sometimes boats were purchased or leased without a customer's spouse's knowledge, or a client just didn't want anyone to know how much he payed for a particular yacht. But this envelope was different. This envelope contained a detailed description and biography of the woman with whom he was currently sneaking around. He didn't want any surprises, so he had insisted, with her knowledge, that a detailed biography be obtained.

He carefully read each page noting that the information Brianna had told him was correct. She was born and raised in New York State. He carefully read the details relating to her parents, her schooling, and her post high school studies in New York City where she studied interior design. The packet included a written evaluation that stated that she was a gifted designer with an eye for detail and a conscientious demeanor with clients. He carefully reviewed each paper in the packet including some medical papers, credit information, and arrest history. He was pleased that Brianna had never been arrested

The papers in the file were spread over his desk and he spent the next hour repeatedly looking at each paper. He sat and looked blankly at his wall while he reflected on his findings. He didn't want Brianna to leave the area yet, and she had a plane ticket to go back to New York in two days. He had to spend more time with her. His body ached to know this young, beautiful girl better.

He thought about the art event that was happening this weekend at Dominic Pepino's art gallery. Noel had volunteered to orchestrate the affair, and there were many of Naples' society who were coming. In fact, the majority of people coming were "invite only", which made the affair more in demand by the people who wanted to be on the A-list. There were also "open" tickets to come to the event, but you had to be recommended by someone who knew the person, and that the person had enough funds to buy items at the gallery. It was a lot like the yacht business, where potential customers had to be vetted and proof of funds supplied to board one of the expensive yachts for sale.

Dave reflected that Brianna might want to experience an event such as this one while in Naples, and it would give him a chance to see her a little longer. He thought about how he might get Brianna a ticket. He couldn't ask his wife, Noel. He decided to call the proprietor, Dominic Pepino, directly. After a few pleasantries were exchanged, Dave asked Dominic if he could get a handful of open tickets to give to some of his high-dollar clients from the marina. Dominic agreed that it was a wonderful idea, and agreed to give him a dozen tickets.

"Do you want to get them directly from Noel?" Dominic asked.

"Well, I could, but I don't know where she is right now. Could I send someone over to your place and pick them up? I have several clients coming in today that I would like to give the tickets," he lied.

Dominic agreed.

"Someone from the marina will pick up a dozen tickets within the hour."

After the call, he smiled and reflected on his little trick. He thought about several clients that he really could offer the tickets, but he would keep one ticket out of the dozen for Brianna, if she accepted.

His next call was to Brianna. He easily convinced her to stay a few more days in Naples. He would cover the expense at the Ritz Carlton Hotel and the cost to exchange her airline ticket. He also told her to buy an elegant dress for the gala. All of Naples' society would be decked out in their finest formal wear, including himself, who would be in his tuxedo. He agreed to pay for all of her expenses.

Brianna was easily swayed to stay.

"I would love to stay longer and go to the gala. Thank you so much," she said excitedly. "But what about Noel? Won't she be there? Will I be able to spend any time with you?"

"Let me take care of that."

"Will I see you before the gala?" Brianna asked.

"Of course, my darling. I will see you tomorrow evening and we can go through some details," he answered.

He hung up the phone satisfied with his decision to ask her to attend Saturday's gala, but he had some arranging to do prior to the gala. He couldn't risk being exposed by his wife at that event. He decided to ask one of his salesmen to escort Brianna on Saturday night. If he could convince his salesman to escort her, he would be able to talk with them at the event.

That should work. Noel, will be busy with overseeing the gala anyway.

He reassembled the packet and placed it in the thick envelope. He unlocked the lockbox in his drawer and placed the contents into it before relocating the box. He hurried out into his sales showroom.

He looked around the showroom trying to remember which salesmen were single.

i can't ask Captain Pete. Pete briefly dated Francine Pacque last year, and since she will also be at the gala, it may draw too much attention.

He approached one of his other single salesmen, Josh Fairmont.

"Hi Josh, By any chance are you free this coming Saturday?"

"Ahh, yeah, I don't have any big plans. What's up, Dave?"

"Well, I have a very personal favor to ask you, but you would have to be discreet about it."

Puzzled, Josh nodded inquisitively. He motioned for him to follow him into his office for some privacy and Josh obliged.

"This is a difficult situation to explain, so I'm asking for your complete secrecy."

When Josh nodded affirmatively, Dave continued, "I have a young woman visiting the area. She is a beautiful woman and about your age. I would like to invite her to an art and antique gala at a private event in Naples. It is a formal event and I'm sure that she would enjoy it. I think you would as well. There will be a number of people there you know, including customers, and of course, my wife, Noel."

He continued, "But Noel cannot know about this woman, so I'm asking if you could accompany her to the gala as her date."

Josh studied his boss' face for a few seconds. Dave looked frantic, but he knew something was wrong.

Why couldn't Noel know about this woman? It had to be an affair, Josh thought.

"Gee, I'd like to help you out, but it sounds a little awkward."

"Yes, it is awkward, but I can assure you it is all 'above board'. I'm sure you would be delighted with your date, and you and she would both have a great time. Josh, I'm in a bind, and I really need your help."

With more of curiosity than delight, Josh agreed to the date.

"Thank you, Josh. I owe you. I will reimburse any expenses."

He explained that the event was a formal affair, but that Josh did not have to wear a tuxedo. A dressy suit would be fine, if he preferred. He suggested that Josh and his date say they met on the internet and that it was their first date.

"My friend, Brianna, isn't from the Naples area, so no one should know her. And, I should be able to come and talk to you and her at the gala."

"Pick her up at the Ritz-Carlton Hotel at 6 p.m. on Saturday. Ask the hotel desk to ring her room when you arrive."

"OK, it sounds fine. Is there anything I should watch out for at the gala with her? Like, Noel?" Josh asked.

Dave's brow furled as he thought.

"I guess you should just act natural. Noel will be Noel, and she'll probably come up to say hello to you and Brianna. Just act natural and don't say too much."

They shook hands before Josh returned to his cubicle. He felt secure in Josh and thought his ruse would not be detected.

What could go wrong? Noel will never notice her, he thought as he sat down and placed his feet up on his desk.

CHAPTER 19

Let It All Out

The women left the art fair site and reset at a nearby restaurant for lunch. Noel could clearly see that Lilly was in awe of her new friends. She observed her looking over each woman's fancy clothes while listening to their conversation, and saw her searching each woman's hand to look at their large diamond rings and glittery jewelry.

Shauna and Babs kept engaging Lilly with a variety of questions regarding her Japanese background and her desires to find work after college. Finally, Noel reached under the table and retrieved a pink bag which she handed to Lilly.

"Is this for me?" Lilly questioned as she observed the bag with wide eyes.

Lilly opened the bag and found the new sundress. Her eyes gazed at her new frock with delight. She loved the yellow dress, and Lilly was excited to wear it during the week. Shauna, Babs, and Lilly talked about several venues during the week that the dress would be appropriate.

Noel was unusually quiet. She knew she would struggle to keep her nervousness under control in case either Shauna or Babs asked about Dave, but she was unprepared for her feeling about this latest robbery. Francine was quiet also, worried about how Lilly felt being in the presence of another theft, since Lilly's mugging had only been a few days ago.

The conversation went to a lull, as no one spoke after Shauna and Bab's questioning to Lilly was over. Lilly suddenly started to cry.

"Are you ok, sweetie?" she asked. "Do you feel all right?"

Lilly nodded that she was feeling fine, but couldn't control her emotion.

"Francine, I can't keep this quiet. What am I going to tell my parents?" Lilly asked, directing her question to Francine.

The women thought she was talking about her mugging, but Francine knew it was about her grandmother's pendant that was stolen.

Francine took a breath and said to Lilly, "You know, I learned the hard way last year, when I lied to everyone here about who I was. I learned that getting the facts out into the open helps a lot."

Noel stirred in her seat, as she was keeping her own secret about her husband's dalliance. But it was Lilly who broke the silence.

"I didn't want to tell anyone, because I was ashamed of disobeying my parents," Lilly confessed.

Noel, Shauna, and Babs looked at each other inquisitively.

"I don't think I got mugged for my purse," Lilly explained. "Remember the beads on the ground when I fell? The ones you found were worthless junk jewelry. I bought a fake jade bracelet back in Chicago. But I also had on a real jade necklace, with an ornate carved jade pendant."

"Oh no, Lilly," she exclaimed along with the other women. She reached out and laid her hand on Lilly's arm.

"The necklace was in my family for generations. It is very valuable and very old. My grandmother gave it to my mother on her wedding day, and my mother was to give it to me on my wedding day. But my mother didn't want me to be lonely, since I was so far away from them in Japan, my parents allowed me to take the pendant with me as a remembrance of my family. It is very expensive and irreplaceable to my family."

Lilly paused and wiped her eyes before continuing, "I think someone hit me on the head and I fell down those steps. I remember someone removing my necklace, but I was too drowsy from the fall. Someone knew my necklace was expensive and robbed me."

Shanua's hand hid her face as she came to terms with what he just heard. Babs sat there and nodded her head back and forth in disbelief.

Noel's hand moved down Lilly's arm and wrapped around her hand.

"Lilly, I'm so sorry, but I have to ask, why were you wearing it here?"

"See, that's the thing. I knew better than to take it out of my safety deposit box, but I wanted to look special for all of you. I wanted to fit in," Lilly admitted.

The women looked at each other and felt a bit ashamed. Each one of them were known for their style and each one carefully dressed and accessorized so they would look unique. They knew their wealth had certain advantages and they each sported large diamonds and other precious stones. But they didn't realize the affect their style may have on others visiting the area. Their feelings were quickly dismissed by the knowledge that they lived in an affluent community and they could afford some of the finer things in life, but how do they explain that to a this young woman.

Francine, Shauna, and Babs returned their gaze to their own plates and started to eat their lunch. Lilly followed their lead. But she felt unusually uncomfortable. She gazed at each of her friends and wondered how she ever turned into such a "bling queen". Noel felt compassion for her young friend, Lilly, who lost her heirloom necklace just to fit into the Naples crowd. She ate her lobster in silence as she silently vowed to herself to somehow get Lilly's necklace returned.

Francine was fidgeting during the entire dinner with the women. The dinner was supposed to be a happy event to have Lilly get a better chance to meet the girls prior to Saturday's gala at the art gallery. But the third theft during the week, and the knowledge that Lilly escaped being badly hurt during her robbery weighed heavily on Francine. Lilly, Noel, Shauna and Babs were nearly finished with their dinners when Shauna noticed that Francine's plate was hardly touched.

"Francine, Is there something the matter with your scallops? You've hardly touched your dinner." Shauna asked.

"No, nothing is wrong with my meal. My problem is that I cannot get over everything that's happened in the last couple of days. I think I may call Officer Breakly tomorrow to see if there are any developments."

"I agree with you," she said. "I'm sitting here thinking that we, that all of us, have to help find this thief. None of us will ever feel the same again if we don't jump into action and help the police.

"Help the police! Noel, are you out of your mind?" Babs asked and continued, "We aren't trained to find a crook. And if we do, what would you do with him?"

"You might be surprised, Babs. I agree with Francine to check what the police have found so far. If they know who it is, then I'll back away. But, if they haven't found him yet, then I think we should jump into action. And I know exactly how to do it," she stated while winking at Francine.

Francine tried to hide her smile, knowing exactly what Noel was suggesting.

CHAPTER 20

The Police Investigation

The following morning, Francine telephoned Officer Breakly for an update on the investigation on Lilly's mugging and on the thefts in general. The officer responded that he could not comment without Lilly Lee's consent, so she put Lilly on speakerphone so they could both hear the update. Noel was sitting nearby and she moved over next to the speaker with the girls.

The officer admitted that the video feeds did not offer any leads on Lilly's incident. The police have suspect lists compiled for some petty crimes, such as purse snatchings, and they looked for any of those known past perpetrators in the videos to no avail. They also looked for similar muggings and thefts in other surrounding cities or art venues. He was is process now of contacting pawn shops in the area to check if the jade necklace turned up and informing them of the risk of selling anything stolen. In other words, letting them know that they will lose their license if we catch them selling the stolen jewelry.

"So, in other words, you don't have anything," Francine said sarcastically.

Annoyed, Officer Breakly said, "I don't call ruling out suspects 'nothing'. It takes long hours of work to go through these videos and compare faces to suspect lists. And, going to every pawn shop in the area takes time. I immediately sent out pictures of the stolen items to

95

them so they were aware. But I personally go to each shop and look at their inventory. I have other cases as well, but I am making Ms. Lee's case a priority because she was physically hurt."

"Maybe I'm being a bit harsh, so I'm sorry," Francine added.

"I'm sorry too. I thought this would be an easy case with some young person making a bad decision for a few dollars. But it looks like this is a bigger operation, or a professional thief," he said.

The women hung up the phone and spoke to each other about the disappointment. But Noel knew that this would not be the end of it. It was time that she and her blingy friends started to do something useful.

Francine announced that the rest of the week had to be focused on Lilly's vacation. It was already Wednesday, and Lilly had not even been to the beach. Lilly was still reeling from the disappointment that her necklace had not been recovered, but she put on a slight smile and said she was ready to have some more fun while in Florida.

The three women talked about the rest of the week's plan. Today would be a beach day in Naples for Francine and Lilly. They were invited to dinner at Noel's house in the evening with the possibility of a ride on one of the Noirty boats. Noel hoped that Dave would be in good spirits and willing to take all of them on a sunset cruise.

Noel knew that her time would be limited the balance of the week as she had to coordinate the gala at Dominic's art gallery on Saturday night. Francine suggested that Thursday should be a shopping day for her and Lilly as well as making sure they had their ensembles ready for the gala on Saturday night. Friday was still an open day for whatever Lilly may want to do. Saturday would be the day that Francine and Lilly would go to the salon to have their hair and nails done with the climax of the week on Saturday night, their formal gala evening. On Sunday, Lilly would be returning to Chicago.

With the daily plans set, Noel left to get her groceries for tonight's dinner. She left a message on her husband's phone stating that they would be entertaining the girls at their home tonight and suggested the boat ride.

Francine and Lilly left for the public beach and set up their towels and umbrella in a beautiful setting. Stately, partially obscured homes lined the beach and Lilly had a wonderful day walking in the sand to admire the homes, and frolicking in the cool gulf waters. She pretended to be fully engaged in the day, and she was truly enjoying herself, but she secretly kept thinking about her lost necklace.

What am I going to tell my parents? It will be such a dishonor to my mother that she entrusted me with the pendant. Maybe I should wait a while to tell them, in case the necklace is found?

She pondered her predicament as she walked in the sand and decided that waiting would be the best idea. Everything felt better as she walked along the beach.

CHAPTER 21

Dinner at the Noirty's

Afer a long day at the beach, Francine and Lilly showered at the condo and headed to Rum Row. Lilly was excited to go to Noel's home as she had heard so many wonderful things about it from Francine. She wasn't disappointed. As they drove in the exclusive area of the Noirty's home, both women gushed over the neighborhood. Francine pulled into the driveway with beautiful flowering plantings on both sides of the drive, but the plantings paled with the grandness of the home.

Lilly was dressed in the yellow sundress that Francine and Noel purchased for her the previous day. Her fair skin glowed pink by today's sun. She had a wide smile when Noel answered the door and gave her a quick hug. If Francine didn't know Noel any better, she would have thought everything was fine. But the briefness of the hug and the dullness in Noel's eyes told a different story.

They walked through the front hallway and stopped momentarily for Lilly to enjoy looking at the furnishings in the front hallway. When they got to the kitchen and family room, Lilly stopped and gasped. She had never been in such a luxurious home and had to inspect each piece of furniture and art before proceeding. Noel was beaming with pride. They headed out to the outside entertainment area complete with a full bar. Dave sat in one of the oversized chairs.

"Lilly, I would like to introduce you to my husband, Dave Noirty."

Dave extended his hand and smiled as he told Lilly how much he looked forward to meeting her. Lilly said she was very happy to meet both of them and was looking forward to their sunset boat ride. Noel scowled as she awaited her husband's reply.

"Well, I'm going to have to give you a raincheck on the boat ride tonight. I have an important client in town tonight so I'll be leaving here directly after eating," Dave answered.

Francine stole a look towards Noel. Their eyes met and she knew that Noel did not believe Dave's story.

Lilly smiled and replied that she understood business came first. Dave glanced at Francine and noticed her smile had disappeared from her face as well as from his wife's face. He wondered if they suspected anything, but didn't know how they would have uncovered anything about he and Brianna. He kept his focus on Lilly, asking her various questions about her family and life in Japan while his wife went to the bar to retrieve some margaritas she had pre-made.

Drinks and appetizers were brought out and put on a table between the group. Lilly appeared to be having a fun time sitting on this beautiful lanai looking over the canal to the Gulf. She commented on how she loved her new group of friends and thought that this night was one of the best times she had ever had as an adult.

"I don't care if there was no boat ride. This day couldn't be more perfect," Lilly stated.

Noel had prepared swordfish and a beef tenderloin for dinner. They ate al fresco rather than going indoors to take part in the beautiful evening. Shortly after dinner, Dave rose from his chair and announced that he had to leave to meet his client.

"That's too bad, darling," she commented nonchalantly. "Where do you have to meet him?"

"At the marina, but we probably will go somewhere for a drink."

Sure you will. Probably straight to the hotel, you prick, Noel thought, while imagining her husband's arms around a young, beautiful woman.

Dave said his goodbyes to Lilly and Francine, and disappeared into the house. She didn't waste any time.

"Francine! This is my chance! Can I use your car to follow him? He won't expect a white Audi following him. You can use my car to drive home and I'll stop at your house on the way home to exchange cars."

Lilly looked confused but Francine explained that she would fill in the details later.

"Of course take my car. Lilly and I will clean up this mess before we go. Be careful, Noel," Francine answered.

Noel dashed into a guest room on the first floor and closed the door while she quickly changed into her disguise. Suddenly, Dave reappeared in the room and asked if they knew where his wife was located.

"Oh, she thought you already left. I think she went upstairs to put on her caftan," Francine lied.

"I guess I'll go then," he answered and he departed into the garage.

The guest room door opened slightly.

"Is he gone yet?"

"Yes. Hurry, before you lose his car," Francine said as she tossed the keys to her friend.

Lilly stood there completely confused when a woman emerged from the guest room. The woman wore baggy, elastic pants and a black tee shirt. She had a brown ponytail, no makeup, large eyeglasses, and nondescript tennis shoes.

"Thanks, Francine," she said as she caught the keys.

"Lose your earrings and rings," Francine suggested.

"I almost forgot about them. Goodbye, Lilly,"

Lilly stared confused but never asked Francine to explain. Francine did not reveal anything to Lilly either.

CHAPTER 22

The Chase

Dave was already turning at the corner when Noel backed out of the driveway. She followed Dave at a safe distance and noticed that he wasn't heading towards his marina. She lowered her body in the car and pressed harder onto the gas pedal to catch up to her husband. When she was a safe distance behind him, she changed lanes and kept the same speed as her husband's vehicle.

Dave drove into the entrance to Highway 75 and headed north towards Fort Myers. As she noticed him exiting on Daniels Parkway, she wondered if her husband was going to the same restaurant as the last time he met his girlfriend He drove past that particular restaurant and continued westward.

She felt her body flush and her pulse quicken as she anticipated what lie ahead. Dave drove until he arrived at Bell Tower Plaza, an upscale shopping center in Fort Myers. She guided her vehicle into the plaza parking lot, carefully watching for Dave's car. She spotted it in a section next to one of the plaza's many restaurants. She continued driving a short distance past his car, and parked in another section.

As she sat in the car, she observed her husband exiting his car and walking towards a mall restaurant. She couldn't see if he went into the restaurant or continued further into the plaza.

"Well, I guess this is showtime. I'm guess I will have to follow him."

Her heart rate quickened and she felt perspiration on her forehead. She took a deep breath and told herself not to be a coward. She checked her disguise in her car mirror and saw that she didn't recognize herself. She looked like most tourists. She got out of her car and walked slower than her usual gait in her tennis shoes, noting how the front of her calfs burned because they were not used to such flat shoes. She grabbed an advertisement paper that she saw tumbling in the parking lot, and folded it up so she would look like she was reading an ad.

Her body felt like it was burning when she spotted them sitting together in an outside cafe. They were so engrossed in each other's conversation that neither of them glanced in her direction. She caught him red-handed with this woman, but she never considered what she should do when that happened. Her heart rate increased further and her mouth felt suddenly parched. She felt as if she was going to faint.

Not knowing what to do, she looked for a place to sit. She hadn't planned on entering the cafe, but the bar in the cafe was the closest place to sit. She walked into the cafe and sat at the bar. She could hear Dave and his girlfriend giggling in the background.

"Thank you, Dave! You're the best," the beautiful young woman said as she flicked her hair behind one ear.

I don't want to hear this.

She shut her eyes to block out the conversation. She continued to feel faint and steadied herself by putting her arms onto the bar. The bartender approached her and asked for her order. She asked for some ice tea. He looked disappointed in her slight selection but left his station to retrieve ice tea from the back kitchen.

The bar seat she chose was close to the outside cafe seating, but it was tucked slightly inside the building. It actually was a great place to do a little surveillance. Her side was towards the couple, and she was able to sit at an angle so they wouldn't see her face. She continued looking at the ads and drank her tea in silence.

When she finished her tea, she paid the bartender and left the bar, continuing into the plaza. Out of the corner of her eye, she noticed that Dave and his date were eating dinner.

"At least he's eating, and not with her at some hotel. Well, he's not at her hotel now, but I wonder how late he will be getting home?"

She felt her eyes well up with tears as she contemplated her husband with another woman. She walked into the plaza and ducked into one of the stores for a quick visit, then hurried to another plaza entrance to backtrack towards the parking lot. She noticed a bench that may offer a view of the outside cafe. She was in luck because the view of the couple was completely visible. She took out her cell phone and pretended to have a conversation while she watched them. The beautiful young woman appeared to be looking back at her, so she turned slightly while she continued to pretend that she was talking on her phone.

Although her glance at the woman was short, her recollection of the woman was vivid. She noticed that the woman was in her early twenties, with possibly an Italian or Latino heritage due to her olive skin, had clear, wide-set eyes and petite facial features. She was wearing a print blouse over white leggings and white high-heeled shoes. She didn't appear to be a harlot type or a showgirl type of woman. In fact she looked very respectable and beautiful.

Just Dave's taste. I'm in trouble.

She got up and returned to the car. As soon as she safely closed the door, tears streamed down her face. She felt her stomach tighten to a hard ball and wished she had taken some anti-acid with her. All she had with her was another bottle of water which she quickly drank. She started the car and drove opposite from the cafe to another lot still in the plaza parking area. She decided to watch Dave leave the plaza and follow him to the next site.

Another half hour passed when she observed Dave and the young woman walk towards two cars parked in the lot. She noticed that they were parked next to each other and wondered if they had planned to park that way.

Dave opened the door for the young woman. The woman was laughing and throwing her head back in glee while she fingered her earrings as they spoke. Dave bent over and they gave each other a hug and she noticed that the woman gave him a slight kiss on the cheek.

Just a peck on the cheek? Maybe they are being careful in case someone was watching them?

The woman got into the car and Dave bent down still conversing with her. Then, Dave dashed to his car door and quickly started the engine. Both cars zoomed off in the same direction. She followed the two vehicles keeping a sizable distance behind their vehicles.

The cars continued down the main avenue that spans Fort Myers, Bonita Springs, and Naples. All three cars traveled about thirty minutes south on the highway, going past car outlets, furniture stores, decorating venues, and many restaurants and entertainment spots, until the first two cars turned right towards the gulf at Vanderbilt Beach Road.

"The Ritz Carlton?" she blurted with surprise. "Of course she would be staying at the Ritz. It's Dave's favorite hotel."

She felt the muscles contract in her throat as she contemplated the next hours. She carefully stayed back several car lengths until she confirmed that Dave and the woman's cars were entering the hotel entrance. Noel pulled her car over to the curb and leaned her head onto the steering wheel.

"I can't follow them into the hotel. What would I do? Confront them in their room?" she blurted.

She sat at the curb until she composed herself enough to drive home. It was nine p.m. She wondered what time Dave would return home, or if he would return home. She put the gear into "drive" position and started a slow journey towards the condo that Francine rented, to exchange her car and return home, but decided to give her friend a call first.

"Hi, Francine, I'm not going to come in by you and Lilly. Can you throw the keys under the front car mat and I'll do the same for you. I really don't feel like talking much right now."

Francine immediately knew that the evening ended badly for her friend, and agreed to leave the key for the car exchange under the mat. She said she would talk to Noel in the morning.

About an hour later, she returned to her home with her own car and parked in the garage. She slowly changed into her nightgown and brushed out her ponytail. Noel carefully folded her disguise outfit and hid it back in the same guest room closet. She walked around the guest room, touching the luxurious bedding fabric and the tops of the polished woodwork. She smiled when she looked up at the painting on the wall that she and Dave purchased several years earlier.

Better years, she thought.

She sat under the picture and her thoughts moved to her impending doom.

I have no skills of my own. No credentials. When we get divorced, I know I'll get some money and could live comfortable on that sum, but the majority of money is in the yacht dealership. Dave's father set it up as part of a corporate set-up to protect his investment. That was fair, but now I realize I won't be able to live my current lifestyle. I'll have to get a job with some health insurance benefits. I need to pay into social security so I'll have something in my retirement.

She did the math in her head.

I'm thirty-five now. If I work until I'm sixty-five, I still can get thirty years into social security. But what can I do? I didn't go on to school and I don't have any skills except modeling. I'm too old for that now. Where will I find a good paying job? Maybe I'll have to move up to Atlanta again to find better work. Oh man, I'm in trouble.

She decided that she had enough trauma for one evening, so she got up and continued walking through their beautiful house with heightened appreciation for past memories. She passed by family photos on various tables and picked them up to look at the faces and remember the pictures' scenes. The process continued from room to room as she tried to grasp some understanding as to what may have gone wrong between her and Dave. When she reached the study, she noticed lights coming down the driveway.

Hmmm. I wonder who that is?

She heard the garage door open. It was Dave.

How long was I wandering around? Noel thought.

She glanced at a mantle clock and noticed it was eleven p.m. She was happily surprised that Dave was home so early.

Dave came into the kitchen and set his watch, keys, and cell phone on the side table as usual. He was startled when he turned and saw his wife standing there.

"Noel! I didn't expect to see you standing in back of me."

You wouldn't expect a lot of things from me, but now isn't the time to come clean, Noel thought.

"I was just walking into the kitchen when I heard you. How was your meeting with your client?" Noel asked.

"It was fine. Nothing special," Dave responded.

"Who did you say the meeting was with?"

Noel noticed the change in the iris of his eyes when she asked this question. She knew he wasn't prepared with an answer.

"Oh, It was with no one you know. Just some guy who might buy a boat."

"Good. I hope he buys it. I just like to know the names of your clients. Sometimes it comes in handy when we run into them at other places," she said to push him for some information.

"His name is Frank. Frank Misner," Dave lied.

He felt ashamed of himself and walked away.

Frank Misner, my foot!

CHAPTER 23

Guilt

D ave felt as if he was walking in slow motion as he tried to move past Noel and enter his study. He was ashamed to lie to her, but couldn't bear telling her the truth, just yet. His limbs seemed numb as he purposefully walked, but he felt awkward. He wondered if she noticed. She did.

He partially closed the door to his study and sat at his computer as he usually did at the end of each day. He usually checked his business email to see if any offers to purchase came through after the end of the day. This time, he did quickly check his business email and quickly went to one of the search engines to surf the network. He wanted to waste time until Noel went to bed. Then he wouldn't have to be subjected to any more of her questions. He started looking up past acquaintances to pass the time.

As he mindlessly surfed the net, he reminisced about his past, stressless life. No worries, easy money from his parents, lots of fun time. There had been so many girls in his youth. He was pleased and yet embarrassed as he thought about his past girlfriends. He couldn't remember some of their names.

It was another life. Another time. We were all out for a good time, and there were plenty of good times.

He sat there and continued thinking about his past. Occasionally a smile would cross his face. He thought about his life with Noel. They had built a very good life together. He had fallen in love with her so quickly. He wondered what their future would hold.

This is a big weekend for Noel, with her coordinating the art gala. I can't jeopardize her mental health this week. But I'm going to have to tell her soon, before she hears from someone else.

When enough time passed, he shut down his computer and silently went into the bedroom. He removed his pants and shirt, and slid into the bed where his wife was sleeping peacefully. He laid with his back towards her and quickly fell into sleep. Noel laid there silently, pretending to be asleep.

CHAPTER 24

Preparing for the Gala

D ominic Pepino opened his art and antique gallery, Vino Antiquity, a little over one year ago at the request of his family, but especially his niece, Angela Fratilo. Uncle Dominic had lived in Italy all of his eighty years and had a panache for acquiring beautiful pieces of art and antiques. The problem was that Dominic was a bit of a hoarder. Actually, he was a big hoarder. His home was so covered in art pieces that no one could recall the color of the room's paint. He had artifacts and art laying on the floor, halls, closets, and garage. When Angela heard that his family found out there were additional storage buildings crammed with art, she came up with a plan.

Angela was the daughter of Dominic's brother who had passed away many years prior. Dominic always regarded Angela as his own "daughter" and he looked after her by visiting the US several times a year. Last year, Angela was ready for him when he arrived in Naples, Florida.

"Uncle Dom, you know what would please me the most?" Angela asked her uncle one evening at her home.

"No, my dear. Please tell me," he replied.

"I wish you would spend more time here with me in the U.S. I live in beautiful Naples, but I really don't know anything about art. I wish you could teach me."

"I would love to teach you to have an eye for art. But I would feel more comfortable teaching you with my own collection, which is superior to what I see in the shops here," he beamed.

He walked right into her net, and she was ready for him.

"I have an important job here that I'm very proud to have, so I can't leave my home. But what if you brought some of your art pieces to Naples for display? I know you have many pieces and could part with some. Maybe you could have your own gallery in Naples, so everyone could enjoy your pieces," she suggested.

Dominic starred at her. His first thought was, *How dare she suggest this*. But as the night progressed and he had some time to digest her suggestion, he started asking some questions.

"If I did do such a thing, as to open a gallery, I know there would be many government questions that I wouldn't know how to answer. I'm not an importer. How would I start such a venture? How would I manage the cost of running a gallery? Who would I know to arrange the gallery to my liking? It isn't that I'm against what you are proposing, but I wouldn't know how to go about getting it done."

"You forget that I'm the Chief Financial Officer for a company. I know who to contact to get the documentation and clearances needed. There are a number of people in the area that have galleries that must have used seasoned architects. I would help you, Uncle Dom. I would be so happy to work with you on this project," Angela answered.

Within the next several months, they came to an agreement. Dominic would handle what pieces would make the trip to the US. He hired someone in Italy to work with him and catalog each art piece in his home and in the storage warehouses. In parallel, Angela worked tirelessly on documentation required to start an import business. It wasn't easy, as background checks had to be made on her uncle and on his art collection. But eventually they received the authorization to proceed with a gallery.

Uncle Dominic wasn't a conventional businessman, and he didn't like the various galleries in the area, despite their beauty and success. Dominic had a vision of his own, and he wanted to create an atmosphere of an art and antique museum with the ability of patrons to purchase the pieces. He visited the Naples area every month to meet with his niece and develop plans for the gallery. On one of his visits he made an announcement,

"I have decided not to rent a building on Fifth Avenue like everyone else. Instead, I want to find someone to create my vision. I want a large building, maybe a warehouse, off the main avenue. In it, I want a showroom that will have some furnished rooms decorated with pieces of art or antiques. We can change the art pieces seasonally so that patrons will want to revisit the gallery. In that way, people can see how art should be displayed in their home. I also want a warehouse section of the gallery to hold lots more pieces. Then the patrons can go into the warehouse, after the showroom, and try to find their own treasure."

He continued, "Spare no expense. I want my gallery to be the talk of the town. I want to have events there every year, maybe twice a year, with the rich and famous of the area attending. So, my Angela, do you think this is possible?"

Angela spared no time in answering, "I have the best possible person to help organize your galas, Noel Noirty. She is the best of the best in coordinating such events. And as for your showroom and warehouse, I will put out a request for sketches from a few people I know. Let's see what they come back with."

Within days, Angela had contacted several architects and business developers to bring in some ideas for the project. She also had an idea to ask her business supplier, and friend, Francine Pacque, for any ideas she may have.

Unfortunately for Francine, Angela was also a distant cousin of Dave Noirty, Noel's husband. Francine had been lying to Noel, Dave, and others in Naples about who she was. She had told all of them that she was a representative for her wealthy uncle in Chicago, and was looking for a home and a yacht for him. Francine was thrust into the group as a welcomed friend, and given the keys to a home for sale, next to the Noirty's own home, sailed around on yachts, and dined and partied with the society of Naples. Eventually, at one of the parties at the Noirty's home, Francine's lie was discovered, when Angela identified Francine as one of her company's suppliers, not as a socialite's representative.

While Francine waited to hear if she was going to be fired from the company she represented due to her lie, she decided to work on the gallery proposal. Her sketches and proposal were flawless. She found locked, glass doored cabinets with adjustable shelves and hard wood frames. She sketched a picture of the cabinets lining up half the length of the warehouse. Between the cabinets, she sketched velvet upholstered benches, so customers could sit and enjoy the art. Between the two long sections of cabinets, an open area was available to display large art pieces. Those areas also had similar upholstered chairs and benches, arranged at various angles for people to sit and enjoy the art.

Francine had access to the art manifests which explained the object, color, size, age, cost, etc. She sorted the manifests by color, and suggested that the cabinets be arranged "by color" so that people could quickly identify accents for their homes. She knew exactly the number of cabinets required for the current inventory manifest.

Francine carefully compiled her proposal and dropped it off at Angela's office before normal working hours. She didn't want to run into Angela who had vowed to never speak to her again. Francine had included two notes along with the proposal.

The first was a hand-written note to Angela saying, "I'm sorry," and the second on an invoice from Francine Pacque LLC. It simply read "No Charge".

Angela had been surprised to find the proposal on her desk when she arrived at work, and she didn't want to share the proposal with her uncle in Italy. Dominic insisted that she send it. He immediately gave Francine the job, realizing that she completely understood his vision.

Francine's unethical lies resulted in a lot of fallout with her work community. But luckily for her, she had already tried to undo her wrong prior to the lie being discovered. Francine did not lose her job or the friendships with her new society friends. Angela was the holdout, but she eventually had to work with Francine on uncle Dominic's project. Over time, they became friends again.

Dominic had a grand opening for his gallery at the end of the Naples' busy season. It was a huge success and the gallery immediately became a favorite with decorators and customers. Dominic frequently visited his U.S. gallery and when he returned to his home in Italy, he became even busier with finding more art and antiques in Europe. The venture did wonders for his own personal esteem. His family was ecstatic that he emptied his own home with clutter. Dominic ended up keeping one of his storage warehouses to keep inventory that would subsequently be imported to the U.S. It was truly a labor of love for him.

He hired a gallery manager and several associates to run the day to day business of his gallery. His niece, Angela, found an appropriate accountant to oversee the paperwork for the business. Dominic and Angela became even closer through the gallery which was the original intention for Angela.

As for Francine Pacque, her input into the gallery became more than her original architectural input. She frequently stopped at the gallery to check the cabinet placements and provide input on any improvements that she could provide. She loved visiting the gallery and was proud that she was a part of the start up of the business. She loved spending time with Angela and her uncle Dominic.

The gala occurring on this Saturday was one of the major events in Naples for the year. All of the past customers, society patrons, decorators, and family were invited. Dominic wanted a party to thank his past customers and friends. If anyone decided to purchase a piece of art or an antique due to their visit at the gallery, well, that would be a bonus.

Noel had much to do the day prior to the event. She had professional movers hired to relocate some of the sections of cabinets to provide a dining and dancing area. A professional party planner was also busy with setting up tables, pedestals for flowers, stand-up beverage tables, a bar section, and access to the kitchen area for the caterers.

She was happy that the gala was keeping her mind busy from thinking abut her own personal problems. She cross-checked her invitation list with the list of RSVPs. There were a number of names that she didn't have on her original list.

"Dominic, I see a dozen names that were not on the original invitation list. Do you recognize any of those names? I need to sit them at appropriate dining tables," Noel asked.

"Let me look. I can't remember offhand," Dominic answered as he reviewed the names.

"These are names that came from your husband. He asked if he could invite some of his customers."

Noel was surprised with Dominic's answer and almost spilled the coffee from her mug. She wondered why Dave didn't ask her directly to add some clients. Her blood pressure rose quickly and she felt herself flush with anxiety. Taking the list back from Dominic, she reviewed the names hoping that there wasn't one extra woman's name on that list. The list was all couples, she thankfully realized. Several names she recognized as major customers of her husband's business. She saw one of Dave's salesmen's name on the list and casually dismissed it as help for Dave with the customers he invited. Satisfied, she revised her table seating chart and inserted the high-dollar customer table closer to a prime position in the room.

CHAPTER 25

The Day of the Gala

Francine and Lilly were so excited for tonight's gala. Their day was packed with spa and salon treatments. In the morning, the girls were booked into a spa for facials, nails and manicures. Francine had a swatch of bright pink fabric that matched the gown she was planning on wearing that evening. She wanted the color to coordinate perfectly with her dress. She had purchased a dress from her favorite designer, Antonio Milano, earlier in the season. Her dress had a Monica bodice and hung tightly on her curves. She had a pair of silver high-heeled sandals that she planned to wear with the dress, along with sparkling silver and pink beaded earrings.

Lilly, on the other hand, wanted a younger look, and wanted flat blue-colored nails for her fingers and toes. Earlier in the week, Francine had taken her shopping at one of the malls in the area. Lilly had fallen in love with a long, flowered dress. The gown had a white background and multi-color designs on the dress. It wouldn't have matched the jade pendant she had planned to wear, but since the pendant was now gone, she didn't feel the need to match the missing necklace. Lilly didn't have designer shoes to wear, but she did have some pretty white sandals with a stacked heel that looked great with her dress.

They finished their facials and the women moved into the nail salon for their manicures and pedicures. Lilly was beaming to receive such grand treatment. It was such a luxury for a young woman just finishing college, but her new friends from Naples, Noel, Babs, and Shauna, surprised her with a gift certificate for the treatments as a graduation present. Francine, who a year ago could never afford such treatments when starting her business, found herself one year later with ample funds to receive occasional spa visits. She was happy that both of them were able to partake in them today.

She and Lilly finished their treatments and decided to stop for a bite to eat before going to the hair salon. Soon afterward, they drove to a salon close to downtown Naples suggested by their Naples' friends. They were surprised to find Noel in the salon when they arrived.

"I have to get ready for the party too," Noel exclaimed.

She stared at her friend in amazement. Noel had her hair half done, with some large loopy curls on the top of her head, and the balance of her hair loosely curled onto her shoulders. She still looked absolutely beautiful with half of her hair ratted and undone. Noel's complexion and makeup was flawless. Jewels bedazzled her fingers and her high-heeled black sandals displayed brightly painted red nails with one diamond toe ring on her middle toe. Her tight black satin pants peeked out of her salon apron.

She looks ready to be photographed for a hair magazine.

It was finally time for Lilly and Francine's treatments, and they were led to their respective hair salon chairs. Francine decided to have her hair pulled off her face in a fancy up-do. It was a different look for her and she felt like she wanted a change. She knew she would have a professional picture taken at the gala and liked the thought of having a different look.

Lilly didn't know what to have done to her board-straight hair.

The stylist suggested pulling just a few front strands up and off her face and fasten them with some fancy hairpins. When she was done, Lilly admired herself in the mirror. She looked young, beautiful, and like she belonged to this exclusive community. Her smile didn't fade on the entire journey back to the condo.

CHAPTER 26

The Gala

The gala at Vino Antiquity began at seven p.m. Noel had a professional party planner stationed at the event for the last two days to ensure that everything would be done correctly. She had spoken to the planner several times earlier in the day, and everything was ready for the event. She breathed a little easier as she dressed for the gala.

This was, in her mind, the event of the year. The fact that she was picked for overseeing the event, gave her a reason to purchase a new gown. She had purchased her gown on a trip earlier in the year in New York City. She carefully chose a color that would stand out in the crowd but not be too overt. She found a beautiful cobalt blue gown with flirty, off the shoulder cap sleeves. Always a vision, she knew she looked like her past model days when she walked out of her dressing room.

"Wow!" exclaimed her husband, Dave. "I've never seen that one on you before."

"It's new. I'm glad you like it," Noel happily answered her husband's compliment.

She was overwhelmed that her husband took notice of her. Although both of them had been busy, their relationship was at best strained this last month. She stole a look towards Dave as he was looping his tie.

"Oh, Dave. Not that tie, please. I forgot to tell you that I bought you a new one to coordinate with my dress. Do you mind?" she asked as she brought a bright blue tie out of the closet.

She hurried over to him and helped him tie the knot. She noticed the Dave was smiling and watching her as she worked. She relaxed a bit more and smiled.

"I bought this Lorenzo Cana Italian silk tie in New York, when I bought my dress. There! Now you're done."

She stepped back to admire her husband. He looked elegant and handsome in his formal black suit and new tie. She stood next to him and studied their image in the mirror. Dave glanced in the full length mirror and nodded with approval. He turned to his wife and gave her a tight hug before walking out of the room. She stood there alone.

I love him so much. I can't believe that our marriage is crumbling.

They arrived at the gala an hour before any of the guests would arrive. A hired valet relieved them of their car and they entered the art gallery. She noticed several large pedestals with even larger floral arrangements flanking the front door. A custom sign stating "Private Event…By Invitation Only" was next to one of the pedestals as well as a temporary valet station with several attendants present. She was pleased with her first impression.

Domino Pepino, Angela Fratilo and her boyfriend, and the event staff were busy checking last minute details when the Noirty's walked in. The front showroom of the gallery was more elaborately furnished than usual, with expensive art and antiques. Usually, only a few high dollar items were kept unlocked in the room, but tonight's invitees were chosen because of their past patronage, or were financially vetted prior to receiving their invitations.

The front portion of the warehouse was reappointed with lavish table settings. Dominic insisted on having bright, Italian fabrics rather than the usual white linen tablecloths. The effect was breathtaking as each table had different ornate fabric, reminiscent of old world Europe, with white dishes and napkins. Dominic chose different antique pieces for each table. Some had antique candelabras while others had small statues adorned as their centerpiece. All tables were full of exotic flowers and candles.

The display cabinets that held the remaining art and antiques also had flower arrangements on pedestals next to the various viewing couches and chairs. Inconspicuous "wish list" notecards were set in various places for partygoers to note future purchase desires.

Noel walked to the small orchestra that were setting up, and asked them to start the music at six-thirty. She knew that guests would start arriving at that time, and wanted a comfortable environment filled with music when they entered the main dining venue.

Liquor was set up on an antique bar that Dominic insisted on using for his event. It was a large bar consisting of two mahogany pieces. One piece was a twelve foot long counter, and the other piece was a bar shelf unit with cabinets holding glasses and liquor. The bar looked like it was always there.

Next to the bar were several large tables set up with appetizers. Dominic spared no expense, as there were large platters of caviar and pates, along with delicious looking and smelling puff pastries filled with meat and vegetables. As she walked along the tables, she noticed that the caterers used various local specialty vendors for some extra variety. She had insisted on that, so that many vendors from the area would be involved in the gala.

Invitees started arriving at six-thirty, just as Noel had predicted. Dominic stood inside the gallery, close to the front entrance door, and proudly greeted each guest. A party event hostess checked each guest against the master invitation list before opening a barrier into the gallery. Angela Fratilo, stood next to the hostess so she could hear the name and whisper it to her uncle prior to the official greet by Dominic.

By seven p.m., the party was in full swing, with patrons lounging through the front gallery, grazing at the appetizer table, looking at art in the locked windowed cabinets, and of course, frequenting the bar. Noel was pleased and everyone looked happy.

Of course, all of Noel's society girlfriends were at the party. Shauna and Tony Delgado, Babs and William Simmons, Mitzi and Paul Vandelooth, and Pepper and Joe Franklin. The friends greeted each other and complimented Noel on arranging the function. Pepper and Joe Franklin were very excited that Noel had contacted their son, Dennis, to provide guitar music during the main orchestra's scheduled breaks.

"We were so surprised when Dennis told us that he was going to perform here. We didn't know that you knew he was a musician. He said he didn't remember meeting you when he performed at the Naples Art Show," Pepper said.

She smiled while nodding, knowing that she couldn't reveal that she was disguised when meeting their son. But she knew that all of her friends commented on Dennis' good musical skills during their lunch after the fair, and thought she could give Dennis some great experience by performing here.

"I didn't meet him at the art show, but I did see him perform. Babs, Shauna, and Francine also heard him and they all liked his performance, so I thought he would be a good addition to this function," she replied.

Joe Franklin gave her a big hug, "This means a lot to us, Noel. Thank you."

She continued talking to her friends when she heard Francine's voice. Turning around, she saw Francine and Lilly approach. Of course, Francine looked beautiful in her gown with her hair partially pulled off her face. She quickly noted that this hairstyle should be how Francine would wear her hair on her wedding day. Now, all she had to do was try to get Francine and her boyfriend on that path. Lilly was wearing her multi-colored floral dress with a white background. She looked youthful and perfect for the venue. Lilly was talking excitedly to the other girls about her new dress and pale blue nails. The women went to the bar to get a refreshment and mingle with their other colleagues and friends.

Noel was, as always, watching the room to make sure everything was perfect and that guests were enjoying themselves. She raised her glass towards her husband and his salesman, Josh Fairmont, from the marina in acknowledgement and returned her gaze to her girlfriends. But something seemed familiar and uncomfortable. She couldn't put her finger on it, so she walked over towards her husband and the small group.

Dave saw Noel coming and his face tensed up. He took a quick drink and looked at his saleman's date with widened eyes. She saw Noel coming too and moved a little closer to Josh.

"Hello, Mrs. Noirty," Josh said and extended his hand.

"Josh, how long have you known me? You should know to call me Noel by now," Noel said and have him a small hug.

Dave smiled but said nothing and took another long sip of his martini. She was disappointed that no one introduced Josh's date. She thought Dave might not know her name and she frowned towards

Josh that he didn't have manners to introduce his beautiful date. She took the opportunity.

"Hello, I'm Noel Noirty," she said to Brianna and held out her hand.

"Its nice to meet you, Noel. I'm Brianna Flagler," Brianna answered with a slightly higher-pitched voice than usual.

"Josh, where are your manners? Why aren't you showing your beautiful girlfriend around the gallery, and introduce her to some of the other people you know?"

Josh didn't know how to answer and looked toward Dave for an answer. He nodded and took Brianna's arm to lead her away. Noel watched them depart into the crowd.

"Josh is acting funny. Is this their first date? He seemed so rigid and nervous. If he's not careful, someone will steal her up with all the alpha males around here," Noel said to her husband.

Dave just smiled but did not respond. Soon he headed towards some of his country club friends, leaving her uncharacteristically by herself. She shrugged off the feeling and mingled with the other patrons.

At eight p.m., dinner was served. Dominic stood at the front table and thanked his audience for the wonderful year since his gallery opened. Dominic was an emotional man and a tear fell down his cheek while he talked. He told the audience that his life had been empty since the death of his wife five years ago, but he now felt a purpose and joy since coming to Naples and opening his business. He raised his glass and thanked God for his good fortune and new "family". The audience clapped and stood up to honor him. Dominic cried while Angela put her arm around him and gave her uncle a kiss on his cheek.

She and Dave sat with major patrons of the gallery. All of them were wealthy people that Dave and she knew for many years. They participated in small talk about their families, vacation trips, and business successes. She smiled and joined in the conversation, but she couldn't get over the uncomfortable feeling she had. She excused herself and went to the restroom. As she walked towards Josh and Brianna's table, Brianna lifted her hand and nervously fingered her earrings while pushing her hair behind her ear.

Hmmm, Do I know her? Noel asked herself. *Maybe she works somewhere I go?*

She thought about the young woman and where she may have seen her before. *Was it at a hairdresser?*

She continued to think about the woman's hair and her motion of flipping of her hair in back of her ear. Noel's eye's widened and her mouth gaped open.

"He had Josh bring his tramp here?" she said aloud, exasperated.

She stormed out of the restroom and walked briskly to the edge of the dinner table settings and stopped. Dave spotted her as she walked. He noticed her fast movements and sudden stop. Her eyes starred at her husband. She was not smiling, in fact, her face was reddened and her bare shoulders and neckline were blotchy.

Oh, oh. Dave thought and stood up.

He intended to walk to Noel and ask her if she needed some air, but Noel was already on the move. She was walking straight towards Brianna.

All the etiquette and poise that she had exhibited over the years transformed into one boiling rage. Her girlfriends and some of the guests noticed her almost running towards a table. The room was almost immediately quiet as the guests quietly watched for whatever was going to transpire.

She stopped directly in back of Brianna and spoke directly to the woman.

"I want to talk to you. Now! Get up so we can let these other people eat. Josh, you stay right here."

Brianna quickly wiped her mouth with her napkin and placed the soiled napkin next to her plate. She turned her head slightly towards Dave Noirty's table. She saw that he was already headed towards her direction. Brianna slowly stood up, knowing that it was Noel talking to her. She stood and slowly turned towards Noel, realizing that her entire body was shaking.

"How dare you come here, you tramp!" Noel said loudly.

"Noel! Quiet!" Dave said, taking his wife's arm and whirling here around.

He took large strides as he guided Noel out of the dining area. Brianna followed with her head down trying to avoid the faces staring directly at her.

Angela put her hand on her uncle's shoulder before he stood up and intervened. She didn't know what the problem was, but interpreted it that Dave was in big trouble. Some of the dinner guests did not know that anything happened and continued with their meals and with their conversation. But Angela could see other guests were turned to watch the trio leave the room. She heard murmurs of gossip being bantered around.

She stood up and motioned that everyone should resume their dinner, knowing that some of them would be too busy gossiping to even notice that she stood up. Angela looked towards Francine and motioned with her head that Francine should follow Dave, Noel, and the woman. Francine obediently got up and hurried out of the room.

"Did you see that?" Babs said to Shauna and Lilly.

"I saw something, but what happened?" Lilly asked.

"I didn't see it. What happened?" Shauna inquired.

"Noel just called some woman a 'tramp' and she, Dave, and the woman stormed out of the room," Babs excitedly related.

"Oh, my God! It must have been the woman that Antonio spotted with Dave. Where was she sitting?" Shauna asked.

Babs motioned her head in the direction of the table and Shauna remembered seeing the young, beautiful woman who was sitting there earlier. Lilly looked confused and worried, and turned to watch where Francine headed off. Lilly took a deep breath and a sip of her wine, hoping that everything would be good for her friends.

Francine left the room and searched the warehouse aisles listening for voices.

She heard Dave's voice saying, "Calm down, Noel. I can explain." Mostly she heard sobbing from Noel and Noel's voice saying, "Don't touch me!"

Francine walked around the corner until she was seen by Dave. She didn't know what to say, so when Dave saw her, she sat down on one of the benches at the end of the aisle and turned in the direction of the dinner guests. Francine thought that at least she could keep other spectators away from the disturbance.

"Noel, Noel, let me explain," Dave pleaded.

He tried to put his arm around his wife, but she shrugged him off. Finally, he pulled a chair over for her to sit.

"At least sit down, Noel."

"How could you do this to me…to us!" she stammered as tears rolled down her face.

She pointed to Brianna but didn't say any of the foul things she was thinking. She wanted to regain her composure before she began.

Dave brought over two more chairs, one for Brianna and one for him. They all sat down. Brianna kept her head down, but continually stole glances of Noel.

"I better go home," Brianna said weakly.

"No, please stay. It's time we came clean, because everyone will be talking now," Dave said quietly to her.

Noel overheard her husband whisper to Brianna. She couldn't believe her husband of fourteen years would treat her so off-handed.

"Of course the tramp should leave. How dare that she stays," Noel exclaimed.

Finally able to control her emotion, she glared at her husband, "Sure. Have her stay. It isn't as if anyone here would notice that you have your mistress here. It isn't as if anyone won't talk about it. I'll probably be stopped by several lawyers in the crowd asking if I need a good divorce lawyer."

Brianna's hand slapped over her mouth hiding her gaping expression. "Dave, please tell her. Please!"

"What's to tell? I've seen this before. I just didn't think my husband would be so callous to do it in front of all our friends and neighbors," Noel blurted.

Dave looked lovingly at Brianna, and then gave the same expression to Noel.

He slid his chair close to his wife and said, "Noel, She isn't my girlfriend. She's my daughter."

Noel's head flew up towards her husband and then towards the woman. She was speechless.

"It's true, Noel. That's why I came down to Florida. I wanted to meet my father," Brianna said softly.

"What? Dave, why wouldn't you have told me this before?"

"Because I didn't know until about a month ago. And, I wanted to be sure it was true before I told you," Dave answered while taking Noel's hand.

Noel's eyes searched Dave's eyes for answers. Tears rolled down her face trying to absorb the truth.

Dave smiled and shook his head that what he said was true. His eyes were filled with tears, worried as to what his wife might think and do next.

She looked towards Brianna and searched her eyes as well. She thought she saw a scared young woman looking back at her.

She rose from her chair and stood for a few seconds making sure her footing was secure because she was dizzy from the news. Brianna stood up nervously looking at Dave and then at Noel.

Noel took a step towards the woman and embraced her tightly. Brianna embraced Noel back and soon both women were crying.

Dave was shocked that when looked at his wife's face again, she was beaming. Her eyes were glowing and he could see goosebumps on her arms. Brianna was holding onto Noel as tightly as Noel was holding her. Tears of joy steaming down her face as she watched her father's expression change from anxiety to happiness.

Francine was trying to give the trio some privacy but as she looked in their direction, she was confused by what she saw. She saw the women embraced with Dave's arms securely around both of them. All three of them were crying.

"What in the world is happening," Francine thought as she saw Noel frantically motioning for her to come over by them.

Francine hurried down the row of displays until she was in the clearing with them.

"Francine, I want you to meet someone. This is my daughter'," Noel said before turning towards the young woman and asking, "Dear, what was your name again?"

CHAPTER 27

The Truth Comes Out

Noel felt confusion and relief through her body as she tried to grasp the information. Francine stood there looking only confused but she linked her arm into Noel's to steady her friend. Dave looked nervously at his wife and reached out to her with no response. He knew he had to quickly explain to his wife the situation. He motioned all of them to some nearby chairs and benches and they obliged.

He explained that he was quite a wild young man in his youth. He had ample funds from his parents so he frequently traveled while he attended college in Boston. One of his favorite haunts was New York City, where he and his friends could go clubbing all night. He explained that he met and had intimate relationships with a number of young women, which he thought wonderful at the time, but now he was regretting his foolish behavior.

He related that he met Brianna's mother on one of his trips and they had an instant connection which led him to going to New York every weekend for about a month.

"She broke off our budding relationship citing that I was too much of a runaround'. I remember that she said she was going to go back with her old boyfriend who was more stable and lived in New York."

He admitted that he felt bad when she cut off things so abruptly, but he was young and stupid, and started dating another girl shortly afterwards.

"I stopped going to New York after the break-up and never heard from her again. Please believe me that I had no knowledge that your mother was pregnant."

Brianna explained that her mother married her ex-boyfriend, and he raised her as his own daughter, even after they divorced six years ago, when she was fourteen. She explained that her mother became ill with cancer and passed away several months ago.

"Her last conversation with me was a suggestion to find my real father, Dave Noirty, and try to kindle a relationship."

Brianna added that she was shocked to hear that her "dad" was not her real father.

"It was devastating news at a time where I was already fragile knowing that my mother was dying. I didn't know what to believe. But I asked my 'dad' and he eventually confirmed what my mother said was true. He knew my mother was pregnant and that he had not been dating her at the time of conception," Brianna said and paused for a moment before adding, "He assured me that he loved me as his own daughter and urged me not to find my real father."

"I waited a month after my mother passed to type in "Dave Noirty" on the internet. I found him easily, as well as photographs of him and his boat dealership."

She explained that she had already found several pictures of Dave and her mother at the time they were dating among her mother's personal belongings.

"It was easy to see that the man in the pictures was the same man that owned the boat dealership. His hair, smile, build...all were the same."

Brianna admitted that she contemplated not reaching out to her real father, but curiosity got the better of her, plus her 'dad' was remarried with several other children of his own.

Brianna opened her small purse and retrieved several items. She had copies of the pictures that she had sent to Dave, along with a copy of the letter she wrote. She explained to Noel that she sent the pictures to Dave at his place of business. Brianna opened a copy of the letter she sent and read the letter aloud:

Dear Mr. Noirty,

We have never met, but we are bound together through my mother, Alicia Banneta. You and she dated many years ago in New York City. I have enclosed some pictures that I found among my mother's things that show that you and she had a close relationship a long time ago.

My mother recently passed away after battling breast cancer for three years. Shortly before she passed, she told me startling news, that I have confirmed with my father verbally. She told me that my father was not my real father. She told me my real father was a wonderful young man she dated briefly, named Dave Noirty. She told me that she knew you now lived in Naples, FL, but that she had never told you about me.

I was shocked and disheartened that the father I had always known was not really my own, and scared to reach out to you. I'm sure you are shocked as well, so I'm sorry.

I am not asking for anything from you but the opportunity to know the truth. I hope that sometime we can talk and meet. I'm willing to share any paperwork or undergo any tests to verify the truth, but if you don't want any contact from me, I understand and will not contact you again.

I hope to hear from you.

Regards,

Brianna Flagler

Francine didn't want to ruin the moment, but she didn't want to see her friends hurt again, so she inquired, "I hope this is all true, for all of you. But have you thought about getting DNA testing to verify?"

Noel's eyebrows raised at the suggestion, but Dave quickly interceded.

"Yes, we have had our DNA tested and I received the results this week. The results proved that Brianna is my daughter. Its one of the reasons I asked her to come here tonight, to get used to this crowd."

"I don't understand what you mean. What 'crowd'?," Noel added.

"Actually, it really didn't have anything to do with our friends and neighbors here. Noel, I didn't quite know how to tell you or how you would react. In fact, I haven't been meeting clients when I've left the house in the evening. I've been meeting with Brianna, so we could get to know each other a bit. I didn't want to tell you until the DNA testing was complete."

"I know what you've been doing, because I have been following you. I even sat at the bar at one of the restaurants where you two were eating. But I thought you were having an affair," Noel admitted.

Dave started to laugh.

"I should have suspected that I couldn't get anything by you. I wanted to tell you a few days ago, but I knew you were so busy arranging this party that I didn't want anything else to interfere."

"The party! We have to get back in there. Everyone will be wondering what is going on," Noel exclaimed.

Noel and Dave walked hand-in-hand back into the dining area

of the warehouse with every guests' eyes on them. Brianna and Francine followed closely behind. When they saw the confusion by some friends, and the desperation for gossip on other faces, Noel quietly walked up to Dominic at the main table and asked if she could make an announcement.

"By all means, Noel. You are in charge of this event," Dominic answered.

She motioned to her husband and Brianna to join her by the table. She took Brianna's hand and asked Dave to take her other hand. The guests looked stunned and the room was quiet.

"May I have everyone's attention please?" Noel announced.

The crowd was waiting with baited breath.

"I want to apologize to all of this community for my outburst a few minutes ago. I hope you will accept it, as it was so opposite of my usual behavior. But most of you know how important I hold 'family'. Dave and I were not blessed with any children so I absorbed myself in community work for this town. I had not had the pleasure of meeting this woman prior to this evening, and I mistakenly thought she was my enemy trying to ruin my family. I was wrong. In fact, she is our family."

She raised her arm holding Brianna's hand and Dave raised his arm as well so the three of them were in unity. She nodded her head towards her husband to continue the speech. Dave took a step forward and started his explanation,

"I'll make this short and sweet. Several weeks ago, I found out that this beautiful, young woman was my daughter from a college day romance with a wonderful woman who had recently passed away. I would like to introduce all of you to Brianna Flagler, our daughter," Dave said while beaming at Brianna and then at his wife.

There were a few gasps in the crowd as well as others murmuring to each other. Francine started clapping and stood up. Soon the community joined in. It was a wondrous sight.

"Oh my God!" Babs expounded and stared at Shauna who nodded in disbelief as she clapped. Lilly Lee displayed only joy as she bounced up and down in her seat.

"Maybe she and I can be friends?" Lilly excitedly said to Francine who had returned to her chair.

"She's about my age and she doesn't know anyone here either."

"You never cease to amaze me, Lilly. That is a great idea. Why don't we wander over to her table when Brianna sits down and rescue her before everyone starts introducing themselves to her."

Francine remembered that Brianna came with a date. Her eyes searched to find Josh sitting at one of the tables. He looked relieved at the news. She watched as Dave and Noel introduced Brianna to Dominic, Angela, and several other good friends. Soon Dave escorted Brianna back to Josh's table so she could continue eating. Her plate was still there, uneaten. A waiter scurried over to relieve her plate and bring a fresh, hot entree. Dave shook Josh's hand and thanked him again for agreeing to taking Brianna as a date. They exchanged a few words before Dave pattted him on the shoulder and looked for his wife among the crowd.

He took a moment to reflect on how lucky he was. He gazed at the crowd and realized that most of the people here were friends, colleagues, or customers. He watched his amazing wife "work" the tables by acknowledging someone at each table and saying a few words. He looked at Brianna who shyly was trying to eat and listen to others at the table. He smiled when he saw Francine and Lilly sit down at two empty seats next to Brianna. Lilly put her hand on

Brianna's forearm and introduced herself. Soon the two youngest women at this party were conversing and laughing as if they knew each other for years.

Dave walked to the bar and asked for a bourbon on the rocks. He enjoyed his drink in silence for a minute until one of his friends joined him in a small toast to what had just transpired.

CHAPTER 28

Another Incident

The party continued until one a.m. with dancing, drinking, and late night appetizers. Dominic's party was officially the event of the season with everyone agreeing on that it was a wonderful event. A band played a variety of music pleasing everyone's tastes. People wandered down the warehouse aisles writing down wish list notecards for potential future purchases. People wandered through the front gallery showroom and sat on the antique furniture and talked about how certain pieces would fit into their own homes. Even street passerby's stopped in cars to take in the view of elegantly dressed people in the lightened showroom.

Dominic met several key individuals in the community which he enjoyed and appreciated. He was happy and a little drunk by the end of the party. When the last guest left at one-thirty a.m., Dominic collapsed into one of the gallery couches and asked the others to give him a few winks of sleep. They obliged as the hired help cleaned up the party for another hour. At two-thirty a.m., Dominic's niece, Angela Fratilo, woke her uncle from his sleep and helped him into her car. By three a.m., only one security guard remained for the balance of the night. Cleanup would continue in the morning with movers arranged to put the warehouse cabinets back into their original display design.

Dominic arrived back at Vino Antiquities at about noon, anxious to see the cleanup progress and pay any overages to the working crew. The crew was about done as Dominic did his final inspection. The art and antiques that were used during the party were carefully stored in one section so that Dominic could direct them back into the proper cabinet or location. He and his store manager were in this process when something looked unusual to Dominic.

He excused himself and walked up to the aisle. He gazed left and right looking at his art inventory in the cabinets. His displays were arranged by color so that customers could easily shop for coordinating accents for their homes. He passed green vases, dishes and pilsners. He looked at the green pillows and jade ended knives. He scanned his green light shades and antique ornaments. He slowly scanned his precious stone jewelry. Alexandrite necklaces from Egypt, green garnet earrings from Asia, and his prize eight-point-nine carat emerald ring. It was all there, but something looked "off". He removed his keys and opened the locked, glass cabinet.

"I think someone jarred the cabinet. They are not displayed as nice as before. Maybe the movers knocked against them," he questioned his manager.

He started repositioning the jewelry when the gemstone on the ring tumbled off the setting. Dominic frowned, not knowing how that could have happened. Picking up the stone, he saw that the stone was a green piece of glass, not the one-hundred-and-forty-thousand dollar emerald that was previously there.

The manager gasped, "How is that possible?"

The manager poked his head in the cabinet as if the other stone had magically rolled off the setting.

"We had a thief. A very good one," Dominic said. "Call the police."

CHAPTER 29

Where Did He Go?

Two squad cars arrived almost immediately with sirens blaring. The policeman from the first car came directly into the gallery with the second one surveying the outside of the building.

The manager greeted the police and explained what he and the owner of the gallery had just found. Dominic was introduced but remained sitting in an armchair. He was ashen and visibly shaking. Dominic was in his late seventies and although his health was excellent, the extent of this robbery made his breath short and loud. One of the moving crew handed him a bottle of water. The head of the moving crew was nervous that he or one of his crew could be suspected of the crime.

The officer took copious notes but he quickly called another officer that he thought had some previous experience in jewelry theft, Officer Breakly. The officer was off-duty, but when he heard of the most recent crime, he indicated that he would arrive there within the hour.

The officers contained the area to ensure that nothing more would leave the premises. They informed the several people working there that their vehicles could not leave until they were completely inspected. Since the emerald was so small, the inspection could take days. They also said that each of them had to be searched before they could leave. There were objections from the small group working, but they also understood. They were allowed to call home to explain that they would be detained for several hours and that they would need to be picked up by someone. The workers scrambled to make their calls all under the watchful eyes of the police.

Dominic asked if he could call his niece, Angela Fratilo, and he made the call thereafter. Angela quickly called Noel.

"Poor Dominic. He was so happy with the gala last night and woke up to this nightmare," Noel said. "I'm going over there. I arranged the party and have the lists of everyone who worked or was invited there."

"I'm on my way there now," Angela reported. "I have to make sure Uncle Dom is ok."

When Angela arrived at Vino Antiquities she saw a sea of squad cars. She hurried in and quickly located her uncle and comforted him. He was still a bit hung over and tired, but he told her that he had pictures and appraisals of the ring that he gave the police. Angela assured him that he was also insured for the loss.

"The police are reviewing my video tapes to see if they can see the theft. If not, everyone at the party will be suspects, including us," Dominic revealed. "These people won't be too happy to find that out, will they? That will probably end my business here in Naples."

"Don't jump to conclusions. I see Noel arrived with the list of people in attendance last night. She's talking to Officer Breakly right now," Angela stated.

Hours passed while the police reviewed facts. Dominic, Angela, and Noel sat patiently in the front gallery in case there were more questions. Finally, Officer Breakly and another officer motioned for the three to come into the gallery office.

"We found your theif on the video. See if you recognize him,"

Officer Breakly asked.

The video showed a man in a dark coverall and wearing a ski mask walk up to the cabinet. He kept his head away from the camera and leaned against the preceding cabinet as he put a small tool into the lock. The door of the cabinet sprung open slightly as he carefully put a gloved hand into the cabinet. They could not see the emerald stone ring in his hand when he closed the cabinet door. The man walked backwards until he was out of camera range.

"I have several videos recording the gallery and warehouse. Maybe you can find him on another one," Dominic stated.

"We are looking into that, but so far, all we see are men in tuxedos or suits on those videos. We are going to have to take the tapes to our office to compare time stamps. Something will turn up," the officer said. "At least all of you are off our suspect list. We know he is a thin man, under six feet tall."

Dominic started laughing. "This is the first time I am glad to be fat!"

All of them had a well deserved laugh.

Officer Breakly interrupted the moment of fun, "It is certain that the theif knew the value of the emerald. There were many other valuable pieces to steal, but he carefully took only that piece. Do you have any ideas as to how someone would know the value?"

Dominic shook his head. It was Noel who started speaking, "The people invited have lavish tastes. Most of them have expensive jewels and art. Some of them are dealers or jewelers. I'm afraid that it could be any of them."

"Well, as I said before, we will compare the time stamps with the video of the theif and see who comes into view on another tape. We will also go through your invitee list to see if anyone has a past criminal affection to jewelry," Officer Breakly added. "By the way, would any of you know who of these attendees may have been at either of the art shows where the other two robberies occurred?"

The group looked at one another and shook their heads and answered in unison, "It could have been any of them."

CHAPTER 30

Lilly and Francine's Confession

Morning found Francine and Lilly packing their clothes as they had to check out of the rented condo. Francine felt bad that she wasn't able to be at Vino Antiquities for the investigation, but Lilly's vacation was ending today. Her flight was later this afternoon. Their plan was to go to her small apartment for the balance of Lilly's trip.

Lilly's experience at the gala was wonderful. It was the first formal event that she ever attended and she had a wonderful time dining, conversing, and dancing. She did exchange email addresses with Dave's daughter, Brianna, and she hoped that the two of them would become better friends. Lilly gushed over all the details of her time in Naples, talking excitedly about the art fairs, beaches, and restaurants. She clearly had a great time.

Francine decided to breech the topic of Lilly's stolen necklace, "Lilly, what about your necklace? It may never get found, I'm afraid. Also, you are going to have some hospital bills that your parents are going to receive. When are you going to tell them?"

Lilly's face turned pale, despite her slight suntan. She nodded and said, "I'm afraid to tell them."

"Then why don't we do it now, together. They need to know."

Although Lilly was scared to tell her parents that she lost her

146

mother's heirloom necklace, she knew that Francine's advice was correct. She knew it would be easier to tell her parents with Francine present so she nodded to her friend and placed the call.

Her parents had been waiting to hear about Lilly's trip to Naples, Florida, so they eagerly listened as Lilly told them about all the things she did on her trip. Lilly carefully explained the white sand beaches, completely pristine, that your feet sank several inches into with each step. She told them that she received a little suntan, which her mother previously warned her against. Lilly fondly related the new friends she met, including the dinner at Noel and Dave's house, and several dinners and luncheons throughout the week. She related the party details, not including the drama between Dave and Noel at the party, adding that she was sending many pictures of her trip so her parents could see the wonderful time she had.

"This is all wonderful news, Lilly. We were worried about you traveling alone. I'm so happy that Francine's graduation present of this trip turned out so well for you," Lilly's mother said.

"Yes, it was a wonderful trip that I will always remember," Lilly said. "But there is something else that I have to tell you, and you will be ashamed of me."

Her mother and father were taken aback by her words. After assuring them that she was fine and very sorry for what she was going to share with them, Lilly continued,

"I wanted to be liked by Francine's friends in Florida. They are wealthy, society women. I was afraid that I would be seen as a silly young girl. I wanted to look like I belonged. These women are flashy and wear designer clothes and expensive jewelry. So, I took your jade necklace to wear."

"You took your grandmother's necklace? That was supposed

to be for your wedding, Lilly," mother exclaimed. "Did something happen? Did it break?"

Lilly started to cry as she stammered some words in Japanese. She looked at Francine as if helpless. Francine motioned to hand her the phone.

"Mr. and Mrs. Lee, this is Francine. Something terrible happened to Lilly," she said as she heard gasps on the phone.

"She wanted to wear her heirloom necklace to the gala last night. But she didn't want to lose it during travel, so she wore it. It was beautiful and I admired it immediately when I picked her up at the airport. I took Lilly to an art show rather than to our condo so she was still wearing the necklace. Lilly was waiting in a safe spot by some stores while I located my other friends. When we came to get Lilly, we couldn't find her."

"What? What happened to her? Where did she go?" Mr. Lee asked.

"This is the terrible part. We found her unconscious on the side of the building. She had hit her head and fell down several stairs. We immediately called for an ambulance and the police arrived quickly. Lilly had to spend the night in the hospital. She luckily did not have a concussion."

The Lee's quickly turned their attention to their daughter's well-being, quickly forgetting the jade necklace. After several minutes of assuring them that Lilly was fine, she continued to explain about the necklace.

"When we found Lilly, there were beads laying on the ground. I assumed that it was here necklace, which I had no idea was valuable. But the beads turned out to be from a costume bracelet she was wearing. Lilly's purse and the jade necklace were gone. Shortly later, the police found her purse and her identification cards, even her charge cards. Only the money was gone. Lilly was frantic because her necklace wasn't there. The police quickly deduced that someone recognized that the necklace was valuable and either pushed Lilly down the steps or hit her on the head before taking her necklace and purse."

She continued, "That's not all. There was another robbery at the art show with jewelry from one of the art booths. It happened again at another show this week. But the worst was that an expensive emerald piece was stolen from the gala we attended last night. It appears that we have a theif in Naples."

"I'm surprised that our Lilly would take my mother's necklace on a trip. But it is only a necklace. Yes, it is an expensive antique. That is true. But it is nothing in comparison to my daughter's safety. I'm so happy that our daughter is well," Mrs. Lee stated.

"Mama, I'm so sorry to disappoint you," Lilly said.

"Lilly, 'You' are not a disappointment. Only this one tiny event is disappointing. You are my daughter and are our pride and joy," Lilly's mother said while crying. "But I want you to understand how valuable that necklace was, Lilly. It was an heirloom, yes, but I never told you the monetary value. That necklace went back centuries. It was passed from generation to generation to the first daughter. The clasp and thread had been changed several times, but the carved pendant was the original. I'm not sure of the value now, but it had been appraised for over fifty-thousand dollars about ten years ago."

"I didn't know that, mama. You never told me it was that old or that valuable," Lilly exclaimed.

"I didn't think I had to, because to my family, it was priceless. It was our link to our ancestors," Lilly's mother explained. "Now it's gone. I hope the police find it, but it probably was quickly sold for a few dollars."

"I don't think so, Mrs. Lee. The police are pretty confident that the thefts are connected. The thief is probably a professional. He probably took one look at the pendant on Lilly and knew it was valuable," she answered.

There were more tears and questions about the robberies until the conversation got around to Lilly's experience at the art gala. Her parents listened intently as Lilly explained the event. Her voice lightened as she spoke about her friends and how they included her in everything from sitting with them for dinner to dancing. She explained the women's dresses and jewels, and explained how the men were primarily in tuxedos. Lilly's parents were happy that their daughter had a chance to experience a different lifestyle prior to getting a post-graduation job.

"Several of them asked if I would like them as an employment reference. They said that they didn't know me for a long while, but it could help me to have some strong, established references. Of course, Francine would be my first reference," Lilly said while looking at her friend.

Hearing that their daughter had an impact on some of the people in Naples, made Lilly's father very happy. The tone of the conversation became much better until they said their good-byes.

Lilly flew back to Chicago later that day with renewed confidence. She had a great life lesson during the last week on how successful people interacted, dressed, and lived. She was ready to start her own job search to build her career.

Francine's phone rang. She looked at the phone and saw that it was her boyfriend, Brian. She gritted her teeth and muttered, "Time to come clean."

"Hi, honey," Brian said. "How was the party?"

"Oh, it was over the top. Lilly looked gorgeous and I think I looked ok too. The arrangements, food, drink, music, everything was amazing. I wish you would have been here."

"I should have been there, but I understand that you needed to spend time with Lilly. Jonathan and I watched some movies and went to the park. We had the usual pizza, not caviar like you," he said with a grin.

They talked more about the party and about Brian's son before she said she needed to talk to him about a few things. In the next twenty minutes, she filled him in on what had transpired with Noel and Dave Noirty. She related Noel's suspicion about Dave having and affair, how they studied how to blend into the crowd, how they practiced their surveillance techniques, and how Noel spied on her husband. She told him about Brianna, and that she ended up to be Dave's daughter, not his mistress. Francine explained that the final confrontation happened in front of all the party guests and how Noel and Dave ultimately introduced Brianna to everyone as their daughter.

"You went undercover with Noel at a Naples' art show? Are you crazy?" Brian asked. "Isn't everyone all 'blinged up' in Naples with glitzy jewelry and clothes?"

Francine giggled, "Yes, they are full of bling."

"You must have been hidden within the bling," Brian added.

"I guess you're right. That's exactly what we did."

"So, did the police find whoever took Lilly's necklace yet?"

Francine grimaced as she knew what she told Brian next would hit a nerve. Finally she took her own advice about owning up quickly to a situation. She explained that there had been two robberies since the original one where Lilly and one art exhibitor had something stolen. She explained that another one involved another art exhibitor at another art fair, but last night had been another one at Dominic's gallery.

"Are you kidding me? Francine, this could be getting dangerous. You are putting yourself in places where there's a potential for something to happen. You need to come home! Now!" he demanded.

Francine could predict the words coming next. She knew that Brian wanted to get married, although he hadn't directly asked her yet. She knew he wanted a stable family life for his son, Johnathan, when he stayed with his dad. She wanted that too. But her business was her first priority at the moment. She knew that in a sales situation, it was very important to be visible to her customers. She had several employees, but they were new to sales themselves. She could not move back to Chicago yet. She needed to be in her territories from Louisiana to Florida, cultivating the relationship with her customers. Brian did not understand.

"I'm going to be home in two weeks, Brian."

"For how long this time, Francine. Are you going to be home for good, or just visiting?"

His words bit into her. He was right. She planned on only being in Chicago for two weeks, and she would be working at her distributor's main office while she was there.

"You know that I can only be home for two weeks. We've talked about this before."

"I've been patient, Francine. But I need more than a couple of weeks every couple of months. I want you to be here permanently.

We either have to make a life for us together, or I have to move on. Maybe you aren't in love with me anymore?"

Brian shuttered as he said those words. He had such a terrible heartbreak with his ex-wife that he didn't date for a long time. When he met Francine, everything changed for him. He felt his heart reawaken and felt the urge for a relationship again. When he made love to Francine the first time, he felt as if all his past hurt lifted. To question if he should move on from Francine was something he never thought possible.

She didn't respond with an answer right away, or quick enough for Brian's liking.

"I guess I got my answer, Francine," he said slowly.

"Brian, I love you.I love you! I just cannot commit to being permanently in Chicago. I need more time," said answered.

"Then let me be blunt. I'm done trying to make this long-distance relationship work. You spend more time in Naples than in Chicago. So if you want me, you're going to have to do the work. I'm done. Its up to you now."

Francine knew he was a man of his word. If she wanted him, and wanted a solid future with him, she would have to be the pursuer.

"I'm going to be blunt too. I love you, and I'll see you in two weeks. But I cannot permanently move back home yet."

She twisted her fingers together, hoping for a good response.

"I'll talk to you later," he said before hanging up the phone before she had a chance to say goodbye.

Brian went to his dresser and opened his sock drawer. He pushed away a sea of socks until he found one that had a different shape. Taking it out of the drawer, he pulled out a small box and opened it. I beautiful square-cut diamond sparkled in his hand. He carefully put the ring back in the box and tucked it into a sock. The box was returned into the sock sea. He walked out of the room distraught.

CHAPTER 31

The Nairty's New Daughter

Brianna's plane back to New York was scheduled to leave on Sunday evening. That left little time for Noel to meet privately with her after a long morning at Vino Antiquities with the police. Dave said he would pick up Brianna at the Ritz Carlton and bring her back to their home for a few hours. Dave was excited for his daughter to come to their home, and so was she.

When she pulled her car into the driveway, she noticed that Dave had just arrived with Brianna. Brianna was casual today, wearing a pant of jeans and a comfortable shirt. Brianna smiled broadly when she saw her, giving her a quick moment of joy. She realized that Brianna was waiting for her to get out of her car before going into the house with her father.

Despite a long night and an early morning visit back to the place of the event, Brianna noticed how put together her step-mother appeared. Noel was wearing a full-length, striped romper over a tank top. Although the romper was casual, Noel had matching clunky jewelry on and high-heeled sandals. Brianna quickly noticed Noel's gigantic diamond ring and layers of diamond bracelets as Noel walked towards Brianna with confidence and grace.

Of course, Brianna was amazed at their beautiful home and Noel let Dave show her around while she fixed a quick lunch for them. She always had some fresh shrimp and salads stocked in one of her gourmet refrigerators for unexpected guests. She served them on a table next to the pool so they could casually talk as they ate.

Brianna explained that she was attending college in New York and living at an apartment close to the school. She had inherited enough money from her mother to pay for her college and that she was taking classes to become a physical therapist. She knew that she would be able to find employment in the health field after college which was her highest priority. She explained that she also was working part-time for an interior designer to help pay her living expenses. She loved that work and knew that design was her passion. Whatever she learned working for the design firm would help her enjoy design throughout her life.

"What a wonderful career plan, Brianna. I'm so impressed. Did your parents help you make that decision?" Noel asked.

"My mother always told me to pick a profession that I could depend on getting a good job. She told me that I was responsible for myself first, and if I found a good job, I would never have to worry about being alone," Brianna replied. "My mother was a nurse and worked up to the last couple of months before she died."

"That's wonderful," she replied.

She quickly thought about her own situation where she depended completely on Dave. She felt ashamed and wished she could do things over again. She quickly refocused her attention, knowing that she still could make her own mark.

"Brianna, now that it is confirmed that you are my daughter, I want you to know that you can depend on us. Noel and I will have to talk, but I plan on helping you with your education," Dave lovingly replied.

Noel nodded to Dave and to Brianna with approval.

"I didn't come here for you to support me. I came because my mother asked me to find you. I didn't know what to expect, but I don't expect financial help," Brianna firmly replied.

"That's nonsense! You are Dave's daughter, and my step-daughter. We were not lucky to have our own children together, but I am over-the-moon happy that you have joined our family. If we had children, we would send them to the best schools they wanted to go to. I feel the same about your education. Please, let us pay for your education and you keep your mother's inheritance as your savings," she said as she put a large shrimp in her mouth.

Brianna smiled and kept eating. She didn't know what to say, but a large weight was lifted from her shoulders.

"Tell me, what about the man you thought was your father.?How is your relationship with him? And does he know that you were meeting us?"

Brianna and Dave had already discussed this, but Brianna answered, "He wasn't happy that Mom told me that I had a different birth father, but he understood. Dad was great to me growing up. He and mom started arguing and they decided to divorce. That was hard for all of us. But Dad remarried a woman he knew from work. She had one young son and they decided to have a baby themselves. Now they have two kids. So Dad has a family again with a wife, two children, and a step-son. I'm always welcome there and I have my own room when I visit." Brianna explained. "When I started college, he knew Mom left me money to pay for it, but he paid for my books and moved me into the apartment I'm renting. I still see him, and my step-sister and step-brothers at least once a month."

"A modern family," Dave smiled and replied as the women nodded in agreement.

At four p.m., Dave indicated that he better leave for the airport or Brianna would miss her plane. Noel was so excited about her new "daughter" that she wanted to ride along, but she decided to give Dave and his daughter a little private time. As they were leaving, she grabbed Brianna's arm and led her down a side hall of the house to an open door.

"This is your bedroom when you come here, and I hope you and your father plan another visit soon," she said as she led her into the room.

Brianna gasped as she looked at the large room and surroundings. She walked into an adjoining on-suite with a walk-in closet.

"This is the biggest bedroom I've every seen," Brianna gushed.

"Well, it's your bedroom now, and you can decorate it however you want. Leave clothes here or buy new ones. This is solely your room now. I want you to feel that you belong here."

"Can I leave a few things here now?"

After Noel reassured her, Brianna quickly retrieved her suitcase and took out the gown that Dave purchased for her to wear at the gala. She also took out a picture of her and her mother that she had brought to show Dave. Noel smiled at how sweetly she placed the picture next to the bed. The joy in Noel's heart was equal to the feeling Brianna had at having a family again.

Dave left with his daughter and had a pleasant conversation during the ride. He handed her a debit card and accompanying paperwork that he had previously arranged for at his bank.

"This card is for you, Brianna. I have deposited ten thousand dollars into your account to help with your expenses," Dave explained.

Brianna looked at him curiously and answered that she didn't want any money.

"That's nonsense, honey. Don't use it if you don't need it, but I know that New York is an expensive city. There is no need for you to be worrying about money. Focus on your education and have some fun while your young. Now…when can you come back down here?"

Brianna was secretly relieved to have some financial back-up. She lived check to check and also had worried about money knowing that her inheritance would only cover schooling. Brianna looked forward to spending more time in Naples with her new family and they tentatively planned another week mid-summer.

Her father reached the airport and slowly took Brianna's suitcase out of the car. He didn't want the time to end. Tears formed in his eyes and in his daughter's as well. They embraced each other and he gave her a kiss on the cheek. She gave him one back which made him tingle with glee. Dave watched her until she was out of sight before he drove away.

When he returned home, he found Noel at their kitchen table with papers laying all over it.

"What's going on/" he asked.

"I printed out information on colleges in New York and on physical therapy and design schools as well. I also printed out info from Florida. Maybe Brianna will want to live here?" Noel said.

"I knew it! You're already a hover mom," Dave said as he took his wife in his arms and kissed her.

CHAPTER 32

Self-assessments

Noel walked down to the end of her circular driveway to watch Dave's car leave with his daughter. She wanted to savor every moment. When she returned into the house her joy quickly changed to concern. She was ecstatic about Brianna and her past month's fear of her husband having an affair completely left her mind. She knew that the recent robberies were weighing in on her mind, but that wasn't what was bothering her.

She poured a fresh cup of coffee and went into her family room to reflect. Although she just experienced great joy with her new "daughter", she felt sad, vulnerable, and irrelevant. The past month had changed her opinion of herself. She could not come to terms with her status in the community, now realizing that it was due to her husband's contribution, not her own.

Sure, I volunteer and chair events, but others could do that in my absence. I haven't contributed anything monetarily to the marriage, haven't paid into Social Security, and don't own my own IRA.

She thought about the consequences if her marriage had been falling apart and didn't like what she saw of her future.

"I have to feel my own self-worth. I have to make a change, but what can I do?"

She pondered her future, knowing that her modeling days were past. She wondered what she could do, what she could add to the community.

A similar self-assessment was happening across town, as Francine wondered how she could retain her business in multiple states and move back to Chicago. She had to find a solution to keep her relationship with Brian. Her business was good and she was employing six regional associates. All of them were making a reasonable wage but there wasn't enough funds to hire a permanent manager to replace herself. She knew without her own presence, some of the accounts she previously earned would be lost.

"What am I going to do? How can I have both my business and Brian?" Francine pondered.

She thought about how lonely life was to her before she met Brian. Even living in Chicago, although she took advantage of many entertainment and shops available, she was busy but remained lonely. She knew that she had to keep her relationship and decided that she needed to make a commitment to Brian when she returned to Chicago.

"My personal life should be more important than my business life. I'll have to find an answer." Francine said aloud before she exited her car and entered one of the dozen businesses she serviced in the Naples area.

CHAPTER 33

The Investigation

A week passed and the police had no leads on the robberies. Officer Breakly had personally reviewed all of the videos from Vino Antiquities hoping to find the man in black coming into view in another camera's video frames. All he saw were people that were on the invitee list or waiters, cooks, and bartenders working the event.

Jason Breakly was disturbed by the videos. He had previously reviewed the videos from the first art fair and found nothing of interest. Those videos revealed hundreds of tourists, some locals, and the exhibitors, food venders, etc. There was no video surveillance of the second art fair robbery since it was in an unused, empty lot. But he knew he would find that same footprint of people; tourists, locals, exhibitors, and food vendors.

"One of you is a thief," the officer said aloud.

He got up and went to one of the detective assistants that were available. Finding two of them gabbing together, he asked if they could take on an important assignment. Soon the two were sitting in a conference room with all of the video monitors.

"I need you to find and mark anyone that appears at both of these events. Mark them on the video, print pictures of them, and post them on the wall. Then I want you to identify those people," he instructed.

One of the assistants gazed at the crowd of people at the first art gala and said, "This will be impossible. There's way too many people here. And how will we know who they are?"

"Look, this is important work. We have a repeat offender in our area who has robbed in three events, and injured one tourist. Naples has a reputation as a safe community. I suggest familiarizing yourself with the people at the Vino Antiquities event. Here is a list of their names. You can pull up their pictures from car licenses and ID's. Then see if you can see them in any frames at the art fair."

The two assistants nodded and quickly got to work, running pictures of the two hundred guests at the event.

The officer left the conference room and noticed that he had received a call from Noel Noirty. He cautiously returned the call, knowing that she was looking for answers he would not have. His call proved him correct, as she wanted an update to give to Dominic Pepino on his emerald robbery.

"I just assigned two associates to identify attendees and compare those people to anyone who might have attended the art fair."

"That'll take them years! I said I could help in any way. Can't I come and ID those people? I know everyone who was there and can easily recognize from the video who was at the art fair."

The officer thought for a few seconds, realizing that she was also at the second art fair and could list the people she knew from there as well.

"I'd happily agree to you assisting, Mrs. Noirty. However, realize that you were at all three events as well, so you are naturally a suspect as well."

"I never thought about that, but that's fine with me. I have nothing to hide. Do you want me to come over now?"

The officer gave her some instructions and they hung up. Noel felt invigorated for the first time in many years, in a way she hadn't felt for years. She was going to do something important. Something that would help the people and community she loved. She anxiously called Dave before she drove to the police station.

"You're going to do what?" Dave asked. "Are you sure you want to be so closely involved?"

"Yes, I do! It would take them forever to put names to faces on the video. I can have that done quickly. Dave, you need to know that I haven't felt that very good about myself for some time. This is a chance of me to do something important."

Dave agreed after realizing that she would be safely inside the police station while she helped.

"Noel, I have to say that I'm proud of you. Not only did you handle the news of Brianna better than I ever imagined, you are tackling the robbery as best as you can."

Noel had tears in her eyes as she heard the compliment. She knew what she was doing was the right thing.

Noel arrived at the police station an hour later, and asked for Officer Breakly. She was ushered into the conference room where Jason and the two assistants were putting up picture identification of every attendee from the Vino Antiquity event. She was surprised as to how quickly they ran everyone's ID's. She suggested putting the attendees pictures into categories, as to who was local, who attended as couples, and who worked there. She easily pulled off the stick pins and put people together into the categories. Officer Breakly was impressed that one event's identification task was completed in a couple of hours.

Noel looked at the conference table and spotted some self-adhesive dots laying there. She opened the pack and started looking at the pictures, putting dots on some of the pictures.

"What are you doing, Noel?" Jason asked.

"I was at the second art fair in downtown Naples. Since you don't have any video feed from there, I thought I could identify some of the people I saw there," Noel answered.

He frowned, recalling that Noel had said she and her friend, Francine, were having a drink in the hotel when the robbery occurred. He didn't like conflicting stories and wondered if he should be involving Noel in his investigation. He liked to trust his instinct and he just caught Noel in a lie.

Noel saw his brow furrow and immediately knew she shouldn't have said anything, but this was a serious crime and she could help. She asked if she could speak privately to him.

A few minutes later, they were sitting in another room which appeared to be an interrogation room. Noel felt uncomfortable as she began explaining that she and Francine were disguised to practice watching her husband's movements. She explained her past months fear that her husband was having an affair and was sneaking around in the evening to meet a young woman. She told him that the woman turned out to be her husband's daughter from a relationship years ago and that her husband had not been aware of having a child until two months ago.

The officer laughed, "Now I get it. I heard something about that when I was interviewing some of the partygoers. One of them told me that it was the best party they ever attended. When I asked "why' they said that it was fabulous by itself, but then, you and Dave introduced a young woman who was his daughter. She said that everyone was talking about it all evening."

Noel nodded and admitted that it was true. She wondered who had told the officer about Dave's daughter but thought again and decided to let the question pass.

"So tell me a little bit about you and your friend being in disguise."

"Francine did some research online to see how to blend into a crowd. She has a whole list of things to do, like avoiding bright colored clothing and fancy jewelry," she said while PoInting to her jewels. "We did a practice run at Miramar Outlets and I couldn't identify her at all, but I needed to tone it down, so we did another practice at the art fair. Our friends didn't notice us at all, but we saw them. Here, I have a couple of pictures on my phone of us in disguise."

He looked at the pictures and was impressed how well she disguised herself after her first attempt. He warned her that going under surveillance can be dangerous if someone finds out that you are following them. He explained that many professional investigators are trained in self defense if things go awry. Noel said she wasn't afraid of her husband's response and that she was only interested in finding out the truth.

The officer was satisfied with her answers so he told her to continue putting her dots on the pictures. She went back into the conference room to continue as he reflected on her contribution to the investigation.

This may open up something. We may get a lead, he thought as he leaned his chair against the wall.

Noel finished her task and the investigative assistants and her started to review the videos from the first theft at the Riverside

Shops Art Fair. The videos were grainy and the crowd was large, so each frame had to be frozen so Noel could study them. Several hours passed with coffee mugs getting filled and emptied during the review. Noel was able to identify some of the locals she knew, including her group of friends, Babs, Shauna, and herself.

The process lasted three days, while the team compared faces from the party to the event. They identified thirty-two people that were at the party and the first art show. Of those, seventeen also attended the second art show.

Officer Breakly and a detective reviewed the team's findings with interest. They knew from the video of the party that the thief was a man, or at least a person of considerable height and weight. They instructed the team to mark in black felt-tip pen a "R" for Riverside Shops Art Fair, an "N" for Naples Art Show, and a "V" for Vino Antiquities, on each picture. They then posted a note card under each of the pictures that attended all three events. The two men reviewed each picture and if the height and weight where similar to what they determined close to the thief at Vino Antiquities they noted "PoI" on the card.

"What are the notecards for?" asked Noel.

"We'll be interviewing each of those people again. But the 'PoI' stands for Person of Interest. Those people will be having a longer investigation into their backgrounds, financial situation, etc."

Noel shuttered at the thought that one of her friends might be the thief. She looked at the cards and found that only six of the seventeen people who attended all three events fit the height and weight range. She didn't think any of those people had any reason to conduct crimes. Suddenly a thought ran in her mind and she turned red and clammy.

"Oh no! Do you think?" Noel blurted out.

"What is it, Noel?"

"I was just thinking. If I was robbing someone, I would be in disguise. So there may be someone else in the crowd I don't recognize."

The officer and the detective looked at each other.

"That makes some sense. But if that is the truth, then we are back at square one," the detective answered.

CHAPTER 34

Losing Love

One week passed since the phone call between Francine and Brian. He had not called her, but answered if she called him. The same happened with texts she sent to him. No texts originated from Brian, only her. Brian's answers were brief and concise. He was sticking to his vow. She was going to have to be the pursuer.

Francine felt sick every day for that past week, as she tried to find an appropriate fix for her problem. She worked tirelessly, doing inventory checks to ensure that her employees in the area were properly tracking inventory. She answered any questions and continued to train her customers and her zone associates on new product features. She met with management to ask how she could better serve their needs. But nothing would fix the ache in her stomach and heart. Finally, she decided that she couldn't wait another week to go home to Chicago. She needed to see Brian as soon as possible.

Francine contacted her customers in another business zone near the Tallahassee area. She explained that she had an urgent personal issue in Chicago and needed to push her visit with them back several weeks. A few of her customers had work-related questions she was able to answer over the phone, and all of them were supportive of her visiting them in a few weeks. Francine also checked with each of her zone employees to let them know that she was returning to

Chicago earlier than expected. Her employees enjoyed the open dialogue she had with them, always treating them as one of her own family. Those conversations lasted longer than with her customers, as each employee liked having the interaction with her as they chatted about their families and their personal lives.

She looked for a flight to Chicago and booked one leaving early the following day. The last thing she did was contact her closest friends including Lilly her roommate, Angela her customer and friend, and Noel her friend and confidante.

"I didn't realize what you were going through," Noel said to Francine.

"There was so much going on, with the robberies and with what you were going through," she answered.

"Yes, but I would always make time to listen to you. You should have told me. I thought everything was going great between you and Brian."

"It is, actually. It is just that he wants me in Chicago the majority of the time. And, I know he wants to get married. I'm happy about that, but it's all too much to handle right now," she replied.

"So, what are you going to say to him when you get back in town?" Noel asked.

"Hopefully, I'll be saying, 'I will'," Francine grinned.

CHAPTER 35

Chicago

Francine's plane landed at noon in Chicago, and she hurried to her townhouse to freshen up. Lilly Lee, her roommate, was anxiously awaiting her when she arrived. They talked about Lilly's job interviews with several firms in the area, and some fun activities Lilly was involved in, until the conversation turned to her accident and theft in Naples. Lilly updated Francine on news that she already knew; that there has not been any leads on her stolen necklace. Lilly said that her parents call her repeatedly asking for updates on the robbery and she felt so ashamed to have taken it along with her to Florida.

Francine told her everything she had learned from Noel regarding the investigation and how the police were using Noel's knowledge of the community to try to narrow down the list of suspects. The girls laughed, thinking of Noel running around the police department in her stiletto heels and diamonds. She ended the conversation, knowing that she wanted to call her boyfriend, Brian, and surprise him that she was in town.

She was ready to call him, but decided to drive over to his apartment instead. She changed into a casual outfit that she knew Brian liked, and jumped into her car. She was nervous as she drove and wondered if he would even be home. Luckily for her, his car was parked in the garage with the garage door still open.

He must have just come home, she thought as she parked in front of the garage door.

Her heart pounded as she walked up to the door. She had a key to his apartment, but since he hadn't called her recently, she opted to ring the doorbell. Soon, the door opened and Brian appeared. Francine immediately noticed how handsome he looked in his tee shirt and bluejeans.

"Surprise!"

Brian indeed was surprised and he smiled. He took a step towards her before he remembered that he was angry about her lack of commitment. He withdrew his step but couldn't contain his smile.

"Francine! What are you doing here? Is everything ok with your parents?"

"Everybody's fine. I thought about our discussion and didn't think you were willing to wait two weeks for me to come back here, so I decided to come back right away."

He opened the door wider to allow Francine to come into his apartment. She noticed that it was not as neat as it usually was. She saw his socks scattered on the floor, an opened and empty pizza box on the coffee table, and an array of clothing laying over the furniture. She knew that Brian tended to get messy when he was upset, so she didn't mention anything, and sat on the couch.

Brain's head was swimming with questions to ask her, but for the moment, he was tongue-tied.

She's wearing that sexy black blouse. She has it unbuttoned just enough to let me see a little of what I want to get into.

He took a deep breath and forced himself to look anywhere other than her cleavage. She noticed his glance and was happy she wore that blouse. Brian didn't pounce next to her on the couch but rather walked into the kitchen. She was shocked. Brian emerged with two beers and handed one to her before sitting on his side chair. He absently looked at the TV and appeared to be intently watching it. She suspected that he really didn't even know what was showing on the TV.

She didn't know what to say or how to start the conversation. She had not seen Brain act this way, so completely apathetic towards her. She wondered if she did the right thing to come to Chicago until she remembered that he told her that she would have to fight to get him back on board.

"I thought you would be happy to see me. I had to change a lot of appointments and have other people cover for me to be able to come here so quickly."

Brian gazed at her and nodded, but he didn't say anything.

"Brian, do you want me to leave?" she asked, fearing for the answer.

"No, I want you to tell me that you are here permanently. If you are just going to leave in a couple days or a couple of weeks, then nothing has changed," he answered.

She looked at him knowing that she didn't have a good answer. She drank her beer and joined him in absently watching the TV. There were several minutes of agonizing silence as both of them pretended to be interested in the television program. Finally, she got up and squeezed herself into the small space available of Brian's side chair.

"What are you doing?" Brian laughed as he moved over a little more.

"I didn't come all this way to sit across the room. I want to touch you, smell you, and do a lot of other things to you," she whispered.

He couldn't control himself any more as he put his arms around her. Soon they were kissing and exploring each other's bodies. Brian started to unbutton Francine's blouse when Francine rose and wiggled her finger to follow her. Brian got up from the chair and they raced to his bedroom.

Afterward, they lay exhausted in each other's arms. They laid there for a long while, satisfied and happy to be together. The rest of their day was spent as it usually was, without any discussions of the future, but in enjoying their time together. Brian updated her on his son, Jonathan's, progress in first grade. He showed her some art work than Jonathan recently gave him with the three of them holding each other's hands.

"He actually has me in the picture," Francine exclaimed. "Look, he drew my blonde hair color, not his mother's dark hair."

"I know. He loves you, Francine, and so do I," Brain answered.

Francine gazed at the picture and felt a warmth within her that she never experienced before.

This must be how mothers feel, she thought.

She smiled and touched the crude painting as if it was the Mona Lisa. She knew that she had to find a solution to her work issue and make a commitment to Brian. Their relationship was more than a relationship between only them. It also involved a small boy who wanted them together as a family.

CHAPTER 36

The Suspects

Noel poured over the grainy videos of the first art fair to find any people she knew who were present. The process took three full days and her eyes were stinging from straining so hard at the video screen. She was able to identify seven people who attended each function. Each of those people were listed as PoI's, Persons of Interest.

She shuttered as she thought of the police going to each one of those six people and demanding full accounts of their backgrounds. She knew that the gossip would be fierce in the community as they were investigated. She sighed with relief that the police cleared herself and her girlfriends as too short to be suspects, per the video of the thief in black from Vino Antiquities.

Officer Breakly thanked Noel for her service and said that he never met anyone who was so generous with their time to volunteer for the tedious review of the videos. He meant that sincerely, as his team would have taken twice as long to find the PoIs and probably would have missed most of them in the grainy film. He hoped that these new leads would be fruitful, but his experience told him that it was going to be another dead end. The robbery at Vino Antiquities was too good, too smooth, to be a local thief. The theft of the large emerald in the midst of a party was more apt to be the work of a long experienced thief. It was someone who probably noticed the emerald some months before while strolling at the shop and planned to be present at the opportune time of distraction during the event.

The officer pondered the word "distraction".

Was it possible that the Noirty's were thieves? Noel was at each event and staged a large distraction which the introduction of Dave's newly found daughter. What if that was all a ruse? Maybe Noel herself had access to the keys of the display cabinets, or maybe one of her friends had access to the keys. A man stole the emerald, and that male fit the size description of Dave Noirty.

The officer's thoughts went to the other two art fairs. Was it possible that Noel herself stole those items because her husband was not present at either of the first art fairs? Why was she so willing to help the police?

He walked back into the conference room and took several stickers off the desk. Soon they were pinned up onto the wall by Noel and Dave Noirty's photo with "PoI" written on them.

Officer Breakly wrote the suspects' names into his notebook. Adding Noel and Dave's names to the list brought the list to eight persons of interest. He looked at the brief descriptions that Noel provided on the PoIs. The names included:

Attendees:

George Farrington - Lives full-time in Naples for over fifteen years, married to Henrietta, originally from Ohio where he ran a business

Ricardo Lemonici - An Italian citizen who has a home in Naples for possibly ten years

Leo Peterson - Lives in Wisconsin, but also has a home in Naples; ran a successful construction business

Norman Jackson - Lives full-time in Naples for several years;

married to Kay, originally from Texas

Workers:

Joe Franklin - Lives full-time in Naples for over ten years; married to Pepper, son is Dennis; organizer of the Riverside and Naples Art Shop

Cal Sullivan - Lives in Estero, FL, lived in various states, worked as a cook at all three events

Other:

Dave Noirty - Lives full-time in Naples for fourteen years, married to Noel, owns a yacht dealership and marina in Naples (note: Dave not at either art fair, but Noel was present)

He scanned the list and decided to start the interviews with each PoI tomorrow morning. When he got to Dave Noirty's name, he realized that there were others that also had the husband or wife attend all three events. He made a mental note that the Noirty's would only be investigated if nothing turned up with the other suspects. If that occurred, he shuttered at the other names that he would have to also investigate.

Officer Breakly decided to approach the list in the order he wrote the names down because he didn't want to alarm the Noirty's unless he absolutely needed to include them as PoIs. He started early the following morning.

CHAPTER 37

George Warrington

Officer Breakly reviewed his notes before he drove into the gated community.

George Farrington - Lives full-time in Naples for over fifteen years, married to Henrietta, originally from Ohio where he ran a business. He carefully reviewed the address before he approached the gate attendant. Announcing his name to the attendant, he showed his badge to the man expecting him to open the gate. But the attendant called the Farrington residence before allowing him access.

"Mr. Farrington wants to know the nature of your business with him," the attendant asked.

He did not want to show his cards to George Farrington, nor tell a nosy attendant, so he answered, "I'm investigating a recent robbery where the Farrington's were attending a party. I need to ask Mr. Farrington several more questions."

The attendant went back into the gate office and briefly talked on the phone before he reappeared and gave directions to the Farrington residence in the large community. The gate opened and he proceeded down the treelined drive. He rounded several bends and saw a large home directly ahead of him. The address matched. He wondered what business the man owned that allowed him to have such a large multi level home in what appeared to be three wings of the house. He drooled as he saw the six car garage.

George Farrington appeared at the front door wearing orange and blue plaid shorts with a bright orange shirt. He was a tall and large boned man, making him a formidable sight. George curtly addressed him stating that he was just leaving for the country club.

"Well, Mr. Farrington, I think you should call your golf partners and tell them you will be a few minutes late," he replied being perturbed at Farrington's "superior than thou attitude".

"I answered your questions the morning after the party, on Sunday morning. I have nothing more to add," Farrington stated as he folded his arms and stood with his face looking down at him.

"Mr. Farington, I suggest you back up and we sit down so I can ask you more questions."

"You can't order me to do anything. Now, I'm leaving in five minutes, so what do you want?" he barked.

"We can do this here or at the police station. It's up to you."

"What? What is the meaning of this? I have a good mind to call my lawyer."

"Mr. Farrington, you were present at the art fair at Riverside Shops, the Naples art fair, and the event at Vino Antiquities. All three venues had a robbery and you match the description of the thief from the tape from Vino Antiquities. As such, you are a person of interest."

"This is preposterous. Does it look like I need a couple of baubles? I could buy the whole fair if I wanted to. You're wrong on this one, and I am calling my lawyer."

"That's fine. I don't think you are the thief, although based on your attitude, I wouldn't mind taking you in custody. Just know that we will be looking into your background, finances, and may ask your neighbors and friends for some character background on you."

"I suggest you leave now. I have nothing to hide, but expect a call from my lawyer to your superior for bothering me this morning. You're annoyance will cost me a good golf score."

He rolled his eyes and closed his notebook. He turned and left the house without saying anything further. He didn't like this man; pompous and rude, but his gut told him this was not the thief.

Ricardo Lemonici

T he description read:

> *Ricardo Lemonici - An Italian citizen who has a home in Naples for possibly ten years*

Officer Jason Berkeley read the description of the next person of interest and saw that he lived close to the Farringtons' home. He drove to the address and found it to be a high rise condominium. He announced who he was into the speaker at the gate and soon was preceding to the condo office. They told him that Mr. Lemonici was at the pool.

He walked through the lobby to an expansive concrete patio with palm trees, tiki huts, a swimming pool and a hot tub.

Not too shabby, he thought as he walked toward a lone man in one of the chairs.

Ricaro Lemonici was about fifty years old, with a tall, thin body tanned from many hours of laying in the sun. He was wearing a Speedo style suit.

"Mr. Lemonici?" he asked.

The man opened his eyes and was surprised to see a police officer staring down at him. He quickly sat upright and grabbed his beach robe, covering himself.

"You startled me, officer. Do you have more questions about the robbery on Saturday?" Lemonici replied.

"Actually, I have questions about three recent robberies. All of them had you in attendance."

"What? Where were they? I have no idea," Lemonici said with his eyes widening with surprise.

He explained the three occurrences and observed the man closely while Lemonici answered.

"Oh, yes, I was present at each of those art fairs, and at the art gala on Saturday. I never miss an opportunity to go to any art show. You see, I'm a bit of a collector. What do you need to know about them?"

Jason felt that Lemonici was answering honestly so he explained that there were several individuals that attended each of the functions and that the police would be making background checks on all of them. He explained that he wanted to extend the courtesy of letting him know that he would be a person of interest in the investigation.

"I undestand. Can I show you something in my condo before you leave? It may help explain my attendance at each of those functions," Lemonici asked.

Soon the two men were going up the elevator to Ricardo's condo. When they entered, Jason was stunned. There was art everywhere. Paintings lined the hallways, leaned against the walls, and of course, there was art hanging everywhere.

"I have a little hoarding problem with paintings, you can see. I attend everything I can from Tampa south to the Everglades and east to Miami and Palm Beach. I can show you my calendar."

Soon, he found himself reviewing a heavily inputted calendar of art events throughout Florida. He watched Ricardo through the corner of his eye as Ricardo lightly touched several paintings from his collection.

"So, it isn't too strange that I attended the three venues you are investigating. It would have been stranger if I hadn't attended them," he laughed.

"Do you live here alone? Can I have a look around?"

"Of course, please, look!"

Ricardo gestured down the hallway.

He looked in every room and found each one full of art pictures. Very few statues, and no jewelry on display. It was apparent that Ricardo Lemonici was an eccentric, but not a hoarder. He would have been more suspicious of Lemonici if he was a hoarder, with uncontrollable urge to have, and to keep everything. That wasn't what Jason observed. Lemonici was a rich eccentric with an eye for art paintings and filled his condo with the paintings he loved.

"Do you wear jewelry, Mr. Lemonici?"

"Why, yes, I do. Let me show you," Ricardo said as he led Jason to a closet in one of the guest rooms.

He opened the closet door and chests of jewelry lined the closet wall.

"You must be asking because of the emerald taken at Dominic's place. I saw it during the event. It was spectacular. I would have loved to buy it." Ricardo added.

"Any idea how much you think it was worth?" the officer asked.

"Not off-hand, but I would guess is was over a hundred thousand. I'm not sure of its size."

"You stated that you looked at the emerald. Do you remember what time that was?" he asked.

"Why, yes. I was walking with Dominic, the owner. He showed it to me. It was right after dinner, so I guess it was about eight p.m.

"Thank you, Mr. Lemonici. I may be contacting you again, but thank you for offering your knowledge."

He didn't think Ricardo Lemonici was the thief, just a kook.

CHAPTER 39

Leo Peterson

T he next suspect was a man named Leo Peterson. Officer Breakly remembered interviewing him at Vino Antiquities on Sunday morning.

Lives in Wisconsin, but also has a home in Naples; ran a successful construction business.

He noted Mr. Peterson's address and drove to his home perched one block away from the gulf.

"This is where I would want to live if I won the lottery," he admitted aloud.

The sprawling house was on an oversized, corner lot and had a high hedge surrounding the property. The officer drove through the open space of the hedge onto a semi-circular driveway. A woman came out of the house, seemingly Mrs. Peterson, and walked up to the police car.

"Is there something wrong? Is my husband all right?"

He got out of the police car and showed her his credentials, assuring her that nothing was wrong. He explained that he had previously interviewed them after the event on Saturday, and had several questions to ask her husband.

"Leo's not here right now, but maybe I could answer for him. I was with him on Saturday at the art gala."

"I will eventually need to speak with him, but maybe you could clear up a few details. Where is your husband now?"

"Oh, Leo is always driving around checking out buildings that are going up. He's a contractor and I guess building is in his blood. He could be home any minute, but I could call him if you want?"

"That's not necessary. I can call him myself. Were you also at the art fair at Riverside Shops and in Naples' downtown area?"

"Yes, we both went. Our neighbor, Joe Franklin, was the organizer of that event, and he told us about them. We really didn't need any more art, but we wanted to support Joe, and wanted to see his son, Dennis, perform. His son is a musician."

He remembered that Joe Franklin's name was also on the list of PoIs, but being the organizer of the event would make him attend both of those events. He wondered about the Vino Antiquities event last Saturday.

"And how about the Vino Antiquities event? How did you and your husband come to attend that event?"

"Oh! That was the best party! We found out about from Pepper, Joe's wife. They live across the street. Pepper and Joe are friends of some of the people that are the nucleus of Naples. They asked if we would like to attend, and I believe Pepper called the woman who was organizing the event for two more tickets," Mrs. Peterson said.

"Would that be Noel Noirty?" .

"Yes! Noel! She and Pepper are great friends."

Jason was heartbroken that this appeared to be another dead end. He would interview Leo Peterson, but Mr. Peterson didn't seem to be thief material.

Just then, a black Mercedes pulled into the driveway. It was Leo Peterson. He quickly parked and jumped out of his car.

"What's wrong?" he said as he ran to his wife.

"Nothing, dear. Just a few more questions about the robbery," she told her husband, reaching for his arm.

Jason nodded and admitted that he had to do a background check on everyone who fit the description of a large man that attended each of the three events.

"Go ahead," Leo Peterson said. "We have nothing to hide. We will help however we can."

He thought he would kill two birds with one stone, so he asked about the Franklins. He needed to do a background check on Joe Franklin as a person of interest.

Why not ask their friends?

The Petersons pointed to a grand house located on the gulf and directly across the street. It was a Tuscany style house with a concrete fence hiding much of its features. The Petersons said that they knew the Franklins for three years, when they bought their own house. The assured the officers that Joe Franklin was one of the pillars of Naples. He belonged to many clubs and attended many charitable functions.

"How come a wealthy guy like he is organizing an art fair?"

"Hmmm, I can't answer that one, but he and his wife run all kinds of charity parties. I think he's just one of those guys that can run events smoothly. He has lots of connections and can get things done," Leo answered.

"How did the Franklins make their money?"

"I think he was in the financial business," Mrs. Peterson chimed in to the conversation.

He said his goodbyes but warned them that there would be some investigation into their backgrounds and to not be alarmed. They understood and wished him well.

He left their home wondering why Leo didn't know how Joe Franklin made his money. Most successful men like to boast about their success. He drove across the street and pressed the gate button. No answer. He decided to call it a day and phone Joe Franklin for an appointment.

CHAPTER 40

Norman Jackson

The next day, he reviewed his list of persons of interest. Norman Jackson was the next name to interview.

Norman Jackson - Lives full-time in Naples for several years; married to Kay, originally from Texas

He drove several miles east from the Gulf until he saw the community where Mr. Jackson lived. It was another gated community but luckily, the gate was open and unattended. He drove into the golfing community and headed to his address. He noted that there was a large group of golf carts at the country club so he decided to head into the club. Maybe he could "score" a glass of soda.

Jason went into the lounge and a beautiful young woman greeted him at the door. He asked if she knew if Norman Jackson was in the clubhouse. She indicated that he was at the bar and she pointed to him.

I'm in luck.

He strolled up to the man, with everyone in the clubhouse watching his movement. It wasn't ordinary to have a police officer inside their club.

Jason introduced himself and Norman Jackson remembered talking to him at the event on Saturday. Jason asked if he could ask him a few more questions and apologized for interrupting him at his club. Norm indicated that it was fine and asked him if he could get him anything. Jason happily agreed to take a cold soda and the two men went to sit down at a table.

"I need to verify the backgrounds of everyone who attended three art events where items were stolen. Unfortunately, your name was on that list," he explained.

"You mean that you are investigating me?" he said surprisedly.

"Actually, you are a person of interest due to the fact that you attended each of the functions and your weight and size corresponded to the man identified at Vino Antiquities. There are seven men who attended each function, to our knowledge. I'm doing due diligence to check each one's background."

Norm Jackson became visually upset and started shaking.

"I can't believe you would be investigating me. I didn't even want to go to the two art fairs, but my wife insisted that I go with her. Do I need a lawyer?" Mr. Jackson asked, clearly upset.

"That's entirely up to you, Mr. Jackson. You are not being charged with a crime, but as a person of interest. The background check will be done by our department and will look into your past finances, criminal background, etc. It will probably be done invisibly to you. We will be reaching out to some of your friends for character references, though, so I want you to be prepared."

"Do you have anything to add to your statement made at Vino Antiquities? Or anything to put on record about the two art fairs?" he added.

"Well, no. My wife bought a couple of knick knacks at the fairs that we didn't need. I don't like a lot of stuff around, but she likes momentos. I do remember one strange thing at Vino Antiquities that I've been thinking about. I don't know if it amounts to anything,"

Norm said.

Jason gestured for him to continue.

"I ate dinner, and got up and went into the men's room. It's embarrassing, but food goes right through me. I have a touchy stomach. Anyway, I was in one of the stalls, and someone came into the other stall and it looked like he put on another pair of pants over what he was wearing. I thought that it might be a catering uniform, but it was all black."

The statement got Jason's attention heightened and he asked, "Did you see his shoes or pants?"

"That's the funny thing. I wasn't really paying attention to the next stall, but I thought it was a catering jumpsuit, or something like that. But the man didn't put it over jeans, like a caterer might wear. They were dark pants, maybe black. And I believe it was black shoes too," he said while rubbing his brow.

"Were they dress shoes or casual shoes?" Jason asked.

"I'm not sure," he answered. "But they were definitely black."

He thanked Mr. Jackson for his time and gave him his card in case he thought of anything else. The man lowered his head as if he wanted to say more, so he sat there waiting for him to speak.

"I need to tell you something before you find out through your investigation," Norm said slowly. "My wife, Kay, and I were originally from Texas. We moved to Naples about ten years ago. No one knew us here, so we thought it would be a good place to retire. We've been happy here."

Norm paused and took a drink of his beer before he continued, "I'm not proud of my past. I did some foolish things when I was a kid. I got mixed up with a group of guys and we did things that

I'm sorry for now. Small robberies, breaking into cars, caused some fights. I spent some time in 'juvi' and a couple times in jail."

"Were you in prison?" Jason asked.

"No, city jail, twice. Once for a robbery until I came up with bond money, and once for a fight at a bar," he explained. "It was a long time ago. I was stupid and poor. Then I met my wife, Kay. She was a real good girl. Went to school and church. Her parents didn't like it that I was dating her, and I decided to get a job and be a better person so they would approve of me. It took years before they did, but Kay married me a year after we met. We've been married for forty years. We have three kids all living around Naples."

"So Naples is expensive. How did you make your money?"

"Kay and I scrapped our nickels together to get by in those first years, and both of us worked. But I stopped to buy a lottery ticket twelve years ago, and I won. I won sixty-five million dollars! That's why Kay and I moved our family out of Texas and came here. Everyone there wanted us to give them money. We heard every hard luck story there is. We gave some people money too, but eventually we moved here without even packing our things. We didn't want everyone to know we were going."

"You lucky devil," he said under his breath. "Thank you for explaining that to me. We will have to verify this, but it is much better that you came forward than to let us find this out first."

"Our friends here know we won the lottery. We were always honest about that. But I never told them about my past record. Do they have to know?"

He was still shaking as he looked sadly towards the officer for his answer.

"I don't see any reason that they have to know any of your past.

It won't come from me, I promise you."

Norm Jackson shook his hand and grasped his arm in appreciation. Jason walked away thinking, *This is not our man.*

CHAPTER 41

Cal Sullivan

Officer Breakly had enough time to visit one more person before his shift ended. The next name was Cal Sullivan. He read off his notes.

Cal Sullivan - Lives in Estero, FL, lived in various states, worked as a cook at all three events

This man was a working man, not a wealthy socialite, so he probably would be working. He called the man and indeed he was working a catering gig in Bonita Springs. Then he drove to the event.

Cal was finished cooking the meal for the catering event and was cleaning up his make-shift kitchen when he approached him. When Cal saw a uniform approaching, he looked sad and scared and glanced in his boss's direction. It appeared that he was more frightened to lose his job, than talk to him.

He explained that Cal was working at every one of the events where a robbery occurred, thus he would be a person of interest, as were some other men. Cal laughed and shook his head.

"Just my luck. I finally got a good job with this catering company, and now something is stolen. Just my normal bad luck. Like I have time for doing that when I cook."

"Just the same, it's my job to do background checks on anyone who was a male of a certain description and size, that attended each of the events."

"What do you want to know?"

"Explain your job at all these events. What were you wearing, where did you work? The other background information will be done by one of our investigative assistants and will involve looking into your finances and criminal record," Jason explained.

"Well, you won't find anything there. I never did anything illegal except a couple of speeding violations. As for financial background, I've never had much money. Never went bankrupt either, but came close several times. That's why I moved here from Nebraska. There wasn't enough money being a cook there. Here, in Florida, I have a chance to make a living. I'm doing pretty well working for Jim Miller, my boss. The people like my cooking, so he's been giving me a lot of events. He'll tell you that himself," Mr. Sullivan said proudly.

"I will verify with Jim Miller. Thank you for being straight-forward on your background," Jason said, noticing his khaki pants and sneakers, "Tell me, is this what you usually wear for catering?"

"Yeah, usually. But sometimes we have to wear a more formal thing. We had to wear that for the big party on Saturday when everyone else was in tuxes and gowns."

"What does that formal outfit look like?"

"Here! I have one in my valise," he said as he pulled out a black jumpsuit. "We have to wear this and black shoes."

Jason noticed that Cal answered this without any hesitation. He didn't appear to be stressed, or answer anything calculating its impact on the officer, but the jumpsuit did correlate with the description that Norman Jackson saw. Jason noted that Jackson saw a man put on the jumpsuit after dinner.

Why would this cook do that, if he already was wearing a black jumpsuit?

Cal Sullivan probably is in the clear.

He called it a day after the interview with Cal Sullivan. The day had been enlightening with one lead, on the black jumpsuit. He wasn't looking forward to the interviews with the remaining two suspects and planned to make formal a appoIntment with Mr. Franklin and Mr. Noirty. He decided to telephone them immediately to set up a time.

Joe Franklin

Officer Breakly met Mr. Franklin the following morning at his breathtakingly beautiful home situated beachfront in Naples. He guessed that the home was in the twenty-million dollar range and knew that his police salary would never allow him a place like this.

Maybe I'll win the lottery like Norm Jackson.

He took a minute to reflect on what he would do with all that money before started his interview.

Joe and his wife, Pepper Franklin, met the him at the door. He was ushered into the house and led to the outside patio overlooking the Gulf. The couple allowed him a minute to take in the sight before Pepper asked him if he wanted a coffee. He never turned down a free offer of food or beverage, so he eagerly accepted.

"So how can I help you?" Joe Franklin asked. "This is a travesty that several of my friends have been robbed. Plus, it is not good press for the Naples' art fairs, which I help coordinate."

"Several friends robbed? May I ask who they were?"

"Why, of course, Dominic Pepino, the owner of Vino Antiquities. We have been friends since he sat up his business a year ago. And the other was the young oriental girl, Lilly, I think. I don't personally know her, but my wife is friends with her roommate, Francine, who invited her to Naples. I also am acquainted with the two art dealers who were robbed due to my work with the art fairs, Jacque Bonfire and Sally Higgins, because I helped coordinate the events. The actual artists are picked by a committee, but I recognize their names.

He wrote down the information. He had almost forgotten that Lilly Lee had her necklace stolen at the Riverside Shops Art Fair. He wondered if Joe knew how she was doing since her fall.

"That's correct. I see your connection with the victims," he answered. "By the way, do you know how Lilly Lee is doing since her fall? She had to go to the hospital, but I remember seeing her at the event on Saturday. Was she ok?"

Joe answered, "I believe she was fine. She spent some time with my wife and her friends during the week before the party. I believe she has returned home to Chicago."

Jason wrote in his notebook that Lilly Lee returned to Chicago. He drew a sad face outline next to the entry and stared at the page as he thought,

Lilly is back in Chicago. I wanted to get to know her better but why would she be interested in me? I'm twenty-five years old and have lived in the southwest Florida area all my life, graduating from Fort Myers High School and college at University of Florida-Gainesville. Here she is, all the way from Japan, beautiful and educated. She's probably going to find work in some high-class institution in Chicago. I, on the other hand, was unable to find high enough wages as a social worker, so I enrolled and was accepted to the Police Academy. I do love my work and find it always interesting and changing. I love helping people in need and love doing my part to keep the community clear of crime. These recent robberies in Naples disturb me. I won't end the investigation until I find the perpetrator.

Jason quickly shook his head back and forth to refocus, but he was not able to put his personal thoughts aside.

Why do I have such an attraction to this lovely young woman who was mugged almost immediately after arriving in Florida? Why do I feel a strange connection to Lilly Lee?

Jason watched Joe looking quizzically at him, so he shook his head a final time and regrouped his emotions. His interview found that Joe Franklin had made his money in real estate, flipping homes in New York at a young age. He invested his money and made a fortune in the stock market, deciding to stop before he lost his gain. He moved to Naples and lived in several homes before acquiring this stunning home several years ago. He stated that his investments are in less risky markets at the moment and he also lends money to some of the known developers in the area. When asked why he coordinates the art fairs, his answer was simple.

"Someone has to do it. I have the time and energy to put into it, so I volunteer. I have committees to do the real work, I just coordinate."

Just like my boss. We do the real police work, and he coordinates and gets the credit, Jason thought.

"So where were you when you heard about the robberies?"

"We had a small office set up in one of the vacant properties at the Riverside Shops. I was there when one of my staff called me. I went to the spot immediately after I was informed, but the police were already there. They interviewed me and took a statement since one of the exhibitors had been robbed. At the Naples Art Fair, I was probably listening to my son, Dennis, perform. He plays the guitar and I hired him, at my own personal cost, to play at the fair. There were tables set around and people standing watching him. I was with him when I heard the police sirens."

What about at Vino Antiquities?"

"Well, that was the affair of the season. We were all excited to attend Dominic's event. I was probably talking to one of my friends when the police arrived. I understand that Dominic walked past one of his cabinets and noticed that his emerald ring was missing," Joe answered.

Jason nodded. Everything checked out, but he asked, "What were you wearing at the event on Saturday?"

"Like almost everyone else, I was in a tuxedo," he answered, puzzled at the question.

Jason thanked Joe and Pepper Franklin for their time and left feeling that he struck out again. He informed them that his office would be doing some financial and criminal background investigations of Joe Franklin, as well as the others who were at all three events. They were not alarmed and said to feel free to ask them any details. Jason left feeling dejected at not having a prime suspect.

CHAPTER 43

Dave Noirty

O fficer Jason Breakly's next stop was at the yacht dealership and marina owned by Dave Noirty. He was hoping for a miracle to find some shred on a crime. He knew that Dave was not at the first two art fairs, but that his wife was present. Could they be a duo crime team? His gut told him not, but he wanted to hear from Dave Noirty. It wasn't every day that he met someone who had an unknown daughter and was able to introduce her at a major gala.

What bothered him was that the job at Vino Antiquities was so smooth. The distraction caused by the Noirty's and their "supposed" daughter could have been done to avert everyone from the glass case that held the emerald. Noel was coordinating the event and had prepared the site before the guests arrived.

Could it be possible that she unlocked the case so that the emerald could be extracted at the time of the distraction? Who would have lifted the jewel? Another person?

Jason's head was swimming from all the details that could have occurred. For now, he just wanted an interview of Dave Noirty and wanted to explain that he would be having background investigations as well as several other people.

The receptionist at the dealership ushered him into Dave's office.

His office was fairly unobtrusive, with pictures of various yachts on the walls. A window faced the marina with a view of the yachts. It was less impressive than the officer thought it would be like. Dave was in an expensive, but casual shirt and pants. He was wearing dock shoes, which seemed practical. Jason reflected on the appearance of Noel, with all her bling, against Dave's more casual appearance.

"Hello, officer. What can I help you with?"

"I have a couple of questions relating to the robbery at Vino Antiquities. I understand there was quite a scene at the event when your wife thought you were having an affair, but the woman turned out to be your daughter."

Dave nodded. He was exhausted from the running around he did behind his wife's back the last few months, and eager to get everything out on the table. He explained the situation and took out his locked box from his desk drawer. Opening the box, he presented the officer with the picture of himself with Brianna's mother taken many years prior. He also showed the envelope containing the blood test taken from him and his daughter. Jason examined the document and nodded approvingly. He believed that the young woman, Brianna, was Dave's daughter, so the distraction was real. It looked like another dead end.

He explained that he was doing background checks on a number of party attendees. He didn't add that the others were all present at all three robbed events. Dave asked as to the nature of the background checks, so he explained that there would be a financial and a criminal check performed.

"You won't find anything at all in a criminal check on me. But I am concerned about the financial check. I have moved large amounts of money and had large sums deposited in my accounts from time to time. It's the nature of the yacht business. We have to pay and we get paid large sums of money, millions. Sometimes I have to cover expenses until the yacht is purchased. But I assure you, you can audit all my books if you need to, and it's all on the up and up."

Dave continued, "Also, I didn't know what to expect from my wife when she would find out about my daughter. So I started a new account and deposited money in it for my daughter. Expect to see that account as well during your financial check."

"Do you or your wife own any jewels?"

"Have you met my wife?" he laughed "that women is made of bling."

Jason had to agree. He had never seen so much wealth dangling in front of him.

He left the marina feeling good that he had completed his interviews and hopeful that something would turn up in the background checks that his department was conducting on the PoIs. He had a feeling that one of these people was the thief, but he couldn't even decide on who that may be.

Maybe I'm not cut out to be a detective, he thought as he strode back to his car.

He took a few minutes to review his notes. He was assigned to lead this case so he didn't have to get back to the police station for a while. His gaze kept returning to one name, one of the victims, not a suspect, but Lilly Lee.

He felt a strong attraction to Lilly the first time he saw her, which was when she was found laying on the cement at the art show. Her small features and porcelain skin looked so different from all the tan skinned girls he knew in Florida. When he interviewed her at the hospital, he found himself staring into her eyes, which were frightened from losing her heirloom necklace. Her sweet voice fascinated him during the interview.

He vowed to find justice for her, and he knew that he would keep trying to find this thief, and hopefully Lilly's necklace, until he was successful. His spirits lifted as he thought about her. He found the contact information she had provided, and dialed the phone.

Lilly answered the phone from the townhouse she shared with Francine in Chicago. He stated his name and asked her how she was doing.

"I am fine. I didn't have a concussion so I healed quickly," Lilly answered, "Although I am still worried that my necklace will never be recovered."

He drew in her words over the phone, wishing he could smell the Jasmine scent he smelled when he first encountered her.

"I wish I would have good news to tell you, Lilly, but I'm just starting the investigation. I've been interviewing some of the persons of interest the last few days," he said, realizing that he probably sounded clumsy and unprepared.

Lilly paused and quietly said, "I know you will do whatever you can to help find the thief, Officer Breakly. I could see your passion in your eyes."

He wondered if she meant passion for his police work or passion for her. Either way it would be true.

They spoke a few more minutes before Jason asked if it would be agreeable if he called her occasionally on updates. Lilly almost giggled, sensing his desire to talk to her. She wanted to talk to him too. Lilly had been dating a young man in college, Corey, but it was only a companion relationship. Corey was sweet and funny, but not the type of man she yearned for. Officer Breakly had the intelligence, mannerism, drive, and machoism that attracted her.

"I would love to have you call me, Jason," she whispered.

He smiled knowing that she already knew the real purpose of his call. They said their goodbyes and he vowed to call her in a couple of days.

CHAPTER 44

Chicago Decisions

Francine stayed overnight at Brian's house for the first three days of her two week "vacation". She still had to go into the office at the distributor that contracted her, Specialty Products Distribution, during the day while Brian worked at his office in the State building. She enjoyed her time at the main office, and learned about some of the new products they added to their portfolio, met some of their new sales representatives, and caught up with her old cronies like Lucas Peterson, who helped her learn the ropes at SPD.

As the weekend approached, she knew she needed to make arrangements to see her parents who lived in Kenosha, Wisconsin, and ran an accounting firm off the main highway connecting Chicago to Milwaukee. She also needed to see her sister-in-law, Chrissy Pacque, who besides being married to her annoying brother, worked part-time for Francine. Chrissy did most of the expediting to get emergency products to customers. She was very adept at understanding the realm of logistics and working with Francine's customers and sales representatives in the South.

Francine called Chrissy and asked if she had time to personally review some of the business, and if she would like to go to Mom and Dad Pacque's house for dinner on Saturday. Chrissy was delighted and said that she, Gerry, and the kids were free on Saturday.

"Darn, I was hoping my brother was working," she frowned, as she had a long history of her brother's bad behavior towards her.

"Oh, come on, Francine. I thought all of that was over now."

"I doubt it. Gerry has the temperament of a teenage boy."

"I can't deny that. Is Brian coming too?" she asked.

"No, not this weekend. He and his son have a sleepover in the school gymnasium. It's training for the kids before they go on a campout this summer," she said, giggling at the thought of all those kids and their fathers in the echoing gym.

She did agree with Chrissy that she and her brother did mend their feelings, but she didn't expect Gerry to hold up his end of the deal. Chrissy reminded her of how proud Gerry was of her business and how pleased he was that she was hired part-time.

"OK, Chrissy. I promise to behave."

When Saturday arrived, Francine drove over to her brother and sister-in-law's home. She walked in the door and was immediately hugged by their two young daughters. Her brother, Gerry, and his son were not in sight. She relaxed as she played with the kids and occasionally talked business with Chrissy.

They were enjoying their time when a loud, booming voice called out her hated nickname, "Fanny Pack! You're here already!"

She grimaced and looked at her sister-in-law who averted her eyes, knowing how much Francine hated being called her nickname.

Gerry was an Administrative Assistant at Northwestern University who worked with their athletic department in recruiting young talent. A past college football player himself, he was a big man with a booming voice, that he liked to use to intimidate people. She had pleaded with him numerous times to not call her that name, usually to no avail. This time, she decided to let it go. It was just a name. Her brother loved her but was too calloused to see that his words affected her. She got up and gave him a big hug.

"Gee, Francine, I thought you'd give me some shit about calling you Fanny Pack."

"I'm over being affected by stupid nicknames. Call me whatever you want," she answered, hoping that he would stop using it if it didn't bother her.

"That's no fun," he answered, pouting as he left the room.

The group left as a family in Gerry's Chevrolet Suburban, to visit their parents. They were met at the Pacque's house with loving kisses and hugs. The children quickly moved down into the basement to play with their toys, leaving the adults in the living room.

She carefully updated them on the robberies in Naples and on the mugging of Lilly Lee. She explained about the police investigation so far, which turned up nothing to date. The family asked about the big gala at the art warehouse, and she quickly removed an I-pad from her purse to show them pictures. She explained about Dave and Noel's daughter, Brianna, being introduced at the gala, and how Noel originally thought that her step-daughter was her husband's mistress.

"That's a lot of information! I thought a lot went on in Chicago, but your friends and their lifestyles make Chicago seem tame," her mother exclaimed.

The conversation eventually rounded back to Francine's business, which the Pacque's kept very detailed accounting records for their daughter. Her father commented on the extraordinary success that his daughter had since she started her business.

"Yes, I have been extremely lucky and blessed to have grown such a wonderful business so quickly. But, that brings me to my next problem," she said with a hesitation.

The family sat quietly, waiting for her to continue.

"Brian and I have been dating for a year and a half. We get along great, and I love him and his son, Jonathan."

Her family nodded in agreement. The Pacque family was very happy that Francine met such a nice man.

"Brian wants a commitment from me. He hasn't asked me to marry him, but he continually uses the words commitment, future, and family. I know that he wants to get married and maybe even have another child."

"That's wonderful, dear!" her mother exclaimed as well as the others.

"Don't you see my problem? I want to marry Brian, but I'm still building my business. The supply business is based on customer service and my name is my brand. They expect me to visit them and croon them. Besides, even if I had someone else to run the business, I couldn't pay myself and pay someone else too. I need another year or so before I feel comfortable with having someone else run the business. I can't come back to Chicago permanently at this time." she explained with a desperate voice.

The room was quiet, waiting for someone to say something. Only her father was nodding and looking directly at her. Everyone else was looking downward.

"Doesn't anyone have anything to say? Can't any of you see it my way?"

"Dear, I want to say something to please you, but love waits for no one. You have to seize it when it happens or you lose it. If you were twenty and asking me what I think, I probably would answer you differently, but Francine, you are thirty-five now. If you lose your business, you will make a living doing something else. But if you lose your love, you will regret it forever," he mother said.

Chrissy agreed with her mother-in-law and forcefully nodded.

"Choose Brian, Francine. After you make the commitment, it will be easier to realize what to do about your business," her mother stated.

She was surprised by the united front of her family. Although only her mother spoke, it was clear that the rest of the family agreed with her mother. She wondered if they had discussed this before, and decided that it probably was one of their regular dinner subjects. She did not commit an answer, and sat there quietly.

The balance of the evening was much lighter with a delicious dinner and conversation interrupted with Gerry and Chrissy's three delightful children. Francine did discuss some business with her father and provided him with documentation and receipts that he could enter into her file. The evening ended on a high note and the ride back to Chicago was uneventful. When Francine got into her car parked in her brother's driveway, Chrissy gently took her arm.

"Let me know if you need something, Francine. I'm always here to help," Chrissy said.

CHAPTER 45

Still Uncommitted

Francine found that her time in Chicago was going by too quickly between work during the weekdays and seeing Brian and Jonathan in the evenings. Brian's son was a distraction to break the elephant in the room between she and Brian, but it also was fun to make meals, play games, and read stories to Jonathan before bed. She enjoyed her new life in Chicago, but still wasn't ready to make a commitment to move here permanently.

By the end of the week, the looming tension between the couple became larger. When Jonathan returned to his mother on Friday night, the tension between she and Brian became unbearable.

They went out for pizza to the restaurant where they had their first date. They briefly reminisced about their date and enjoyed their pizza and draft beer. Brian was much more quiet than normal, and she knew it was because she was going to be leaving to return to the South. She had appoIntments on Monday in her first zone territory she opened, so she was flying directly into Louisiana rather than return to Naples to retrieve her car. She had decided to rent a car for a couple of weeks while she visited several of her six zones.

The pizza was eaten and the waitress was preparing the check when Brian asked for another beer. She recognized that he was going to stay here until they talked about their future. She told the waitress to bring her a beer as well.

Brian sat gazing directly at Francine and she smiled back at him. She slid her arm across the table towards him but he did not respond.

D-Day, she thought.

The speech her mother gave the preceding weekend had an impact on her. She knew that her mother spoke the truth and if she asked for more time, Brian would leave her forever.

With a deep breath and a sip of beer, she started her dialog, "I know that you are waiting to hear what I'm going to do. If I'm going to give up my business and move back to Chicago."

Brian sat without emotion looking at her, but his pulse quickened and she noticed his face reddening.

"You are the best thing that ever happen to me, Brian. I want to spend my life with you. I hope to have a family with you. I guess what I'm trying to say is, I choose you."

She could see the relief sweep across his face and he took a deep breath. She smiled and slid her hand again, out towards him. This time, he took her hands into his.

"This is for real? You're not going to change your mind? You are sure you're choosing me over your business?" he asked in succession.

"Yes, yes, and no," she returned. "I am committing to you and committing to living in Chicago. I will tell my employees and my customers next week that I'm moving back here permanently. But, I still am hoping to keep my business as long as I can. I'll try to run it from here, from Chicago. I'll lose some customers, but not all of them. Maybe I can find a solution before all of them go."

"And when do you see yourself moving back?"

"I should be here by the end of June."

Brian squeeze her hand, delighted with her answer.

"Are you going to move back into your townhouse, with Lilly? Or are you going to stay with me?"

"I will stay at your house often, but I don't think I should live there. What would Jonathan think? I plan on keeping my townhouse lease going until we decide something different."

Her eyes twinkled as Brian leaned forward and gave her a long kiss.

"I love you, Francine."

"I love you, Brian."

They paid their bill and returned home to his apartment arm and arm. He was anxious to get home and get into bed with her. He had been controlling himself so as to not appear too eager. He was now eager to satisfy his urge.

She lit some scented candles in the bedroom knowing what was to occur. She was anxious too. Soon, Brian emerged with a couple of glasses and a bottle of champagne. She really didn't need any champagne after several large beers, but she didn't want to ruin the mood. He popped the cork and filled into the two flutes.

As she accepted the flute of champagne, he said, "Wait, don't drink it yet."

He got down on one knee, and Francine's eyes grew large. She felt goosebumps on her arms.

"Francine Pacque, you are one extraordinary woman. I was intrigued the first moment I met you and quickly fell deeply for you. I am so lucky to have you in my life and want to ask you to be my wife. Francine, will you marry me?"

His eyes probed hers awaiting her answer as she took a deep breath and answered, "Yes, I will."

He withdrew a small box from his pocket to her surprise. She looked stunned as she opened the box. It held an exquisite square cut diamond solitaire. Brian slid it onto her finger, knowing that it would fit. He had taken one of her costume rings to the jeweler to get the correct size.

Francine stared at the ring as she admired it. She knelt on the floor so she would be equal height to Brian who was still kneeling. They kissed and started removing their clothing. They never made it into the bed.

It was already late, so she didn't call anyone to tell them about her engagement until morning. She knew who to call first. It was her mom.

"You are engaged! Oh, Francine, I am so happy. We are both so happy," her mother said while yelling the news to her husband.

She had the same wonderful reaction from everyone. She called her sister, Genevieve next, then her brother's wife, Chrissy. Later she called her roommate, Lilly, who was so very excited at the news. She subsequently shared the development with some other Chicago friends, before dialing her Naples friends.

"You are what? You and Brian got engaged? Francine, I'm so happy to hear that," said an excited Noel Noirty who also yelled the news to her husband, Dave.

Other calls were made too, to her business employees and friends. She was anxious to change her status on Facebook, but she wanted to make sure her good friends found out from her directly.

Brian did the same type of calls to his parents and friends. He decided to go to his ex-wife's home to tell Jonathan directly. He knew his ex, who was remarried and had another child with that husband, would be happy for Brian to get married again. He called her first and told her over the phone. He was correct in that she was happy for him. She said that her family was going to go to the movies in the afternoon, but they would be home until noon. She suggested that he come with Francine so they could tell Jonathan together.

The engaged couple drove over to Brian's ex-wife's house in the late morning. Francine was a little nervous to meet Brian's wife in person, but she quickly realized that his perky wife was genuinely happy for their engagement. She said that she and her husband would give them some privacy by going upstairs while they talked to Johnathan. Brian yelled to his son to come downstairs. Soon Jonathan came running into the living room and gleefully ran into his daddy's arms.

When the three of them were alone, Brian said he had some news for him.

"What, daddy?", he asked as he plopped onto his dad's lap.

"Francine and I are going to get married and she will be living in Chicago again," Brain announced while bouncing him gently.

Jonathan gave a gasp followed by a big smile as he looked at Francine.

"Will you give me a baby brother then?" he asked her directly.

"I didn't expect that question," Brian said.

"Johnny, one thing at a time, please. First, Francine and I have to get get married," Brian explained while kissing his son.

Francine was beaming with happiness.

CHAPTER 46

Back in Naples

Two weeks had passed since the robbery at Vino Antiquities. The Naples Police Department had finished getting the background information on all seven persons of interest without finding anything different than what the PoIs had already told the police. Officer Jason Breakly was running out of options. He had hoped that leading this investigation would lead to his detective's badge, but instead, he reported that he didn't have any more leads to his superiors.

The robbery victims had all been insured and the insurance investigators were calling him regularly for updates. He had wondered if there was some insurance fraud happening through the robberies, but the victims had different insurance coverage and there was no indication of past fraudulent activity. He sat in the conference room staring at the storyboard with the robbery timeline and pictures of people at those events. He knew he was missing something. He was so intent on finding the thief, or thieves, that he had stopped sleeping well. The case was consuming him. He had to find the missing thread that tied these robberies together.

He had called Lilly twice in the last two weeks to give her updates. He hadn't done that for the other victims. He liked her and the calls were nice to hear her voice. He hoped they were becoming friends but since they were a thousand miles apart, he knew it could not be more. But he still hoped and dreamed that he would get a chance to see Lilly again under better circumstances.

His phone rang while he was still looking at the storyboard. It was Noel Noirty. He hadn't seen her in a week and expected that she wanted an update, which was awkward, since she was not a direct victim. She asked if she could talk to him privately at the police station. He was intrigued and said he was available all afternoon.

Noel hung up the phone, and anxiously got her phone and keys to leave the house. She quickly got into her little Mercedes sports coupe and hurried to the police station.

The last week was a pivotal week for Noel. Her adrenaline had been so pumped the last few months agonizing about her husband, coordinating the Vino Antiquities gala, and dealing with Lilly's traumatic mugging and the robberies. She kept that high going after the robberies by helping the police identify people on videos that attended the three art events. But last week was a week of discovery for Noel.

When she was worried about her husband leaving her, Noel realized that her status in the community was due to her husband's yacht business. Sure, she ran some charity events and had some great parties, but someone else would do that in her absence. She realized that if she and her husband were getting a divorce, they would split their joint finances, but not her husband's yacht dealership business. The business was where the money was. He and his father had the company incorporated at its beginning, so that they wouldn't be personally liable. Her husband was the President of the business and his father was the Financial Officer, although, Dave actually had an accounting department as well as an outside accounting office for audits.

Noel was a model in her youth, but gave that up when they moved to Naples. Without her husband, she would have no insurance, no wages, no retirement. Sure, she could sell their house and pocket a large sum, but she wouldn't be able to live the Naples lifestyle. She realized that she was vulnerable and that had to change. She racked her brain to think of something she may be good at. Spending money wasn't a profession. She could do party planning, but she had been doing that gratis for so long, she didn't think she could charge those same people.

Luckily, her husband wasn't divorcing her, and she hoped they would stay together forever, but she vowed to make a contribution and get a substantial job. She would keep thinking until she found a perfect fit for her. She thought about her friend, Francine, who needed someone to run her business, but she knew she wasn't right for that job. It had to be something else.

Noel was led into the conference room by another officer and found Jason still staring at the conference room bulletin board.

"You're still racking your brain, aren't you?"

"Hi Noel. Yes, so far everyone checks out. I was hoping you had something for me," he replied.

"I've been thinking about it almost non-stop. I'm not in your business, but I have a feeling that the thief is someone on this storyboard. I can't shake that feeling."

Jason stared at her. He thought the same thing.

"I've done some research about professional thieves. They tend to have collectors already lined up. It's like a black market crime. I don't expect to find any of these items at a local pawn broker," he stated.

"Do you think that the thief may have been 'warming up' with the other crimes before stealing the emerald? I would think that Queen Josephine's emerald would be something a collector may have wanted," Noel inquired.

"Hmmm, it's possible. But why the other robberies? Why mug poor Lilly?"

"Maybe he didn't mean to mug Lilly. Maybe he pushed her to grab the necklace and she fell. The EMTs thought she hit her head on the planter," Noel answered.

"It's a possibility. Lilly said her great-grandmother's necklace was very valuable. She said it was valued at $50,000. I saw a picture of it, and it was a beautiful carved Jade pendant," he added, confused that he was offering too much information.

"I had no idea her pendant was that valuable. The poor dear. No wonder she was afraid to tell her parents about losing it."

"You mean having it stolen. Lilly didn't lose it," he corrected.

Noel smiled and nodded. It was clear to see that Officer Jason Breakly had a weak spot for Lilly Lee.

"I came here with an idea," Noel exclaimed.

Jason sat upright and motioned for Noel to continue.

"What about trying to bait the thief with another substantial jewel show? I'm aware of some jewel trunk shows that travel to wealthy cities such as Palm Beach, New York, and Beverly Hills. Maybe I can orchestrate having one come to Naples."

Jason looked at her inquisitively. He was surprised she would come up with such an intricate event, but how would it attract the thief? And how would they catch the thief?

"I admire your perseverance, but there are entrapment laws that the police need to follow."

"I know, and I think I have a solution for that problem."

Intrigued and desperate, Jason asked what her plan involved.

"Simple, my friends and I would do the surveillance. We would catch him in action, and then we would call for your police help," she said with a grin.

"What? Noel, I know you did a little spying on your husband, and I have to say, I was pretty impressed with your disguise. But to involve your friends would be crazy. Plus, some of your friends' husbands are persons of interest, including your's," he answered while his head was thinking of some way that her plan could work.

"I've put some thought into this, Jason. I wouldn't involve those friends. But, I have several others that I would use, Francine Pacque would be one of them. And, Angela Fratilo. Her uncle is Dominic Pepino, so she has an interest in this case," she answered. "I'd also use Mitzi Vanderlooth. She's a high-end real estate friend who was in Europe when all of these robberies occurred. She can keep a tight lip."

"But how would you bait him? He might not be interested."

"Dominic Peopino has other antique jewels that are back in Italy. I would make sure those pieces were included. The thief wouldn't know that the jewels were Dominics, but would think they were part of the trunk show. We would advertise them to be such," Noel explained and hesitated to allow him to think.

Noel continued, "But I think if he was interested in Queen Josephine's jewels, he would be interested in Cleopatra's as well," she said with a wink.

Jason frowned and stared at her.

Where is she coming up with this? But, if she really could pull this off, it might work.

"I have to think about this, Noel. There still may be some entrapment issues, and I would have to get permission to proceed. Your plan may draw in the thief, but I'm not sure you women would know what to do if you caught him in action. The police would have to be close by to step in."

"I know. These types of jewel trunk shows have security and the thief would know that. He would know that the Naples police would be there too. That's why it would have to be a big catch for him. 'The bigger the catch, the bigger the risk'. I saw that on a TV show once." Noel said.

"I tell you what. We don't have anything to lose. Why don't you check on the availability of one of those trunk shows coming to town and I'll check some things on my end. Maybe start getting your spies committed." he said. "I may regret those words."

Noel laughed, "I will get back to you soon if I have any luck finding a show that has open dates."

She left the police station feeling proud and helpful. It was a feeling she hadn't felt in a long time.

Noel went home and started doing some research on jewel trunk shows. There were a few online that she found in New York. She even found a listing for a trunk show that had occurred in Naples in 2014. That set a precedence for a trunk show so it wouldn't look suspicious. She was in luck. She also found an artifact trunk show that was taking place in Charleston.

"Maybe that's a better option to include some antique jewelry," she said aloud, deciding to do a search of museum trunk shows as well.

The following day Noel contacted the organizer of the Charleston show and several museums shows. She found that the Charleston show had artifacts and some antique jewelry. She asked if they would be open to do a show in Naples, and if they would be willing to include some other important jewelry from an undisclosed dealer. The owner said that he was willing to do it if Naples picked up the expenses. Noel asked for some open dates and he provided them. All she had to do was to contact Dominic and ask if he would be willing to use his Cleopatra jewels as bait.

Noel wasted no time in contacting Angela Fratilo, who not only was Dominic Pepino's neice, but also a distant relative of her husband, Dave. The two always considered themselves to be "cousins" although many times removed. She told Angela about her plan and asked for her consent to go into disguise during the event to snag the thief. Angela agreed immediately. She said that she would support the plan with her uncle, but thought it prudent to have Officer Breakly present when Noel discussed with uncle Dom. Noel agreed and called the officer.

"I think I found our trunk show," Noel announced.

"Already! Boy, you work fast, Noel."

They discussed the possible trunk show that Noel found and said that she and Dominic's niece would like to talk about it with Dominic, but wanted him to come along with them. He agreed and said that he would be ready at their convenience. This may lead to the break he needed.

CHAPTER 47

Back to Work

Francine left for Louisiana knowing that she had to come up with a plan to hand off her business oversight. She spent the entire flight to Monroe, Louisiana, wondering how she could keep her business running, but she knew that the business would quickly revert to its old suppliers without her. She looked lovingly at the large ring on her finger. She was engaged. She had spent years stealing a peak at other women's hands, searching to see if they had a ring. At thirty-five, she wondered if she would ever have one herself. She rubbed her forefinger of her other hand against the sparkling stone. Brian picked out an exquisite ring. She smiled contentedly that she made the right decision.

She met with her sales representative, Bill Hanson, a man that she hired by meeting his wife working in a diner. Billy, as he was known, had skills in computers and was liked by the suppliers. He excitedly showed her some of the inventory improvements he had made by looking at several of his customers and standardizing some of their supply options. Through this, he was able to reduce each of their inventory levels, thus freeing up money.

Francine was very pleased. Bill's standardization was something he came up with on his own. The customers loved his service and boasted about him to Francine, as if he worked directly for them.

Maybe Bill's zone can sustain itself without me, she wondered.

She spent three days in zone one before moving to the next zone, several hundred miles away. She repeated this for each of her zones one through four. Some of her representatives struggled at resolving customer problems, but all in all, all the customers were happy with their service.

Zone five was in the Ocala, Florida area, and zone six was the Naples/Fort Myers territory. She knew that zones five and six were in good hands with the man she hired to service them. She found Tom Bender at the Ritz-Carlton Hotel in Naples, where he worked as a waiter. In talking with Tom, she found that he was eager for a job in his field. He had a business degree but couldn't find a decent waged job and settled as a well-paid waiter. Tom was thrilled to get a chance to work part-time as a sales representative her Francine. His job grew into a full-time job when he took on both zones, but he continued to work weekends at the Ritz-Carlton as a waiter.

"The tips are just too good to pass up," Tom had told her.

She had visited all her zones north of Florida in a whirlwind two weeks, leaving her tired and depleted. She was happy that she was once again in Florida, and was ready to stay in the small apartment she leased in Naples.

Francine reflected, "Well, I'm half way there. I've been staying away six weeks before I return home to Chicago. I've just proven that I can get that done in three weeks. Half-way there!"

She wondered if Brian would be agreeable to her traveling every other week. She knew he would not.

Driving down Highway 75 in the spring rain was a delight for her. It was cold yet in Chicago, and each of the last two weeks were delightful being in warmer weather. She drove directly to one of her customers, Creative Fabrication, where her friend, Angela Fratilo, was the Chief Financial Officer. She knocked on Angela's open door and surprised her friend that she was back in town. Angela was thrilled and the two of them made plans to go out for lunch to catch up on each other.

"Yes, of course I will go," she said, "But, first, let me show you something."

She held out her left hand, displaying her gorgeous ring.

"That's what I wanted to see. I was so happy that you called me after you got engaged. When is the wedding?"

She admitted that they hadn't settled on a date, but she expected that it would be this year. The women decided to leave for lunch now since there was so much to talk abut. Soon they were discussing wedding plans that drove Francine into hyper gear.

"I have some other news to share that affects you, Angela. Brian doesn't want me doing this traveling anymore, so I'm not sure how to handle my business yet. I plan on keeping Tom Bender as my sales representative, but I won't be down here to oversee and support him," she admitted.

She explained how Brian has a son and he would like to have a family with her. Angela smiled, clearly not upset. That was a little disturbing to her.

Angela asked her if she had spoken to Noel lately, and she answered that she had called her to announce her engagement. Angela decided to let her know about Noel's plan to catch a thief. The thought of doing surveillance at the show excited her. She said she was "all in" and would make sure if she would be available. She wondered how her fiancé would react and decided that he may be a good person to include on the "team".

She called Noel and thought she heard a stronger, renewed

voice in her friend. Noel explained that she had offered to do some undercover work for them, enlisting some of her friends. It would be a small group, only Noel, Angela, Mitzi, and her.

"Why not the other girls?"

Noel hesitated before she answered, "Because, it is possible that one of their husband's is the thief. So I need to keep this quiet from them. In fact, I'll probably say that I'm out of town when this show occurs, so it doesn't look strange that I'm not there."

"But, I don't know how you're going to get another show here after season. Also, how are you going to organize it? You don't even know where the show would take place."

"I know. That is a problem. I've spoken to the show promoter and he understands the discretion. Dominic is going to include some fine jewels from his collection, but to the audience, it will appear to all be coming from the promoter. I have to make sure it looks legit and not involve myself. I think I'll have the promoter call Naples Events, LLC, like the normal shows call, and they'll find an organizer."

Noel had already contemplated the risk of getting personally involved with the trunk show. It had to be scheduled and planned through regular channels. She thought about the challenges ahead of her to get this done and she liked how it made her feel. She felt more alive than ever.

CHAPTER 48

Another Exhibit

Several discussions occurred between the Naples Police, Noel Noirty, and Artifacts Unlimited, who was the trunk show owner from Charleston. Noel, with her husband's permission, offered ten thousand dollars to the promoter, plus expenses, but strict discretion was necessary. Officer Breakly was present at all phone and video meetings with the promoter and offered his gratitude to the promoter. Simple contracts were drawn, with the help of Dave Noirty's attorney and the first draw of the fee was given to the promoter.

Jessie Gerin and his partner, Sal Rifton made several comments that they were thrilled to do a show off-season in Naples. Their business slump occurred in the summer months, although they did bring their show to various affluent communities in the Northeast. But the chance to get an up-front ten grand, plus revenue for their show was a fabulous contract for them.

She arranged to have Dominic Pepino contact the promoters with the inventory list of what he was going to have them include in the show.

"Noel, my inventory is in Italy now, but I will have the items brought to Naples by courier. I have a number of gems that were from the Egyptian dynasty times. There will be a crown, bracelet, swords ladened with jewels, a necklace, and of course, a large ruby ring, worn by Cleopatra herself."

Jessie and Sal looked at each other and gasped when they heard the contents. Their artifacts were not as valuable as the one's that Dominic was including. They spoke about their trunk show items and that Dominic's jewels would outweigh anything they owned.

"It doesn't matter. No one has seen my items before and no one knows how I came to be in possession of them. You need to include them as if they were part of your own," Noel explained.

"I would feel better including a brief that the Egyptian items were on loan from an undisclosed owner. It is normal protocol to include other items, so it shouldn't draw attention." Sales mentioned.

Dominic agreed and said that he would disclose some information and value of his items for them, so they could discuss with visitors at the trunk show.

"But you do understand that my display has to look transparent. We are trying to lure a professional jewel thief and we have to be above suspicion," Officer Breakly added.

The following day, Jessie and Sal called Noel to say that they had telephoned Naples Events, LLC. They announced that they would be bringing their trunk show to southern Florida, with a stop in the Naples area and later in Palm Beach. They explained that they would have fifteen glass kiosks with all of their artifacts, including Renaissance pieces, and a special exhibit of Egyptian Dynasty jewels from the days of Cleopatra. Naples Events LLC was thrilled to have an opportunity to display this exhibit in their area on short notice. Naples Events would find a proper venue for the event, do necessary advertising, and find a coordinator to run the event. They agreed on a twenty-five dollar fee to attend the event and a two-thousand dollar retainer paid to Naples Events to start the process. Jesse and Sal paid via their business credit card and informed Naples Events to quickly identify the date, so they could plan their next show in Palm Beach.

Naples Events started calling hotels in the area to see if they had any openings for a trunk show. Although it was past busy season, weddings and company events were plentiful, but several dates were finally presented.

"Where else should we call? Should I start calling country clubs?" one of the workers asked.

"Why don't you see if Joe Franklin has any ideas. He's a high-roller. He may even help us with the coordinating," a male worker suggested.

The woman called Joe and asked if he had any suggestions. He didn't think his usual venues for art shows were right for the event.

"This could be a special event for us. We have never had such old pieces on display. Maybe we could use the theatre building? Or even Dominic Pepino's place, Vino Antiquities, although after his robbery several weeks ago, he probably wouldn't be too willing." Joe replied.

"We will check out the opera house and the theatre lead. Thank you," the man replied.

Joe hung up the phone and turned to his wife, explaining the unique opportunity Naples might be having with an antique artifacts show. She was excited to hear that something substantial was being planned in their community.

"Why don't you help them, dear? You know how to do these things. Maybe Dennis can play at this event too? It would give him some more exposure," Pepper asked.

Joe mulled it over. He had two things in abundance, time and money. Maybe he could coordinate for Naples Events. It would get his name mentioned, and he may be able to include his son's musical talents. He answered his wife that he would consider it, but after the police put him as a person of interest for the past robberies, he would rather stay away from this event. Pepper Franklin agreed that staying away would be a good idea, but maybe he could still get Dennis a gig doing some of his instrumentals on his guitar.

By the end of the week, the trunk show was scheduled. Naples Events would be the coordinator for the show that would occur at the Inn on Fifth Avenue, in downtown Naples. The Inn on Fifth Avenue was a perfect spot, as tourists and locals wander down the main downtown street. The show promoters, Jessie and Sal, were given a suite at the Inn for the duration. The police were happy too, because there was a limited number of exits and streets from the hotel, if indeed there was a thief. The show would occur in three weeks. Notices were put in the local newspaper, online advertisements, as well as posters in various shops. Naples Events were already receiving calls and selling tickets for the event.

CHAPTER 49

Practicing for Their Big Ruse

Noel was able to convince Angela Fratilo and Mitzi Vandeloof to participate as undercover investigators for the event. She asked them to come over to her home with disguises so they could critique each other. Noel decided to use her same disguise from spying on her husband over a month before.

How the time flew since that nightmare! she thought.

The two women arrived at the same time at Noel's house and Noel answered the door in her disguise.

"May I help you?" a disguised Noel asked.

Mitzi frowned and looked a bit surprised at the housekeeper answering the bell, "Hi! Is Noel here?"

"Sure, Com' on in," she said with a southern drawl.

The women spoke to each other and followed Noel into the family room, chatting with each other. Noel went over to one of the cabinets and took a cloth rag, pretending to dust. The women sat down and waited for their host to appear.

After several minutes, Mitzi asked, "Does Noel knew we are here?"

She hadn't seen the housekeeper notify anyone that they were there.

"You bet your sweet ass she does," Noel said loudly turning around to meet their gaze.

"Noel! Why, I never would have known that was you!" Angela exclaimed.

Mitzi stood there, shaking her head back and forth. She never would have guessed that Noel could look so different.

During the next few hours, Noel explained how to blend into a crowd. She took the paper that Francine originally wrote with tips, including wear no jewelry, wear neutral colors, wear a hat or wig, avoid direct contact with people, etc. Angela and Mitzi took out their disguises they brought from home and the three women critiqued them.

"Angela, You are very thin. Francine wrapped herself with tape to appear heavier and that worked well. Maybe you could try that." she suggested

"Mitzi, Your hair is very unique to you, with your black and white spikes. I have several dark haired wigs you may want to try," she said while handing her friend several hairpieces.

Noel was in full swing. She was confident and forceful in her suggestions. Soon her two friends appeared from one of the bedrooms wearing their new disguises. Noel was happy that both women looked different than normal. She was confident that their neighbors and friends wouldn't identify them unless they made direct contact with them.

"I understand that The Inn on Fifth Avenue is going to hold the event. It's a gorgeous hotel, but not a large venue, so running directly into someone may be a problem. So, I think we need to have some practice. Are you ready to take a ride and do some surveillance?"

"What about Francine? Is she going to be undercover too?"

"Francine and her fiancé, Brian, will come as a couple. Francine, of course, will be in her disguise, but no one knows him, so they can do surveillance as a couple."

"That's wonderful, and we get to finally meet him."

"Yes, it is. But bringing him is the only way that he was open for Francine to join us. He wants his lady 'home' and 'safe. I had to speak to him at length to convince him to come with her."

The women headed to the car. Their first stop was Waterside Shops.

Officer Breakly had given them some practice assignments to gain their investigative knowledge. The first was to pick out someone and look at them for three seconds. Then each woman was to separately write down everything they could remember about that person.

The women picked their target and watched a man coming out of the shops. He walked towards them on the sidewalk so they observed him for probably about ten seconds. After he passed, they took out the small notebook Noel gave them and noted what they remembered.

Noel started, "White male, fifty, brown hair with flecks of silver. Wearing khaki pants and a blue golf shirt."

"That's good, Noel," Mitzi said. "That's what I wrote down. What about you, Angela?"

Angela looked embarrassed and answered, "I wrote male, Caucasian, with rugged lines in his face. Brown or gray eyes, mole on side of his nose, fifty to fifty-five years old. One inch hair cut with side part and shaved sides and back. Khaki pants with cargo pockets, light blue Nike shirt, Air Johnson gray sneakers with dark blue stripe. Went to late model, white, two-door Lexus with FL plates."

The women looked at each other and shrugged. They were no match for Angela Fratilo on identification.

The three of them practiced their identification techniques on several more people, improving each time, and observing the person for shorter intervals.

"This is something we can practice ourselves until the trunk show. We should get better and better."

They had dressed in their disguises and posed for Noel. She wasn't an expert but she knew that Mitzi still needed some work. Mitzi was a small lady so that made her a little unique. She wondered what they could change to make her look a little different.

"How about making her older?" Angela suggested.

"I'll hate it, but it would make me look different, like I was shrinking like all older ladies. I'd have to get a grey wig." Mitzi replied.

"I love that idea. You could still look wealthy so it wouldn't look strange that you were at this show. I, myself, have to change my disguise a bit. I look frumpy in this outfit, so I need to polish it up a bit." she said.

"And I'll take your advice and wrap myself in gauze or layers so I don't look so thin." Angela added.

"Then its set. Let's practice next weekend at the mall and see how we do. We can observe some people and write down their features too."

"But I still don't know how we are going to catch the thief, even with our disguises," Mitzi said.

"I don't know either," she admitted. "But Officer Breakly will teach us that part."

CHAPTER 50

Francine and Brian

Back in Chicago, Francine was trying to run her business remotely from her home. It wasn't working out too badly, but she worried if it wouldn't be long before customers started leaving her as a supplier. Knowing that customer service kept customers, she set up a regular schedule of internet/phone conferences using a business service similar to Skype. Hopefully that would help retain a personal relationship.

Brian's work as a manager overseeing the City of Chicago highway construction was booming. His expertise in Civil Engineering led him to doing audits on the road construction to verify that the various contractors were doing things properly. Brian had a team of engineers reporting to him and could have opted to stay in his office, but he enjoyed going on the job site to see for himself.

Their relationship was at an all-time high. The couple saw each other several times during the week, and always on the weekend. Every other weekend was Jonathan's weekend with his dad, so Francine either slept on the couch or went to her own place overnight.

Francine brought up the idea of going to Naples with Brian over dinner one night. She could almost see the hair on his neck raise up. She explained that it would not be "for her work", but rather to attend a trunk show of jewels and artifacts. The show was legit, but it was being planned to entice the jewel thief.

"I'm not sold on this, Francine, but I'm going because I know I won't be able to stop you," Brian said.

Francine grinned. He knew her too well.

"The best thing is that no one will know you, so you don't have to come in disguise. We can be a couple and enjoy the show."

"What about you? How are you going to go?"

"I hope you like brunettes," she said while wrapping her arms around her man.

He kissed her gently on her neck as he couldn't quite reach her lips. Soon she was sitting on his lap and they were able to properly share a long kiss.

She felt happier than she ever had been. Her mother was right when she said to choose her heart over her job. Although she was happy, it still did little to help her anxiety about her business, Lilly's missing necklace, or the other robberies. She pretended to be concentrating on Brian who was tugging off her clothes while she thought of all her problems.

CHAPTER 51

Advice for the Spies

Officer Jason Breakly met with Noel prior to meeting Angela and Mitzi at the mall. He wanted to go over a few ground rules with Noel.

"I want you to remember, that if you see something peculiar or see the thief in action, you are not to interact with him. When a thief is in the midst of a robbery, they are likely to do anything. Their adrenaline will be pumping and they may even be armed. So you have to push the button I will be giving you and an officer will come to you. Do you understand?" he sternly asked.

"Yes, but if it is someone I know, I could probably detain them," Noel answered.

"Noel, listen to me. This isn't a game. These professionals don't get good by being gentle. They don't care who they use. Anyway, you will be in disguise, so the guy won't know you," he reminded her.

"Oh, that. I forgot. I won't do anything. " Noel said, but her head was thinking otherwise.

"I will have a panic button for every one of you. Keep it in your pocket or in your handbag and press it if anything seems wrong. I have a screen that will identify who has each device and I will know where you are by watching the screen."

"Now, I know I'm going to meet, and test, Angela and Mitzi

today. But what about Francine and her boyfriend? When will they be here?" he asked.

"I don't know when they arrive, but I will let you know."

"OK. Now, let's get down to business. We will know who purchased tickets for the event shortly, so we will be able to compare those names to see if any of our persons of interest are attending. With such an important show, I expect that most of them will attend." he said.

Noel nodded in agreement. She already knew several who were going, as she had run into Ricardo Lemonici, who told her he was attending. She also knew that Pepper Franklin was attending with her husband. She was disappointed that Joe hadn't volunteered to be the coordinator, because she knew he organized events smoothly, similar to how she did, and she did not want any organizational hiccups.

The officer continued, "My plan is to have each one of you assigned to a particular PoI. You can mingle with the crowd, but continually watch one person. I want each PoI watched 100%. So, when we get the list, we can assign you to that PoI. Does that sound reasonable?"

She agreed, understanding now how their surveillance could work. She knew her friends would be relieved to know they would have a particular assignment.

"One problem, however, is 'door sales'. If one of the PoIs doesn't buy a ticket up front, we may not know that he's coming until he arrives. I may use Francine and her boyfriend as an 'extra' in case that happens. Just assure your friends that we will have police nearby if they press the button. We won't have anyone in the Inn during the show. We will rely on the usual security provided by the organizers." Jason said.

"What will happen to the robber when he's caught?" she asked.

"He'll go to prison, where he belongs. He will immediately go to our jail, where he will no doubt try to post bond. That's an issue of concern for me. These guys are some of the pillars of the community, so the judge will be hard pressed not to give them the chance to post bail. But, if we catch them red-handed, then the thief will know that he doesn't have a chance to not be sentenced. We may have some leverage to get the stolen items back for a reduced sentence. That's what I'm hoping for. I want to get Lilly Lee's necklace returned to her."

Jason quickly added, "As well as getting the other jewelry returned."

"That sounds good. And I'm sure that Lilly would be very appreciative."

The officer blushed.

She and Jason left the police station and went to Gulf Coast Mall, where Mitzi and Angela were waiting for them. They discussed the actual surveillance, just as was presented to her, which delighted the two women. They felt much more comfortable having to watch one particular person than an entire crowd.

The officer looked around the parking lot and identified three people from three different vehicles who were entering the mall. He assigned each woman to a particular shopper and said to follow them and report back in an hour everything that person did. If they got caught by the person, to notify him on his cell phone and he would come to explain that they were not "stalkers". The women left to start their test.

Angela Fratilo volunteered for the first person entering the mall. It was a man in his early fifties who was carrying a bag from one of the local stores. Angela had disguised herself as a frumpy tourist, or local. She had bound her thin frame with yards of fabric and put on a body shaper to hold it in place. The effect made her twenty pounds heavier. She wore a simple tunic dress that she usually wore when she worked in the garden. It had a simple beige and white print that was non-descriptive. She wore a simple pair of flat shoes that she had in her closet. Her short hair was pulled back and secured by hairpins. She looked like any soccer mom or casual tourist, and definitely not like the polished executive that usually wore designer clothes.

She followed the man carefully, staying a minimum of thirty feet behind him. The man walked into one of the stores and walked to the counter. He was returning a shirt that he had bought previously. She looked at the apparel on display as if she was purchasing something. She noticed that the man took out a charge card to scan the returned item. When he was done, he walked out the door and headed to a coffeehouse across the mall aisle. Realizing that he would be in the coffeehouse for a few minutes, she approached the cashier at the counter.

"Excuse me, but I think the man who just left was an old co-worker of mine. Was his name Tom, or, maybe it was Dave?"

The cashier was happy to help, and reached in her drawer for the credit card receipt.

"No," she said while looking at the receipt, "that wasn't his name."

It only took a moment while the cashier had placed the receipt down for Angela to read the man's name, Mike Ferris. She apologized to the cashier for wasting her time, and left the shop towards the coffeeshop. He had already received his coffee and was heading out the door. He gave her a short look as she was entering the store when he left. She knew she had made a mistake being noticed.

She waited in the coffeehouse until she saw where Mike Ferris was walking. She felt comfortable enough to leave to follow him. He walked through the mall while he drank his coffee and proceeded to his car. She followed him two aisles down and took out her phone. When he got into his car, she ducked down between the cars and moved towards his aisle. She was able to take a picture of the back of his car as he headed out of the lot. She enlarged her picture and was able to get a clear license plate number. Pleased with herself, she headed back to the squad car where Officer Breakly was waiting.

She told him many things about the man. She could clearly identify his hair, eye color, clothing, size and weight, age range, etc. When she told the officer how she learned of the man's name, Jason was very impressed.

"Angela is a natural for this type of work. I can trust her surveillance at the upcoming trunk show."

Mitzi Vandeloof's assignment was to follow a woman who was getting out of her car in the mall parking lot. Mitzi's heart was racing, as she was apprehensive about following someone. She had chosen a light grey pair of pants with a simple, gray blouse. She wore a short wig to disguise her tipped and spiked hair. She had on a pair of simple, dark sunglasses and carried a small clutch purse. She also had found a pair of flat shoes and was cursing to herself as the shoes were a bit tight to wear.

She followed the woman at a safe distance behind her. The woman window shopped down the mall, and she did the same to keep here distance. Finally, the woman went into one of the stores and started looking at one of the sales racks. She entered the store and proceeded to the same rack, but in the section for her size. The woman took several items into the dressing room. She did not enter the dressing room, but continued to look at items in the store.

When the woman reappeared, she put back one of the items on

the rack and proceeded with the other item towards the cashier.

As she passed by, she said, "Mitzi, is that you?"

She was astonished that someone would recognize her and her mouth gaped open. Soon, she realized who the woman was. The woman was the sales clerk at the wig store where Mitzi purchased her wig.

"I was wondering if you would recognize me," she said to cover up her ruse.

"The wig looks great on you. I hardly recognized you," the woman answered.

She and the woman talked for a few minutes until the woman said her goodbye. Her cover was blown.

When she returned to the squad car, she related her story to the officer.

"Did you get her name? What did she look like, what did she purchase?"

She realized that she made another mistake. She still should have continued to get information. The woman may have recognized her, but she at least could have gotten the woman's name.

Noel was the last assignment made by the officer. He assigned Noel to watch one of three young women entering the mall. She frowned, as she didn't want to follow some high school girls, but she grudgingly followed the three into the mall.

The girls were giggling and texting while they walked. Texting made them bump into each other as they didn't watch where they were going. She made a mental note of what her assignment was wearing: shoulder-length straight blonde hair, five foot five inches, sixteen or seventeen years old, white spandex pants with a cropped red top, red flip-flops, multiple bangle bracelets and bangle-type earrings.

The girls wandered into the Victoria Secret store.

Oh, great, complained Noel as she entered the store.

She was greeted by a cheery sales girl who asked her if she needed any assistance.

"I'm looking for something for my daughter. Thank you, but I don't need any help."

The sales girl hurried away.

Noel watched the girls as they continued to giggle, bumping into each other, as they spoke to each other. She was annoyed at their behavior and wondered if she ever acted so foolishly when she was in high school. The girls were looking at a table of cute panties and thongs as they conversed. She continued to look at a side rack but her eyes were watching the girls through her sunglasses. She noticed something wrong. It looked as if two of the girls would talk while the third placed panties into her purse. The sales crew's vision was blocked by the two girls so they could not view the theft. This practice continued for a few minutes as the girls would move to another rack and continue to do the same sequence.

She was steaming. She could see that these young women were well clothed and probably came from good, law-abiding parents. She slowly walked up to the panty display and started looking at the items on sale. The girls stopped their conversation and started to walk away, but she stepped in front of the girl she was watching.

"I will not allow you to leave this store without you paying for those panties," she said softly.

The three girls looked at each other and she could see their expressions change to fear. The one girl, who had the panties in her purse tried to move past her towards the door, but she took a large side-step and told her to stop, blocking the door.

The manager of the store quickly moved towards the group.

"Is something the matter," she asked as she looked back and forth at the three girls.

Noel said as cool as a cucumber, "No, my niece found the panties she wanted. Dear, do you still want them?"

Noel extended her hand to the girl's purse, opening the top and pulling out five pair of panties. The three girls stood there frozen, looking at her.

"Are these the ones you picked out, dear? If so, lets go to the counter so you can pay for them with the money I gave you," she said while staring at the girl.

"I think I changed my mind," the girl said while looking at her friend.

"OK then, this woman can put them back," she said handing the manager the panties.

The manager looked confused but took the panties from her. She thanked her for her time and turned around. The girls had already left the store.

She returned to the squad car and explained what she found. The officer praised her for taking the initiative to stop the crime. Angela and Mitzi hugged Noel, truly in awe of their friend.

It was the second time that Noel felt like she had a purpose. She remembered the first time, identifying the attendees at the art shows. Noel felt taller and more alive than she felt for a long time.

"Your posse is ready to be deputized," Noel exclaimed as her friends applauded.

The officer said the women needed to practice a bit more to get comfortable.

"It's one thing to observe strangers, but quite another to watch and identify one of your friends," he cautioned them.

The women looked surprised at his comment until it sunk in that the thief might well be one of their own society friends. They left the officer in silence as they thought about his words.

Office Breakly returned to the police station and to the conference room where he stared at the pictures on the same bulletin board he had been studying for weeks. He wondered if he was doing the right thing by involving Noel's "posse".

He considered the advertisement in the Naples newspaper promoting the trunk show. It was a tasteful and elegant ad announcing the venue at the Inn on Fifth Avenue. Besides the ad, the newspaper had a half page article on the Charleston trunk show promotors with some pictures from a past exhibition. Anyone who looked at the ad would never suspect that the exhibition had been planned by a local woman from their area.

CHAPTER 52

Hurray, There's Another Event

"I don't know if I want to work at another art event," Cal Sullivan said to his employer. "I got questioned by the police about the other events, since each event I worked at had a robbery. Heck, I wouldn't even know what to do with jewels. I think I'll pass on working at this one."

"But Cal, this is a high-class event and you make those great canapés and shrimp fondue. I think you should reconsider. I could even sweeten your wages a little on this one," the employer begged.

Cal needed the work as the busy season was over. He could continue to cook for weddings, but those affairs were not the same caliber, or the same wage.

"I'll do it, but I want to make sure that I'm always working with someone. I don't want any question as to where I am, in case another robbery occurs."

His employer was grateful that he accepted the position. It was difficult to get dependable chefs and this particular assignment might pull in some big dough for the company. Cal's request was readily accepted.

Another Naples resident, Ricardo Lemonici, was already deciding on his outfit for the exhibit. An excellent, but flamboyant dresser, Lemonici planned his attire carefully. He needed to make an impact on the other attendees. He gazed at his wall, wondering where he could fit in another piece of art. He would worry about that later. He had some planning to do at the moment.

Tickets to the exhibit were limited, so people were already coming forward to purchase their tickets. One of the first tickets purchased was from Pepper and Joe Franklin. Although Joe did not want to be involved as a coordinator, his wife, Pepper insisted that he try to get their son a job playing some instrumentals on his guitar. Joe obliged her and called Naples Event, LLC. They were not asked to provide any music for the affair. Joe did not want to disappoint his wife and son, so he asked if he could donate funds for music, anonymously. After a call to the trunk show hosts in Charleston, a phone call was made to Dennis Franklin.

"Sure, I'm free to perform at the show," Dennis answered happily.

At twenty years old, Dennis was starting to venture out of his home to find musical gigs around town. He was thrilled that Naples Events called him, not realizing that his father had arranged it. Dennis was a gifted musician that was eager to play string instrumentals rather than the rock and folk tunes that he usually played. He planned to make music his career, either as a musician, songwriter, or music store owner.

Pepper Franklin was excited to learn that her son was performing, and she quickly purchased tickets for the exhibit for her husband and her to attend. Joe was beaming as he saw how excited both of them were. He provided a lavish home for his wife and son, but he knew that at some point his son needed to make it on his own.

By the end of the week, the exhibition was nearly sold out, as the Naples society group salivated to attend another function. The ticket list of names were presented to the police, who had asked for the list as a precaution. Jason Breakly examined the list noticing several of his PoIs attending.

"Mr. and Mrs. Joe Franklin, Mr. and Mrs. George Farrington, Mr. Ricardo Lemonici. Well, that's three of the seven PoIs. I better check on the caterer list. Yep, Intoxicating Tidbits is the caterer, and Cal Sullivan is listed as working as a chef at the exhibit. That makes it four PoI's so far," Jason said, realizing that the bait was set and wondering if the remaining tickets would be purchased by any of the remaining suspects.

CHAPTER 53

Planning for the Future

Chrissy Pacque, Francine's sister-in-law, called her with the bad news.

"I hate to tell you this, but there is a shipment in Monroe, Louisiana, that got mixed up. Billy ordered it correctly and I expedited it to the Monroe Airport. But when Billy went to pick it up at the terminal, they said they didn't have it. I don't know what to do. It's a specialty electrical control box that I arranged modifications per the customer's design. Billy said that the plant is down and the customer is ready to pull us as a supplier."

"Who made the modifications, Chris, and can they expedite another quickly?"

"I already checked and the answer is 'no'," Chrissy answered. "What would have happened to the one we sent? I have the receipt that it was put onto the plane in Chicago."

Francine was afraid that something like this may happen. Monroe is a pretty large city, but not that large that there may be some insiders trying to jeopardize her business. She was aware of two previous attempts while she was still actively in the territory.

"I suspect that someone at the airport may have been paid to 'lose' things of ours. It has happened before, but it didn't have the plant down. Let me get into it a little more," Francine said, asking her sister-in-law for product numbers and descriptions.

Chrissy emailed Francine all the information she had on the electrical control box, including the specification that the Chicago supplier modified. When she understood the product, she called Billy, her sales rep for the zone.

She asked Billy if he could ask the plant if there was anyone else in the area that could supply this part on an emergency basis. She stressed that he should sound sincere when he asked if anyone could help. Billy already knew the answer. He had already heard that the plant's past supplier happened to make a "cold sales call" to the plant and they stated that they may be able to get the plant the needed control box.

"Sounds suspicious, doesn't it?" she asked Billy.

"I thought it was plain old good luck, but maybe it was too good of luck," Billy confessed.

"Our first objective is to get the plant back running."

Billy reminded her that the plant was very angry with their company, so Francine said she would contact the owner directly. A few minutes later, she was on the phone with the owner, coordinating the transfer of the other supplier's control box to their company. The plant should be running within the hour. He was not impressed, as he already lost several hours of production, and threatened to take his business to the other supplier.

After she was notified that the plant was running, Francine called Billy and asked him to take a picture of the control box. She suspected that something was awry since the box was so unique. She looked at the picture on her phone screen. It looked identical to the box that Chrissy had gotten made, but with the other supplier's identification sticker on the box front. She asked Billy to get someone to open the box to take one more picture. Billy asked the plant electrician to open the box. When he did, the electrician immediately saw part of the wiring diagram stating Francine Pacque, LLC, and the Chicago electrical company's name.

"Well, I'll be darned. How would that happen?" the electrician asked the sales rep.

Billy knew that the other supplier must have had someone at the airport take his company's box and label it as their own. He kept his thought to himself, as Francine instructed him to do.

Unfortunately for Francine, she knew she had to make yet another trip down south. Brian would be furious, but she needed to explain personally to the plant owner what happened, and she needed them to confront the supplier or this would continue to occur.

Brian came home from work exhausted from dealing with various road construction crews. Francine could see that he wasn't in a good mood, but she needed to explain her unplanned trip to Monroe. The discussion didn't go well. Brian said that nothing had really changed.

"You may be in Chicago more often, but your head is still wrapped around your business. You're glued to your computer screen even when we watch TV or eat dinner. What about our wedding, Francine? We said we would get married this year, but you never have time to talk about it, yet plan the wedding. You are here physically, but not mentally. This isn't the commitment I was expecting," he ranted forcibly.

Francine sat without moving, as Brian continued his outburst. She knew he was right.

"And another thing, now we have to go next week to this exhibit in Naples. At first I thought you wanted me to meet everyone, but instead we are going 'undercover' like your some super spy. I don't get it with you, Francine. I thought that Johnny and I were in your future, but your actions speak otherwise."

Francine shook her head. She felt herself give way to tears.

"I don't know what to do. I'm sure I want to be here with you and Johnny. But I'm trying to keep my business too. Yes, I do want you to meet my friends. I wish we were going to Naples only for fun. But these robberies loom over my friends in Naples and they asked for 'our' help," she said between tears.

Brian, always a soft heart, understood his fiance's problem. He was the same with his customers. He quickly remembered that one of the things that he fell in love with was Francine's commitment to her friends. He didn't like it, but he understood it.

"I better eat something and relax. Sorry to jump down your throat," he apologized as he strolled off to the kitchen.

Francine sat on the couch with her knees tight to her chest. She didn't have an idea what to do to solve her dilemma.

She flew to Monroe the next morning and immediately went to the plant. The owner was pleasant but kept a stern demeanor as he motioned for her and Billy to enter his office. Losing assembly time was very expensive for any plant and he expected to have to pay overtime to his employees to make up for the several hours of downtime they loss. Francine got right to her point.

"Mr. Mueller, of course we are sorry that your plant experienced a shutdown due to our missing control box."

He interrupted to explain the seriousness of the downtime and finished saying, "This is completely unacceptable. If it wasn't for our old local supplier, my plant would still be down."

"Sir, I believe that your plant was down 'because' of your past, local supplier. I'd like to show you something."

Francine presented the tracking notification from Chicago that the control box had been put onto the airplane to Monroe. She explained that somehow their box was removed from the incoming freight and given to their past supplier.

"Here is the proof. Bill took a picture of the box that they installed for you. Notice their company logo sticker. But when you open the box, here is the custom work sticker and ID number for the customized work we had done in Chicago. They appeared to resticker our control box and pass it on as their own," she explained.

He carefully looked at the documentation and pictures. Then he called his maintenance supervisor to verify that this box was the one installed last evening. He excused them from his office until he had gotten his confirmation.

"We verified the box and believe you are correct. I don't know what to say, except that I will never do business with my old supplier again," Ms. Pacque.

Francine and Billy thanked him and shook his hand. She asked if there was anything else that they could do for them while she was here. He was stunned and ashamed that his old supplier would stoop for something so low.

"How are you going to handle this other firm?"

"Things like this happen more often that you would think. I'm going to let Billy talk to them. He knows those people and he has the proof to show them. If they try it again, we have this as a precedence and we will contact the police."

Billy was happy to hear that he was going to handle the other supplier. He played in a pool league with some of those people. He knew they wouldn't want their company name trashed all over town.

"Just make sure you pay us for the control box, not them. And maybe you want to charge them the cost of the downtime they created."

The owner thanked them again before Francine and Billy left his office. They could hear their customer rant as they left the building.

"Why should I have to eat this overtime cost? It was their fault. I'm going to give them a piece of my mind, and tell them that they are going to owe me some money."

Francine flew into Louisiana only for that one day. She spent some time with her sales representative, Billy, at several other plants before she had to leave for her flight. She was anxious to return home to her fiancé.

This was an anxious time, but, somehow I had a clearer head knowing that I had someone waiting for me at home. I've never felt so happy.

CHAPTER 54

Preparing for the Trunk Show Exhibit

O fficer Breakly met with a team of policemen to talk over the event. He had a map of the downtown Naples area posted with red marks for every city video camera. He explained that the police were to stay away from the immediate area of the Inn on Fifth Avenue, but were to be available on several side streets. He pointed to several unconstricted streets where they could react quickly, and stated that only one police car was to be positioned directly on Fifth Avenue, about a block west of the Inn. He explained that the absence of any police would scare off a professional thief, who would expect some local presence.

Security within the hotel would be handled through the hotel security team. He explained that the hotel had contracted for extra security for the event, including several undercover agents stationed in the exhibit, not identifying Noel and her small team of friends as the agents.

"This exhibit contains many valuable artifacts and includes some jewels worn by Egyptian royalty. It is a good chance that our thief will not be able to resist, and we will close in on him if a robbery occurs. Please, make sure you handle this day as if it is any ordinary day. This thief probably lives among us, so we don't want to tip him off."

The police team spent some additional time going over the map and the potential suspects. The exhibit was in a few days so detailed planning was necessary.

He reviewed the final list of people who purchased tickets. One more person of interest was on the final list, Mr. and Mrs. George Farrington, making the number of people to watch as "four" persons of interest.

He gazed at the list searching for another name, Lilly Lee. He knew that she wouldn't be on the list, but *a guy can hope, can't he?* He tried to regroup his thoughts away from Lilly and back to guarding the exhibit. He was having trouble keeping focus so he telephoned Noel and said he had the final list of names and which of the undercover agents should watch which person.

"I want Angela to watch Ricardo Lemonici. She has an eye for detail, and that man is liable to do anything. Next, Francine should watch Cal Sullivan, who is signed up to work as a chef. He might not come out of the kitchen, but she will have to keep moving around to watch for him appearing through any interior door. Mitzi should watch George Farrington, who I do not think is the thief. He'll be attending with his wife. And last, you, Noel. Keep an eye out on Joe Franklin. He'll also be with his wife, and I understand that his son, Dennis, is performing as well."

"OK, I'll tell the girls their assignments. I'm not so happy watching our good friends, the Franklins. If I get too close, they will surely recognize me. We've been friends for years."

"I don't think Joe Franklin is our thief either, Noel, but he's still a PoI and should be watched. You can stroll around and enjoy the exhibit while keeping one eye on him. It shouldn't be too difficult."

CHAPTER 55

The Egyptian Exhibit

A ritifacts Unlimited owners, Jesse Gerin and Sal Rifton, arrived in Naples one day prior to the event. They were given an address of a secured parking garage to keep their large truck with the exhibits. Naples Events provided 100% security plus contracted the police to stay outside the garage. The men felt secure with the arrangement, realizing that the likely attempt of a robbery would occur within the hotel, during the exhibit. They understood that the Naples Police would also do regular drive-bys during the night for extra protection.

The owners stayed at the Inn on Fifth Avenue during the night. They loved the smaller boutique hotel but questioned how their displays and the participants were going to be secure during the event. The hotel featured a small lobby and one small hall for the exhibits. They were told prior to the event, by Noel Noirty and Officer Breakly, that extra precautions would be made the day of the event.

"They have paid us in advance, and we are insured, so don't be so worried, Sal."

"I know that our items are secure, but what about us?"

Jesse shrugged as he answered, "There will be undercover police. What could happen?"

In the morning, draperies were hung on the windows of the hotel, limiting spectators on the street to look at the exhibits without a ticket. Although the dark drapes were pre-approved by the hotel manager, the effect was stark. There was very little light in the front lobby for the hotel to run their regular business.

Velvet ropes were hung to divide off the hotel from the exhibit areas, and the exhibits began to be placed in their well-designed cabinets. Jesse and Sal were known in the business to have very fine artifacts, but having Egyptian jewels brought them to another level. The men spared no expense in making displays for the various jewels. A large glass cover was placed over the cabinet as protection.

Various professional posters were hung on the draperies surrounding the exhibit. Some showed artifacts in the archeological place where they were found. Others showed museum displays of additional period pieces. A separate display was made featuring the Egyptian jewels entitled, "Egyptian Dynasty". It portrayed a picture of a woman posing as Cleopatra on her lounger. She was wearing some of the jewelry that was being featured in the show. Dominic Pepino had paid for the large poster after Jesse and Sal suggested that it would fit in with their own items.

The back of the exhibit hall featured period pieces that were for sale. These pieces were not part of the exhibit, but a very important part for the owners. It was how they made their money. It was seldom that someone actually wanted to purchase one of the expensive artifacts. And, of course, the Egyptian Dynasty pieces had a marque that read "not for sale".

By noon, the exhibit was ready. The owners walked through the exhibit one last time before they allowed security or others to go through their show.

The Egyptian display was directly in the lobby area, by the request of the Naples police, who said that the hotel cameras would be utilized to watch the exhibit. It was a breath-taking display of four cases, each featuring beautiful Egyptian art. The forth cabinet held the huge ruby diamond ring. A small picture, similar to the large poster on the wall was laid next to the ring, so attendees could imagine the ring on Cleopatra's finger. Jess and Sal could not believe the vast value of these pieces that were in Dominic's possession, but they acted as if they were their own for the event.

Their own artifacts were beautifully displayed in matching cabinets in the small hall, in front of the artifacts for sale. This room was also artfully and beautifully decorated. Jesse and Sal looked at each other and gave each other a high sign. They were ready to bring in the others working the event.

Security was led through the displays as Sal talked about the period pieces. The three guards nodded and talked among themselves as to best watch the crowd. It was decided that one guard be stationed at the exhibit entrance, one at the hall entrance, and the last near the cash register in the sales area. The cooks, servers, and bartenders were brought through the exhibit next. They were not given a detailed account of the items by Sal, but rather, instructed where to set up their tables and cash bar. The hotel hallway was determined to be the best area.

"I don't know how we are going to handle two hundred people in here? It's crowded already," Jesse asked Sal.

CHAPTER 56

Meeting the Society Group

The flight from Chicago to Fort Myers, Florida, was uneventful. Francine read some magazines that she purchased from the airport. But, her fiancé, Brian Sherman, was fascinated flying over the fields and cities. For the past three hours, Brian was fixated on the landscape far beneath him, realizing how small we all are in the realm of everything. He recognized some of the cities below by their location on the Mississippi River. They appeared in his window but were quickly gone as the airplane flew its route.

We are nothing but a mere speck. Heck, our big cities are a mere speck in relation to our planet.

He turned towards Francine to discuss his new revelation, but realized she was too engrossed in her gossip magazine. He turned back to his window and continued to observe the land below.

When they arrived at Southwest Florida International Airport, they quickly rented a car and sped down the highway towards Naples. Brian had been to Florida several times, but never on the west, Gulf of Mexico side. He was disapointed that he couldn't see the water from the car, but knew that the land adjacent to the water was too valuable to have a highway.

A half hour later, they arrived at the Naples exit. They arrived at the small one bedroom apartment that Francine leased. It was clean and nicely furnished, but most importantly, it held many of Francine's hot weather clothes. She intended to end the lease in November, when its term was over.

They were invited to Noel and Dave Noirty's house for dinner, along with Angela Fratilo and Mitzi Vanderloof. Noel wanted time for the undercover girls to talk. She wanted to share the information that Officer Breakly provided to her, as well as the girls' assignments at the exhibit.

She knew that Noel was excited to meet her beau, but unknown to Noel, knew that Brian was just as excited. He had spent the last year and a half hearing about "Noel this, and Noel that". She knew he was anxious to meet her husband, Dave, and hopefully see one of his yachts, and possibly board one of them.

As she drove down Rum Row, the exclusive street where the Noirty's house was located, she could see the change in Brian's behavior. She observed him sit upright in his seat and look back and forth to observe the homes on both sides of the street.

"This is so posh. How do you know where to turn? There's so many intricate streets and so much foliage, it looks like a park, not a residential street," he asked.

As she turned into the Noirty's driveway, she heard a sound come from Brian's mouth.

"It's beautiful, isn't it?"

"I knew it would be, but until you see it yourself, you can't imagine. Where was the house you rented last year?"

She pointed next door, to another similarly stunning house. Brian nodded but didn't comment further, since he knew that Francine had lied about her bio and gained access to renting that house on a ruse.

They arrived a half hour before Mitzi and Angela at the request of Noel. She wanted to meet Brian before the others arrived. Noel came to the massive front door and swung it wide open. She hugged her and gave Brian a hug too, carefully looking him over before the hug. Noel could tell that Noel approved. He was tall, powerfully built, with a slight rugged look to his face.

I can see why Francine would be attracted to Brian. Any woman would be, Noel thought.

Soon, the four of them were in the outside entertainment area getting drinks made by their bartender and host, Dave. Brian's eyes kept looking around the yard, to the pier where two beautiful boats were docked, and to the house which Noel artfully lit up with tasteful lights and accessories.

A while later, Mitzi and Angela arrived, and more drinks were poured and introductions given. Noel motioned with her head towards her husband for he and Brian to leave the woman for a while.

"Would you like to see the boats?" he asked.

"Of course!" Brian said jumping off his chair.

The two men left for the pier and soon entered the smaller, pleasure craft. Dave was saving the yacht for last.

Noel took the opportunity to explain the assignments of each woman. She gave copies of the pictures of each assigned person of interest to them, explaining that they were to watch their particular person assigned. Noel explained that if the PoI makes a direct move to steal an item, they should press the alarm button in their pocket, and the police will quickly enter the hotel to make an arrest.

"Officer Breakly said to make sure to press the button only if the crime occurred. If not, there would be no evidence to make any arrest," Noel explained.

The girls understood and took their assigned color-coded buttons.

Noel added, "The officer wanted me to express his gratitude for volunteering for this. He said that nothing may happen at the exhibit. The thief may be long gone, but if a robbery is to occur, we have to remember that a thief will do anything to escape. We are not to intervene. Just press the button and the cops will know which PoI corresponds to the button. There are cameras in the hotel which should capture the theft. Again, we cannot do anything. The thief could be hiding a firearm or knife and we could get hurt, or worse."

The girls nodded that they understood.

The rest of the evening consisted of wine for the girls and beer for the guys, with a shot of whisky occasionally. Brian was so in awe of Dave's yacht, that dinner was brought onto the ship for the group to enjoy. It was no problem, as the ship had a full, gourmet kitchen with a dining table for eight. Dave and Noel entertained flawlessly, as Noel moved from the galley to the dining table in her Dolce and Gabbana heels with her long caftan dress flowing as she walked. Brian noticed her huge wedding ring as well as several other diamonds on other fingers. He glanced at Francine's ring. He thought a one carat diamond was big, but it was dwarfed by the rings on the yacht.

The group left about nine, knowing that they needed to be in top shape for tomorrow's surveillance. Mitzi left in her convertible BMW and Angela in her stately Lexus. As Francine and Brian got into their compact rental, he began jabbering.

"You're friends are great, but, Oh my God, all that wealth! It has to be tiring."

She laughed and nodded.

"Such a burden, but what a way to go," she replied.

The Exhibition

The day started as most do in southern Florida, sunny and beautiful. The forecast called for partly cloudy afternoon skies and a temperature of ninety degrees. Normal for early summer in south Florida.

Officer Jason Breakly read the forecast and was pleased. He didn't want rain to interfere with the electronic buttons he gave to the women going undercover. He hadn't slept last night. His head raced from detail to detail, suspect to suspect. He wanted to catch this guy. Not only so he would be closer to his detective's license, but so that his community would be safe again.

He thought briefly about Lilly Lee. It was one of his favorite pastimes to think of her. He hoped for a lead to get her necklace returned, even if it was a long shot.

At least I'd have another reason to call her, if there is a lead.

The exhibit was to run from two p.m. until five p.m. Three hours to hope for an alarm signal. He expected the guests would walk through the exhibits first and then move to the hallway to get appetizers and drinks. He liked his odds that the exhibits would be less trafficked from four to five o'clock. It would be easier for the women to notice something.

Everything was going smoothly, almost too smoothly, when

he remembered his mentor, Officer McQuaid, tell him that 'too smoothly' means something is 'off'. He scratched the back of his neck thinking if he missed something.

"Too smooth," he said aloud while shaking his head.

Several unmarked police cars were borrowed from surrounding stations for the officers to use during this sting. The officers moved to their respective cars, with him picking a shiny black Mustang. One marked police car drove to its identified position, about a block and a half from the Inn on Fifth Avenue. That officer was to appear very normal, and exit the car occasionally, to get a coffee or sandwich. Everything was moving too smoothly.

Inside the event, the high-top tables were cloaked with black and gold striped tablecloths, reminiscent of the cloth used by Egypt's dynasty. Solid black chairs were perched next to each table next to the portable bar. A small area was cleared next to the bar for the musician to set up his gear.

Dennis Franklin set up his small amplifier, stool, guitar stand, and his favorite Martin guitar. He was nervous to play entirely instrumentals. His normal gig consisted of light rock with some old folk tunes, and he was a novice at performing to an audience. But he was hired to perform instrumentals today for this high-crust crowd. He sat and tuned his strings, hoping to create the best tone.

This show will be good on my resume, he thought as he quickly thought ahead to moving to Nashville one day.

He continued to strum as he became comfortable in these new surroundings. Several of the waiters and kitchen help left their positions to listen to his tunes. Several of them clapped as he finished, alleviating some of his nervousness.

Exhibit attendees started to arrive before two p.m., anxious to get a first look at the displays. But Jesse and Sal stood firm at the entrance of the exhibit, not allowing the ticket girl to accept any tickets just yet. When the Inn clock struck two, they opened the velvet rope to allow patrons inside.

The attendees began to surround the displays and oohs and aahs could be heard throughout the crowd. Noel overheard several patrons comment on their wonderful luck to view these artifacts. She provided her entrance ticket to the ticket girl, and hurried through the crowd, hidden from her real identity by her disguise. She walked through the displays casually, continually looking for her PoI, Joe Franklin, but he and Pepper had not yet arrived.

Mitzi entered the event with a flashy cane, helping to create the illusion that she was a wealthy, elderly woman. The ticket girl asked if she needed any assistance, looking at her cane when she entered.

My disguise must be working, Mitzi told herself, while moving forward slowly looking for her mark.

Angela entered the exhibit and immediately noticed a man wearing a bright red suit with a yellow polka dotted ascot. She walked towards the man, looking at the displays until she could identify his face. It was Ricardo Lemonici. She thought that her time observing Mr. Lemonici would be interesting, but hardly thought that someone wearing such an outlandish outfit would dare to rob the exhibit.

Noel spotted Joe and Pepper Franklin entering the ticket gate. They were their usual, elegant selves. Joe was wearing a formal men's suit with a tie matching his wife's beautiful robin egg blue dress. Pepper's dress was one that Noel had seen once before and she wished she had it for herself. The fitted dress showed off Pepper's ample curves with a pin tucked bodice. Noel almost forgot that she was in disguise as she moved towards her friends to greet them. She quickly retreated to look at one of the displays while Joe and Pepper spoke with some other well-known Naples socialites.

Brian Sherman entered the ticket gate with a sassy looking brunette on his arm. Francine was disguised but her fiancé was unknown to the Naples group, so he didn't require a disguise. Francine wore a dark straight skirt with a simple blouse tucked into her skirt. She padded herself a bit to appear to be heavier than she really was, but not too heavy to appear pregnant. She and Brian spoke quietly to each other as they looked at the displays. They appeared to be an interested couple, probably wealthy tourists, and no one gave them any attention.

Angela had trouble keeping up with her person of interest. Ricardo continually moved from display to display, veering suddenly to the bar to purchase a martini. He drank his cocktail quickly and headed back into the exhibition hall. He quickly moved to the artifacts that were for sale, looking for anything interesting to him. It appeared to Angela that he liked everything.

Mitzi walked through the exhibit looking for George Farrington. She found him chatting with neighbor, Joe Franklin. They were chatting with an occasional friendly pat on each other's arm. Soon they approached the bar while their wives teamed up to look at the exhibits. The men ordered drinks and chose two chairs close to where Joe's son, Dennis, was performing.

This is too easy, Mitzi thought as she found a chair by another table to rest.

Soon a waitress came and took her order. She ordered a coffee and asked for a couple of appetizers, trying to imitate what an older women may do. She continued to rest while her mark sat drinking his Manhattan.

Francine took a quick peek into the kitchen each time the door opened for a waitress. She spotted Cal Sullivan moving pans on the stove. He was in high form, shouting some audible orders to his other cooks. It appeared to her that Cal took his chef position as an honor, and suspected that this particular event of Naples' royalty may be his ticket to a full time chef position. She suspected that he also wanted to impress the management of the Inn on Fifth Avenue who stood impassively in the kitchen,

She noticed Brian nibbling on appetizers and joined him for some of her own. She could keep a watch on the kitchen door in case Cal left his position. She could also watch the main door in case he would leave the kitchen through some back exit and reappear at the main entrance. She smiled as she realized that her person to observe was an easy task.

George Farrington finished his drink and wandered back into the exhibits to the back hall where the store was located. He found his wife, and they moved in unison to the archeological artifact displays. They looked intently in the cabinet, trying to identify unique pieces and match them up to the artifacts on the giant posters that lined the walls.

Mitzi positioned herself in the store area, looking at items while observing the couple. Again, she was asked if she needed some assistance by one of the waiters.

I'll have to take a cane anytime I'm looking for a seat, she thought, laughing to herself.

She quickly composed herself and continued watching Mr. Farrington.

Joe Franklin listened to his son for several songs, clapping at the end of each one and motioning to his friends to clap as well. Occasionally, someone Joe knew would stop to talk to him, and they engaged in friendly conversation. Noel continued to mingle behind other patrons who were looking at the prize display, the Cleopatra ruby ring. She watched her mark with one eye, but also watched every person looking at the display. She did not want to miss anything.

White male, five-foot-eight-inches wearing cream silk pants. Next, a six-foot male, dark hair thinning at his brows, about sixty, Noel thought to herself as she tried to memorize every person's details.

She was supposed to watch Joe Franklin, but wondered if someone else, unknown to the group, was the thief? She realized that she needed to focus on Joe.

Where is Pepper? she questioned, scanning the room.

She spotted Pepper talking with the trunk show promoters, Jesse and Sal. They were deep in conversation about their show and the displays they were showing.

Good. Nothing unusual is happening. Everything is going smoothly, Noel thought.

Ricardo Lemonici returned to the front of the exhibition where the Egyptian artifacts were displayed. The Cleopatra display was most viewed by the patrons attending the event, but as the time passed, the crowd died down. Angela looked at her watch and noticed that it was three-thirty, half way through the event. She was getting more anxious as the time passed. If there would be a robbery, it would have to be in the next hour and a half.

Lemonici walked around the display, lightly touching the glass all the way around the display. Angela wondered if he had some type of diamond tool that was cutting a line through the glass top. She moved closer to the display, as to also look at the large ruby and other jewels.

"Beautiful, isn't it," Lemonici said to her from the other side of the cabinet.

Angela nodded, remembering not to engage in conversation. She quickly looked at the glass and did not see any cut line. She also stole a glance at his hand and saw that he did not have any tool. She moved to the next display hoping to get a little distance from her mark. Angela looked through the next cabinet's glass, still able to watch Lemonici. He continued to look at the jewels and touched the glass frequently.

Soon, another man, much less flamboyant, joined Lemonici. They gave each other a small hug and Lemonici began describing the jewels to his friend. It appeared harmless. After a few minutes, they moved to the next cabinet and began the discussion again.

Angela looked at her watch again, three-fifty.

Francine was also growing more anxious as the time for a robbery closed in. The exhibit would last only slightly more than one hour longer. She shifted in her chair to steal another peek at the kitchen. Cal Sullivan was still preparing appetizers for the crowd. As most of the patrons had finished looking at the exhibits, the bar and table area where the appetizers were displayed was booming. Francine knew he would be busy for at least the next half hour until clean-up would begin. She took another canapé from the table.

"These are delicious," she said to Brian.

"Yeah," Brian replied softy. "Your guy is one heck of a chef."

Noel continued to watch Joe Franklin as he walked around the exhibits and spoke to people he knew. She knew he was a great communicator, and he was used to being a great host. She knew that Naples Events had asked him to be the coordinator for this event and Joe turned it down, but even though he turned it down, he volunteered his special communication skills as he worked the room.

She admired him and felt awkward watching him as a PoI.

Joe joined his wife, Pepper, to talk with another couple that Noel knew from Naples. Soon, the four of them were coming towards the appetizer area to get some more snacks. Noel continued to move around the exhibits but always kept one eye on the Cleopatra display and one eye on Joe Franklin.

Mitzi's mark was very easy to watch. George Farrington did not seem very interested in the displays, but it appeared that he came to satisfy his wife. He sat at one of the high-top tables listening to Dennis Franklin play guitar almost the entire time. At three-thirty, his wife came to the table and they briefly spoke before they bid their friends good-bye and left the exhibition. Mitzi's job was done. She used her cane to slowly walk to the bar.

"Give me a dry martini," she said. "And only show the glass the vermouth."

She took a plate of appetizers and found an empty chair at the bar. Her undercover day was complete.

Officer Breakly sat in his unmarked Mustang and watched the clock. Four-ten. Nothing unusual and no buzzer alerts from the undercover girls. He had been nervously communicating with the other four unmarked squad cars every fifteen minutes. There had been nothing to report except for one officer's wise crack remarks about a scantily clad woman parading down his street.

"I guess the plan didn't work," Jason thought to himself. "The thief is probably long gone."

He knew that he would get the blame for costing undue overtime. It may cost him his detective's badge. He watched the clock, waiting for his four-forty-five check in with the other squads.

Back in the exhibit, some patrons were getting ready to leave, others were chatting with the exhibit promotors, and some listening to Dennis while having a final cocktail. There were still about fifty patrons wandering through the exhibits or in the artifact sales area. The event was a big success for the promoters. They had a sell-out crowd and had a number of sales. They were even approached to do another exhibit next season when the Naples'crowd was back in town.

Noel realized that the exhibit atmosphere was perfect, with patrons talking, laughter, and good music. It was going very smoothly.

BANG! BANG! BANG! BANG! BANG! BANG! BANG! BANG!

A quick series of loud bangs went off in the hall.

"There's a shooter!" someone shouted.

BANG! BANG! BANG! BANG! BANG!

Another series of apparent shots were fired. This time the sound appeared to come from the hallway, near the kitchen.

Suddenly, smoke filled the areas, with occasional sound of more gunfire.

"Run," someone shouted. "Someone's shooting!"

Panic filled the area as the lights in the hotel went out, leaving the area almost completely black with the heavy exhibit draperies on the hotel's windows. People were screaming and running for the door. Brian grabbed Francine without asking and almost lifted her by her arms to get her moving towards the door. Angela was knocked down by a man as he climbed over her to get out of the exhibit. All she could see were a bit of red pants climbing over her. Someone else helped her up and she proceeded out the door.

Little Mitzi forgot her cane as she sprinted ahead of most of the patrons, knocking a few of them away. Her experience as a high-end real estate lady taught her to be the first one at a property for sale, or in this case, the first one out the door.

Chaos abounded as several more shots were fired, one in the front exhibit area. People were screaming as they knocked over one of the first Egyptian display cabinets with its precious contents scattering on the floor.

Francine pushed her buzzer as Brian led her towards the front door, alerting the police that something was happening. The police cars surrounded the back parking area as patrons were running.

"We need to keep these people in one place. One of them could be the shooter or a thief," Officer Breakly shouted in his radio to the other officers. They quickly started to corral the scared patrons, leading them to a safe area away from the Inn, but under watch by the police.

Several patrons ran down Fifth Avenue shouting, "There's a shooter at the hotel!".

The half asleep officer stationed a block away from the hotel started to run towards the area. He instructed people on the street to go into any of the shops that lined the streets and to tell the shop owners to lock their doors.

"We need back-up!" Officer Breakly shouted into his microphone to the police station. "Active shooter and possible robbery at The Inn on Fifth Avenue."

Oficer Breakly glanced at his watch. . "Had only one minute passed since he did his last check?"

The simple alarm sounded at the Inn, alerting all their guests to exit the building, not being able to differentiate that their guests may be shot as they exited.

Access to the front door was limited, because part of the lobby was roped off for the exhibit. Some people were coughing due to the smoke and others were coming out of the Inn. Noel frantically tried to see through the darkness and the smoke, but could not make out anything but shadows. She occasionally heard familiar voices calling for their loved ones. One of the voices she heard was Pepper, as she shouted to her son, Dennis,

"Dennis, Dennis!" she yelled

"I"m ok, mom, I'm still at the stage. Are you and dad ok?"

Pepper must have gotten close to the stage and could spot her son, "Oh, thank goodness. Leave your stuff and lets get out of here."

Noel was happy to know they were not shot.

BANG, BANG, BANG, BANG!

A second round of shots were fired and people began screaming again as they tried to get out the door.

Noel was against the draped window, standing between two exhibit cases. She crouched to the floor and held part of her blouse up over her nose to shield the smoke fumes. Her eyes were glued to the case in front of her, the Cleopatra ring case. She was not leaving it.

Sirens were heard in the background to her great relief, as she suddenly caught a black shadow in front of her. POP! POP! POP! The glass case shattered, but she remained silent. She hoped her crouched position gave her the advantage she needed to remain hidden.

She saw an arm stretch out into the cabinet and knew that the person had taken the jewel. She silently watched as she saw something put into a small container in the person's hand before the person walked forward towards the bar area. She crawled on her knees forward and stretched out completely laying on the floor. Although she was quiet, she noticed the thief stopped and quickly turned around. As he didn't see anyone standing there, he quickly proceeded by the small stage.

The smoke was clearing just enough to see a hand reach out to the face of the guitar leaning on its guitar stand. Then the body quickly moved forward, dashing out the door, with the remaining people. The police were outside the Inn, directing everyone to a safe place away from the inn. No one was allowed to leave until the exhibit could be checked, and if necessary, until each patron was checked. Some people left through the back emergency entrance, and they were also met by the police.

A fire engine arrived and the firemen started fitting their hose to the hydrant. Additional police cars were raced onto Fifth Avenue, blocking traffic and setting up a safe perimeter. There was a strange silence as the smoke from the inn dissipated and the inn's main doors were open without a sound.

The Chief of Police arrived and took control of the situation. He carefully led a team into the building, being uncertain if anyone had been shot or if the thief, or thieves, were still in the hotel. They advanced with several officers carrying bright lights since the electric was off in the building. Other police had their weapons drawn as they carefully moved into the inn.

About fifty feet into the lobby, they saw a woman laying on her stomach. Jason recognized Noel's disguise. He ran over to her a knelt down, expecting to see blood. His stomach tightened, expecting the worse.

"Noel, can you hear me? It's Officer Breakly."

She continued laying down but answered, "Jason, I saw him. I know who took the ruby."

Jason saw blood oozing on the other side of Noel's body.

"Get an ambulance. This woman has been shot!"

"Don't let him leave, Jason. Promise me you won't let him get away."

"Who did you see?" he whispered in her ear.

Noel was approaching unconsciousness. She didn't see the thief's face. She took one hand and pointed towards the guitar.

"The guitar singer?"

"No, not him," she weakly answered, pointing to the guitar a final time. She strained to keep conscious.

Jason went up to the stage and lifted the guitar, expecting to find something rattling inside. It didn't make a sound.

The Chief yelled an "all clear" and more police and firemen rushed into the lobby. Yellow tape was tied to keep the crime scene intact, with the Chief giving only five police officers the ability to enter.

Noel was carefully put onto a stretcher with Officer Breakly overlooking her care. Despite their friendship, the Chief gave the instruction that Noel was to be checked for any jewels on her person. Jason frowned at the Chief's instruction, although understanding that it was the right call.

Jesse and Sal were summoned back into the hotel to check their exhibit inventory. They gasped when they saw the front Egyptian cabinet glass shattered. They immediately noticed that the large Cleopatra ruby ring was missing, but all other jewels were still present. The promoters checked their own displays and found their glass cabinets intact.

"Oh, no", Jesse said as he realized there was blood on the floor. "Was someone shot?"

One of the officers who was present when the EMTs put the woman on a stretcher answered him.

"No, it appears she wasn't shot. She cut herself multiple places when she crawled on the broken glass."

The ambulance left with sirens blazing. The exhibit patrons and other spectators were frantically trying to find out what happened, but the police didn't have enough knowledge to tell them anything yet. Francine, Angela, and Mitzi had been led to an area in back of the shops. They wondered where their friend, Noel, was located, but knew that other patrons were led to another safe zone.

There was a small group of people standing in Fifth Avenue, which had traffic blocked off. These people were also to be questioned. Pepper, Joe, and Dennis Franklin were among those people.

"Officer, is it safe to go inside and get my son's musical equipment? We are afraid that the sprinklers might be engaged by the smoke and his equipment ruined," Joe said.

"Yeah, especially my guitar," his son added.

One officer led them towards the door and asked the Chief. The Chief nodded his head in agreement saying, "Let one of them in to get their stuff."

Joe looked at his son and motioned for him to stand with his mother, as he preceded inside the Inn. He walked slowly and directly to the stage, and picked up the guitar.

Jason noticed him and yelled, "Hey, who let you in here?"

Joe pointed to another officer who nodded that it was approved. Jason returned to his investigation and started writing some notes, as he remembered Noel's pointing gesture.

He paused. He had checked the guitar and it was empty.

But, something was bothering him. Something seemed wrong. He turned around and walked towards Joe, yanking the guitar away from him.

Joe looked surprised, "The Chief said I could take my son's guitar. It is very valuable and could get ruined or taken."

Jason took a light and looked inside the guitar's cavity. It was clear. He gently shook it but nothing sounded. He handed the guitar back to Joe.

Joe smiled and nodded. He turned and walked towards the door.

Jason watched as he thought of how Noel's hand had pointed to the guitar. Her hand seemed to cramp as it bent severely. He frowned as he positioned his hand as she had demonstrated. *I wonder if she was showing me what to do?*

"Joe! Stop!" he yelled as the other officers stopped and looked his way

He grabbed the guitar away from Joe who looked confused as he let it go from his grip. Office Breakly slid his hand under the strings and into the sound hole. He bent his hand as remembered Noel's gesture.

He felt along the inside of the cavity when his hand hit something. He placed his two fingers on each side of the item and tugged. The item released. It was a small pouch with a fine velcro strip on the back. Jason unzipped the front of the pouch. A gleaming red ruby was inside.

Joe Franklin tried to look surprised, but his face did not fool the police. Joe was told he was under arrest, read his Miranda rights, and led to a squad car.

"This is preposterous!" Joe screamed. "I just came back for my son's guitar. I have no idea how the ring got in there? When my attorney gets a hold of you guys, you're going to be sorry."

Noel observed the arrest happening as she was being prepped for transport by the paramedics. She halted them and motioned for Officer Breakly. He quickly moved over her as she whispered,

"I coated the back of the ruby with transparent paint. Get my purse. I have a small black light in there. See if he has any traces on him."

He stared at her in disbelief. They hadn't talked about any paint or a black light. He started laughing and shook his head as he got up and approached Joe Franklin.

"Hold out your hands, Mr. Franklin," he demanded.

Joe thought he was going to release his handcuffs and quickly moved his hands and arms towards the officer. Jason switched the small black light tube on and waved it over Joe's hands. Joe's right hand glowed in the dark.

Jason waved the light over the ruby and the pouch and it matched with a bright glow. He then waved it over the guitar and found remnants of glowing paint.

Joe Franklin's eyes widen with despair. He looked at the woman laying on the stretcher without any recognition of who she was, but he thought to himself that she was one heck of a detective. He put his head down and was led to an awaiting police car, much to the dismay of his wife, Pepper, and his son, Dennis.

"Joe, it's all my fault, all my fault," she repeated as she placed her outstretched hands on the car's window.

The officers looked at each other and back at her.

"Mrs. Franklin, I think you need to take a ride with us," the Chief stated. "Arrest her."

Dennis stood there completely confused. His father and then his mother were arrested directly in front of him. He didn't know what was going on or what to do.

The Chief and he talked with Dennis for a few minutes. They explained that his parents were arrested for the suspected theft of the Cleopatra ruby. It was found in a small pouch in his guitar's cavity.

Dennis' mouth quivered and tears formed in his eyes.

"I don't know about a pouch," he replied weakly.

"Dennis, we do not believe you were involved, but it appears your parents may have used your guitar as a way to get small jewels out various places," the Chief explained.

"But why? They don't need the money. There must be a mistake."

"I hope so, for your sake. But we will have to confiscate your guitar. I'm sorry, son," the Chief replied.

CHAPTER 58

The Aftermath

Jason Breakly's heart was beating quickly. On one hand, it appeared he may have found the jewel thief, or thieves. On the other hand, the Inn on Fifth Avenue was a wreck of broken glass, broken artifacts scattered on the floor, and the remnants of smoke. This wasn't what he envisioned when he dreamt that one of the women would press their pocket alarms and he would rush in to apprehend the thief.

He had been apprehensive to allow the women to go undercover, but continued with the plan at Noel's insistence. Now, poor Noel was covered in blood by the shattered glass of the Cleopatra display. He marveled at how she kept her cool in such a stressful situation. Although the cuts appeared to be shallow, there was a tremendous amount of blood on her due to the multiple places she was struck by glass.

Jason wandered out of the hotel to find the other women. He found them in the back parking lot. They started to wave madly in his direction so he would notice them. The women did not know what had happened inside the Inn, only that shots were fired.

His first words were, "Thank God that all of you are ok. The 'shots' you heard were mostly fire crackers, but a real gun was used to shatter the glass of the Cleopatra display."

"So it was a robbery?" they asked in unison, followed by, "Have you seen Noel?"

"Yes, I've seen Noel, and she is going to be fine, but she was just taken to the hospital for many glass cuts. She did lose a lot of blood."

The women gasped and Mitzi quickly had tears in her eyes. He wasted no time in explaining that Noel stayed hidden among the exhibits to safeguard the Cleopatra ruby display. He explained that she saw the ruby taken and where it was hidden.

"Who's idea was it to coat the back of the ruby in blacklight paint?" he asked.

Angela stepped forward and said, "It was Noel's idea. She spoke to my uncle about it as another way to identify a thief. Uncle Dominic agreed and so she bought a blacklight and fluorescent paint. Why? Did it help?"

"Oh yeah. We recovered the ruby, but since the hotel was so dark and smokey, Noel couldn't identify the thief until we ran a black light over his hands," he said. "It was brilliant!"

"Who was it?" Angela asked.

He explained that they had to keep this confidential for a while, but Joe and Pepper Franklin were arrested. Mitzi stood speechless as Angela clutched onto her arm. Francine's hand quickly grabbed Brian's arm, who continually shook his head. He was proud of these women who went to bat for their community. Unfortunately, the thieves may turn out to be one of their own group.

"Can we go, Jason? I'd like to get to the hospital where Noel was taken," Francine asked.

"Yes, I'll be heading to the hospital after we get done here, and I'll take your statements then. I need to call Noel's husband, before he hears from someone else about his wife."

He dialed his phone and Dave Noirty answered on the first ring. Jason informed Dave about his wife's involvement in the police sting. He called Noel a "hero", as she stayed in harm's way until she observed the theft. He explained that Noel sustained multiple cuts from spraying, shattered glass when the display glass was shot, and that she sustained additional cuts by crawling on the floor to see who the robber was, and where the ruby was being hidden.

Dave Noirty burst out in tears. He had no idea that his wife would do anything so brazen and dangerous. He was informed of what hospital Noel was taken to and darted out the door, much to the surprise of his employees.

One of his contracted boat captains, Captain Pete, called to him. Dave said he had to get to the hospital because Noel was badly cut in a robbery attempt.

"I'm driving you!" Pete yelled as he grabbed Dave's arm. "Jump in, my Ferrari is right here."

Angela called her uncle, who lent the ruby to the exhibit to tell him the news. Dominic Pepino was an elegant, but stern man. He slumped into his chair after learning that his ruby had actually been stolen and already found.

"I owe all of you girls so much thanks," Dominic said.

"We all pitched in, but the credit goes to Noel. She wouldn't give up."

Dominic knew this was true. He had seen Noel organize his art gala several months ago, and saw the fever she had to ensure everything went well. But knowing that her community was being threatened by crime launched Noel into a quest to get her town back to normal.Dominic was no stranger to people and personalities. He made his fortune finding other people's weaknesses and taking over their companies. He had that same fever himself, until he retired.

CHAPTER 59

The Confession

J oe Franklin was quickly booked for robbery and led into a cell at the Naples police station. He wasted no time in calling his attorney who said he would be getting him out of there within the hour. Joe's wife, Pepper, was also booked as an accessory in the crime with the attorney assuring them that Pepper would be leaving there with Joe.

The Chief of Police and Officer Breakly knew they would be released, but intended to question both of them when the attorney arrived. Attorney Jay Stein wasted no time in speeding to the station and was given some time with his clients separately before they would be questioned together.

Throwing Attorney Stein off guard, Officer Breakly said that he was going to question Pepper Franklin first. Pepper was led into one of the few interrogation rooms in the Naples station.

Pepper had been crying continuously since the arrest. Her face was striped with black lines from her weeping mascara. She appeared small and scared behind the interrogation desk.

Attorney Stein immediately spoke, "Mrs. Franklin is too distraught to be questioned at present. I demand that she be let free and allowed to see her personal physician."

"That won't be happening until we get a few facts straight," Jason said sternly as he stared directly into the attorney's eyes.

The attorney sat down and held Pepper's left hand on top of the table to stop her shaking.

"Mrs. Franklin, do you understand the seriousness of the crime for which you are being investigated?

She nodded and was informed to answer.

"Yes, I do" she answered softly.

"Mrs. Franklin, you made several statements at the scene of the crime, telling your husband. To quote you, you said, Joe, its all my fault.' Can you tell me what you meant by that?" Jason asked.

The attorney started making an objection, but she put her finger to her lips to silence him.

"I will tell you everything, if you let my husband go," she blurted out, completely to the dismay of her attorney.

"Mrs. Franklin, this isn't a courtroom and I'm not the District Attorney. We are just trying to understand the facts at this point."

Pepper started shaking uncontrollably and crying as she stammered, "It's all my fault. I brought him into my family. I introduced him to my father and this lifestyle. It's all my fault. Arrest me, but not my husband."

Jason looked at the two-way glass expecting his Chief to burst into the door, but there was no reaction. Jason looked at the attorney, who was shaking his head that his client would say so much to the police.

"Mrs. Franklin, please help me understand what you are saying?"

"Franco Fabrese! Franco Fabrese! That's who is to blame. He's my father. I never should have let anyone into my life," Pepper cried, finally folding her arms and putting her head down onto them while sobbing.

"Who is Franco Fabrese?" he asked the attorney.

Attorney Stein shook his head and answered, "I have no idea."

Jason motioned for a police woman to come into the room.

"Maggie, take Mrs. Franklin back to her holding cell and give her a damp towel and some water. If she continued to shake, please call her physician."

He indicated that he was going to take a short break before bringing Joe Franklin into the interrogation cell. The attorney appeared grateful for a break as well.

He quickly returned to his desk and looked up the name "Franco Fabrese" on his criminal database. He didn't see any name listed. He telephoned one of the assistants to do a little research on the name in the international database. About five minutes later, his phone rang.

"Franco Fabrese is a big name in international jewel thefts. There are many reports of suspected heists that he conducted using various names and disguises. He lived in Madrid, Spain, but he is deceased. He died in 2005," the assistant reported. "I'll email you the report."

Jason sat there and rubbed his head wondering if Franco Faberge was really Pepper's father. Could he have taught his daughter and her husband how to become jewel thieves? Was that why the Franklins had so much money?

He realized that there would be no reason for Pepper to lie about something like this. It must be true. As he sat there, he wondered how many other thefts were the result of Pepper and Joe Franklin.

CHAPTER 60

Is It Enough?

Brain Sherman could not be in any more of a hurry to get Francine back to Chicago. Their current plans were to fly in for the weekend to attend the exhibit, and fly home on Sunday night. He now wondered if she would try to convince him that so should stay a bit longer.

He knew that he was the more practical one of the two, and that he had simpler tastes than his fiance. Brian was happy in his small, two bedroom, one bathroom apartment in Chicago. He knew that Francine lived an "uptown" lifestyle in Chicago when he met her, but he hoped that the simple life that he and his son, Jonathan, enjoyed would be enough for her. Her could see now that the lure of Naples and her blingy friends may be the real pull for Francine. Brian decided that he needed to discuss this with her as soon as possible.

The couple had raced to the hospital to see Noel as soon as they were released from the incident. They were surprised to see that Dave Noirty was already in the surgery waiting room when they arrived. They learned that Noel had to have several of her many lacerations stitched. Dave explained that he was immediately informed that his wife would need some plastic surgery to repair more delicate tears on her face, but the doctors were stitching and taping her up presently just to stop the bleeding.

After an hour passed, a physician appeared and told the group that Noel was resting comfortably. She had lost quite a lot of blood and had many lacerations, so she was going to be sedated for the balance of the day. She could have visitors, but they need to prepare for what they were to see.

The group waited outside Noel's room until Dave gave them a sign that they could enter the room. When they entered, they saw their friend completely wrapped in gauze and tape from head to toe. She had several IVs hanging by her bed and a nurse was monitoring her vitals when they approached her.

Being sedated, Noel managed to say a weak hello to her friends. Dave continued to hold her hand as he stared at her with tears in his eyes. Francine, Angela, Mitzi, and Brian all spoke a few words, telling her how brave she was and that she would be back to normal soon. No one spoke directly about Joe or Pepper Franklin. The door opened, and a grateful Dominic Pepino entered the room at the delight of everyone.

He almost stumbled getting up close to Noel as he lightly gave her a kiss on her forehead. Noel managed a slight smile through her foggy haze. Dave suggested that Noel get some rest so the group left the room leaving Noel and Dave behind. Dave tugged his wife's blankets gently around her and sat down still staring at his wife. The love was undeniable.

The group disbanded and Brian felt compelled to begin a discussion with Francine about their future.

"I know this isn't the best time, in fact, its a horrible time, but I have to ask you this."

Francine looked quizzically at him.

"I can see your attachment to your friends here. It's a bond that I don't know if I can compete with. Are you going to be happy living in Chicago, Francine? I can't provide a mansion for you, or jewels like your friends here have. I just want to make sure you know what you are getting into. It's a middle class lifestyle," Brian said while driving.

Francine could understand Brian's concern. She had thought about it from time to time as well.

"Brian, I came from a hard working middle-class family. I am that kind of person too. I like nice things, but I never aspired for a wealthy 'yachting', for lack of a better word, life. I need someone who shares my values. You and I are exactly alike in that way. I do look forward to getting a house someday, hopefully in a nice Chicago suburb, and I look forward to having a baby or two," she said nervously while looking at Brian.

Brian's fears subsided as she spoke the exact words he hoped to hear. He nodded and smiled at her. The discussion was over. Francine reached across the seat and touched his shoulder.

"Does this qualify for make-up sex?" she inquired.

"Well, it really wasn't a fight, but I guess you may convince me."

She lightly hit him on his arm as they laughed. He sped towards her apartment.

Francine continued smiling as they drove, but her mind was reeling to the anticipated police statements, trials, Noel's recuperation, and her business. She knew the next months were going to be busy. She had no idea when she would have time to plan their wedding until next year.

CHAPTER 61

Dennis Franklin

D ennis Franklin returned home without his parents or his guitar and equipment. He drove his truck into the garage, opening and closing the polished gates quickly. He wondered if the media would soon be outside his home.

He walked into the massive living room of the mansion and looked around, taking in the furnishings, paintings, and sculptures. He continued into the kitchen and took a cold beer from the beverage refrigerator. Opening the beer, he continued toward the loggia overlooking the Gulf of Mexico. He slumped into the first chair and began crying.

Dennis wondered if his parents would be home soon on bail.

On bail!

It was too difficult to believe that his beloved parents who raised him to be participative, kind, and honest could possibly be jewel thieves.

How could they possibly be involved in these robberies? Why would they do that?

He thought about the specially designed pouch, stuck to the inside of the guitar and wondered why his parents would risk involving him through the use of his guitar. He suddenly stood up and threw his beer against the outside wall. He put his palms over his face in despair, and sat again, staring blankly at the Gulf.

After a long while, he got up and went upstairs to his father's office. He knew where his father kept his passwords and combination to his safe. He looked through his father's library for a particular book and opened it. Inside the cover, he peeled back a false lining and removed a sheet of paper containing his father's passcodes.

He nervously approached the wall of his father's paneled office. He jiggled a corner and one panel popped open, revealing a safe. Dennis used the combination code he just obtained and opened the safe, his fingers shaking as he hoped to find nothing.

CHAPTER 62

Out On Bail

The paperwork was completed and bail money was posted late in the evening.

"Joe and Pepper Franklin have clear records and have reputations as upstanding citizens," their attorney vouched to the judge who was irritated for being interrupted at dinner.

Eventually convinced, the judge approved paperwork allowing the couple be freed as a "no flight risk". The Naples' Police Chief violently protested to no avail. At eleven p.m., Joe and Pepper left in their attorney's car.

Early the following morning, Officer Breakly and four other officers headed to the Franklins' mansion with a warrant to search the house. Jason rang the gate and waited until Dennis Franklin opened the gates. The officers were already standing at the front door with Jason holding the search warrant when Dennis opened the door.

"Boy, you're early," Dennis said while rubbing his eyes.

It was obvious that he had just awakened by his glassy eyes and disheveled appearance. Jason noticed the smell of beer on Dennis' breath and knew that the man had a difficult evening.

"We have a search warrant, Dennis. You need to let us in and notify your parents that we are here. We'll try to be fast, but this is a big place to search," he instructed.

Dennis held the door open to allow the officers inside. They quickly scattered and began opening cabinets and drawers, quickly looking inside before replacing the goods back in their original position. Dennis stood there quiet and confused as the officers invaded his home.

"You better let your parents know we are here, Dennis," he repeated.

"But they are at the station. They aren't here," Dennis answered, confused at the question.

"What?" he exclaimed as he quickly turned around and faced Dennis.

"Your parents were released late last evening and left in their lawyer's car. They had explicit orders to remain at their home."

"I didn't sleep last night so I know that my parents didn't return home."

Dennis added, "Not even a phone call."

He checked Dennis' cell phone for verification and found no call was received during the night.

Dennis led him to a small room containing surveillance videos of the home. Jason quickly backed up the tape and fast forwarded it, expecting to see a car driving up to the residence. There was no evidence that the Franklins returned to their home.

He looked at Dennis who stood awkwardly by one of the ornate columns in the house. He felt truly sorry for the young man, who was only a few years younger than himself. His life had been turned over. He could see that Dennis had no knowledge of where his parents were located. He looked scared and severely hurt.

He decided to take another tactic, forgetting the search. He led

Dennis to some chairs and asked him some personal questions about his life and his musical career. Dennis relaxed as he spoke about his passion. He eventually would need to lead the conversation back to the day before.

"I've heard you play at one of the bars on Fort Myers Beach. You're good. You play some mean instrumentals although you do a good job with singing, too."

Dennis continued to relax and spoke about his desire to relocate to the Nashville area eventually to pursue a career as a musician. As he spoke, reality again stepped in, and Dennis' voice cracked, realizing that he didn't know what was going to happen next, where his parents were, what was going to happen to them, and if he would ever see them again. Dennis stopped talking and lowered his gaze to the floor.

"I can't imagine what you are going through, Dennis. We will try to stay out of your way and finish this fast," he said sympathetically.

Dennis stopped him as he was leaving the room.

"I can speed this up for you," Dennis said.

He looked quizzically at Dennis and followed him up the stairs into his father's office. There was an officer looking through the desk when they arrived.

"Can you give up a minute, Tom?"

The officer nodded and left the room, leaving Dennis and him alone.

Dennis retraced his steps from yesterday, releasing the false panel and revealing a wall safe. Soon the safe door opened, and Dennis withdrew some boxes from the safe. The two men moved to the desk and the Officer Breakly opened the first box. Inside, was an intricately carved jade necklace. Shivers went down his arm as he realized he was looking at Lilly Lee's stolen necklace.

The remaining boxes revealed the other jewelry stolen at the Riverside Shops Art Fair and at the Naples Art Fair. There was no sign of Dominic Pepino's stolen emerald from his Vino Antiquity gala. Other items in the vault were personal to the Franklin family such as social security cards, passports, and birth certificates.

As he reviewed the passports, he realized that there were multiple sets with unfamiliar names. Joe and Pepper Franklin have used false paperwork when they travelled, he noted, as he jotted down the passport country and date stamps. He wondered if these dates corresponded to international theft dates. He would bet his paycheck that they would.

"Thank you, Dennis. I don't know if we would have found this safe without your help. I can't imagine how difficult this must be for you, but the owners of these items will be so grateful to hear that they were found. Especially this jade necklace. The young woman who owns this has been devastated for losing her grandmother's necklace. But I have to ask you, have you seen a large emerald which was taken from Vino Antiquity?"

Dennis shook his head negatively, and Jason expected as much. He knew that Dominic's emerald theft was probably a pre-arranged heist. His research discovered that collectors who want that particular jewel sometimes look for someone to steal the gem. He assumed that the Franklins received the contract. The other small jewel thefts at the Art Fairs were probably "practice" for the real theft, and the Cleopatra ruby was too much of a desire to pass.

"I know that a girl was hurt at the Riverside Fair. I heard about it on TV," Dennis added, looking nervously at the officer.

He knew that his father was the coordinator of that event and had a small office along the stores in that property. He was ashamed for his parents and hoped that the girl wasn't injured too badly.

"The girl, Lilly Lee, probably bumped her head when she was pushed down the steps. We believe that her injury was an accident, not the intention."

Dennis appeared to be relieved, while still wondering what other terrible things his parents might have done.

Jason went downstairs to inform the other officers that Dennis found most of the items in his father's wall safe. The officers continued to look for items another hour. They also photographed all the art in the home, in case it was stolen elsewhere. About two hours later, their search was finished and they left Dennis standing in the driveway alone, wondering what to do next.

CHAPTER 63

Feeling Proud

Noel's wounds healed during the next few weeks. All that remained were several swollen scars on her face that would need some plastic surgery in another month. There were many articles in the local and even in the national news about the "housewife" that saved Naples. Pictures of Noel were included with the news that featured a luminous woman wearing Dior with multiple layers of jewels hanging from her neck.

"Some 'housewife', Dave Noirty would exclaim each time he saw Noel's picture posted.

Noel felt proud of herself for staying put in the hotel until the thief was revealed. She had never felt the thrill of being a success for something she did on her own.

So this is what it feels like to be proud of yourself.

Suddenly her future seemed somewhat brighter. She knew that the novelty of her celebrity would wear off eventually, but she knew that her personal pride of solving this crime and making her community safer would never end. She thought about Dave, who she thought at one time did not love her anymore, and how she felt so desperate and alone. Now, she had a family, with Brianna as her step-daughter, and knew that her husband loved her dearly.

Her thoughts drifted to the Franklins, Pepper and Joe. The

investigation by the police revealed that Pepper was the daughter of a renown jewel thief. Originally born in Portugal, Pepper, or Joanna Fabrese, as her original name now was known, grew up as a student of her father's skill. Whether it was willingly or unwillingly was unknown, but Joanna worked along side of her father on several international heists. She met Joe Franklin when he was studying abroad and they got married. Not much more of Joe Franklin is known, but it was suspected that he got involved in the family business as well. They moved to Naples when Dennis was a small boy, already wealthy and keeping to themselves.

The investigation found that Joe Franklin often travelled abroad and it was suspected that he met with his father-in-law on those trips. Sometimes his wife joined him, but she usually stayed home with their son, Dennis. High profile robberies took place during the same period of times that Joe was traveling. It was too much of a coincidence.

Something changed when Dennis turned about ten years old. The Franklins didn't travel as much and blended into society in Naples. Joe and Pepper often led charity events and Joe coordinated a variety of art and social events gratis for the community. It appeared that the Franklins wanted a normal life for their son so they gave up the "family business". It was unknown why the sudden change leading to the recent jewel and art thefts.

Noel knew Dennis Franklin for the past twelve years as her friendship with his parents grew. She felt terrible for the young man, but didn't know how to help. She asked her husband to ask Dennis if he needed a job, suggesting that Dennis become involved in the yacht business. Dave convinced her to leave the young man's future alone until he came to terms with his parents.

CHAPTER 64

Jewels and More Jewels

Officer Jason Breakly wasted no time to notify Lilly Lee that her jade necklace was recovered. She couldn't believe her good fortune and thanked the officer profusely. He sat up a little higher in his chair as Lilly complimented his investigation. She hoped that his detective badge would be given to him soon after solving such an important case. He beamed as she spoke, knowing that her words would probably be true. He expected his promotion to detective soon.

"I was hoping that you could come down here to collect your necklace."

"Oh! I'm not sure if I can do that," Lilly answered.

His disappointment was hard to contain.

"We will need to retain the necklace for a while as evidence, but I'll get back to you when it can be released."

"Maybe by then I'll be working and could afford to come down there to pick it up," Lilly offered.

Jason quickly smiled and the two of them started talking about every day things. They had become friends over the past month. Both of them hoped that there could be more than friends between each other, but for now, friends would be fine.

The emerald ring stolen from Vino Antiquities was not recovered, but Dominic Pepino was elated that he didn't have to worry about other robberies now that the thieves had been identified. The emerald had been covered by insurance so his investment in the jewel was secure. He thought about the events that unfolded that led to solving the case.

We would have never known what happened if it wasn't for Noel.

He sat on his lounger, smoking one of his fine cigars, as he contemplated on Noel Noirty. She organized his event, added clientele to his business, and solved the crime. He reached for the phone.

"Good day, Noel. I have a business opportunity to discuss with you."

"Really? I can't imagine what that may be."

"Any way you can come to Vino Antiquities today?"

A few hours later, Noel appeared at Dominic's business. She arrived carrying a fresh bouquet of flowers to place in the antique vase at the beginning of store. She walked in confidently, not expecting anything from him for helping the police solve the robbery. Dominic led her into his office, filled with beautiful antiques and works of art.

"Dominic, your office is beautiful," she exclaimed as she sat in an exquisite velvet chair.

"My dear Noel, What can I say more than 'thank you' for your help. This business wouldn't be what it is today if it wasn't for your input into how it was designed and getting your Naples' crowd to come here as customers. You arranged the most elegant appreciation event a month ago which exceeded my expectations. You went undercover to solve a great mystery and solve a crime. I owe you so much."

She thanked Dominic and rose from her chair, thinking they were done talking.

"Please, Noel, sit down. I haven't gotten to my proposition," Dominic explained while he pulled a document out of his drawer.

"First, I want to thank you by having another grand event. The guest list would be up to you, as this party would be one of gratitude for what you accomplished. Second, this paperwork is a draft of a proposition. Please take your time to review it and discuss with your husband. Take your time, but I hope you accept. I'm not a young man anymore and I want to spend more time with my family in Italy."

Noel curiously took the paper and quickly read through it. Dominic wanted to be equal partners with Noel for Vino Antiquities. His draft outlined that Noel would take control of running the business and he would continue to send antiques and art from Europe to the US to sell in the business. The inventory would continue to be purchased and owned by Dominic, but an equal commission would be given to them, with the balance of funds used to run the business.

"Dominic! I can't accept this! I'm not trained on how to run a business and I don't have funds to purchase a percentage of your business."

"Nonsense, Noel. You have guts and brains. I need someone of your caliber to oversee the operation. We have a store manager and sales people to run the daily business, and my niece, Angela, can continue to oversee the accounting aspect. You are perfect to be my partner, and the only person I would trust with my business."

Noel sat there stunned. She wanted desperately to accept the partnership on the spot, but agreed to discuss it with her husband.

"Dominic, I cannot thank you enough for your generosity. I will take the paperwork and discuss with my husband. But as for the thank you party, I do accept that gift, and I know exactly what I would like to do with that."

She leaned over and whispered into Dominic's ear. He smiled and enthusiastically nodded in agreement. They shook hands and embraced. She left the business, briefly looking back at the marquee.

"This might be partially mine."

She raced to her husband's office at the yacht dealership and marina to show him the proposal.

CHAPTER 65

Plans in the Works

A week later, Noel and Dave Noirty met with Dominic Pepino at Dominic's lawyer's office. Angela Fratilo was also present to witness the event. The final paperwork was signed and notarized. It was official, Dominic and Noel were partners in Vino Antiquties.

Noel had been quiet about the partnership, waiting for the paperwork to be signed before telling her friends and family. She and Dominic had carefully drafted an article for the Naples newspaper announcing the partnership. That draft would be given to the paper today.

The group went to a local restaurant to celebrate the business venture over champagne and dinner. Several of the Noirty's friends were at the restaurant, so the word was "out" about Noel's new position. She was so proud of herself to be involved in something she loved.

"I didn't say anything about the other 'thank you' that Dominic presented to me. He offered another grand event at Vino Antiquities as a 'thank you', but I have a better idea.

Dave and Angela exchanged a curious glances at each other before she continued. Dominic smiled and nodded before Noel explained,

"I would like to offer the party to Francine and Brian for their wedding venue."

Angela gasped and clapped with delight. Dave gasped in disbelief until he saw that Dominic was already apprised and happy with the suggestion.

"Francine has been involved with Vino Antiquities since it began, as the designer and supplier of the cabinets and beautiful chairs that line the warehouse. I thought it would be wonderful if her family saw what Francine helped create. And, as you know, Brian has been after her for not having time to plan their wedding. I thought us girls could help her by doing the arranging. She and Brian's family just have to show up."

"I love that idea, Noel!" Angela exclaimed.

"Well, I like the idea," Dave said, "but with one change."

Noel, Angela, and Dominic all frowned inquisitively at Dave, waiting for him to continue.

"How about a double ceremony?"

"What? Who else?" Noel asked.

"You and I, my darling. I would like us to renew our vows."

Noel's tears rolled instantly down her cheeks. She leaned into her husband's arms seated next to her. Noel couldn't stop crying.

"I think that is a 'yes', Dave," Dominic chimed in with a grin.

CHAPTER 66

A Most Important Plan

F rancine was shocked when Noel telephoned her to offer Vino Antiquities as her wedding venue. She and Brian had expected to be married in Southern Wisconsin or Chicago. They had never discussed a destination wedding, but as she thought about it, it solved several problems.

Of course her largest problem was the time to arrange a wedding in the North and where to have the wedding reception. This would be solved immediately and everything from the actual church ceremony to the menu, flowers, and music would be planned by their friend, Noel. Noel had indicated that she would have Francine and Brian approve everything, but the actual work of it would be done by Noel.

Noel had thought about everything and had a quick answer to every obstacle she raised during their phone call. She had already called her favorite hotel, The Ritz Carlton, to arrange for a bank of guest rooms and the bridal suite, at a discount due to her long relationship with the hotel. She explained how the guests would themselves have a vacation as they stayed at the hotel.

Another problem for her was to plan a honeymoon. Noel and Dave offered their yacht with a crew to wait on the couple as they cruised the Caribbean.

"All you have to bring is your wedding dress," Noel said. "Or, if you want, us girls can go with you to find your dress, and I'll make sure it gets to Naples."

Francine quickly thought about other obstacles such as making arrangements for Brian's son, Jonathan, during the trip. She wondered if Johnny should stay with them or if he should stay with someone else.

"Oh, for goodness sake, Francine. Let Brian decide. Maybe he'll even suggest inviting his ex so he has someone to take his son. No wonder you haven't planned your wedding yet. You worry about everything."

She smiled, as she knew Noel was right.

"OK! I'll ask Brian. It all sounds so wonderful. And then we would be there to see your wedding renewal also. What a grand idea."

She didn't waste time asking her fiancé when he arrived home after work. He sat there stunned as she related everything that Noel offered.

"I think its a great idea. We can whittle down the list a bit more easily too, if we have a destination wedding," he answered. "Who are you going to ask for your maid of honor?"

She didn't hesitate as she said her sister-in-law, Chrissy's name. Chrissy had helped her with her business and remained a steady friend.

"What about your best man?" she asked her beau.

Brian answered with one of his life-long friend's name.

"I would like to involve Jonathan, though. What about as ring bearer?"

"I love that idea," she answered, along with a long, passionate kiss.

CHAPTER 67

Another Match Made

The Saturday after Thanksgiving was chosen as the wedding date, to make it easier for the wedding attendees to travel. The Pacque family used several cars and travelled as a group the eleven-hundred mile trek to Naples. They arrived at the Ritz Carlton in time for Thanksgiving, and they enjoyed a delicious meal and a fantastic time enjoying the pool.

Lilly Lee was invited to attend the wedding. Lilly, was now working as a consultant in a treatment center in Chicago. Francine said she would arrange for someone to pick Lilly up at the airport.

Lilly walked down the terminal until she spotted a driver holding a sign with her name. She hurried over to the driver.

"Hello, I'm Lilly Lee."

"Hi Lilly, I hope you are glad to see me," the driver said, taking off his baseball cap.

It was Officer Jason Breakly. She was overjoyed to see him and she quickly gave him a hug.

"I was hoping that I would see you," she admitted.

"Me too. I was happy when Noel Noirty called to ask if I could pick you up. And I have something for you," he said, holding out a box containing Lilly's jade necklace.

She embraced him again and he nervously leaned in to kiss her. His lips were greeted with her soft, wet lips as she pressed against his mouth.

"Are you off of work on Saturday? I would like to bring you to Francine and Brian's wedding," Lilly asked.

"Yes, I was hoping you would go with me. Noel sent me an invitation to come." he said, leading to another hug and kiss.

Lilly shook her head, realizing that Noel had been playing matchmaker. She took a hold of Jason's hand as they headed towards the exit door.

CHAPTER 68

The Weddings

On a beautiful, bright sunny day in Naples, about one-hundred and fifty guests sat in the air conditioning of Noel and Dave's church. White orchid bouquets aligned the center aisle of the church as violin music began to play. The crowd quieted and turned in their pews watching the mahogany door.

The door opened with Dave and Noel Noirty standing at the entrance. Dave was wearing a light beige tuxedo with a lavender orchid boutonniere. Noel, was wearing an exquisite Pnina Tornai dress. The dress was one of Pnina's bustier dresses, tight in the waist, but Noel had a white lining altered into the dress to make it appropriate for her taste. She had her hair in her normal upsweep as her husband preferred, fastened with some elegant pearl hairpins.

The attendees rose as Dave and Noel proceeded down the aisle. The violinist continued to play as they walked. Noel's friends nodded and shook their heads in approval for their beautiful friends' appearance.

Dave's daughter, Brianna, sat in a pew in the second row, behind Noel and Dave's aging parents who were flown in for the ceremony. She attended with her New York family, consisting of the man who raised her that she thought was her father, and his second wife and their other children. She was so thrilled that the entire family was invited so they could become one, happy family. She had been able to meet her real grandparents, Dave's mother and father, earlier in the week. She sat lovingly behind them now, as they watched their son renew his wedding vows. She wished that Noel's parents were still alive to witness the renewal, as she had learned that they had both passed away several years earlier.

Dave and Noel exchanged personally written renewal vows, each one worded appropriately and beautifully. At the end of the ceremony, Dave gave Noel a long kiss, which prompted a few cheers from their family and Naples friends. Noel was beaming as she turned to face the crowd. They held their hands upward, clasping onto each other as the audience clapped. Then, Noel and Dave proceeded to the second pew, alongside their daughter as they waited for the next wedding.

The violinist began another song as a side door opened and several tuxedoed men walked towards the front aisle. The second man was holding the hand of a seven year old boy in a miniature tuxedo. It was the groom, Brian Sherman, holding his son's hand. The best man and the ring bearer were wearing beige tuxes, similar to the one Dave was wearing, but with a light orange cummerbund. The groom was wearing a white, long-tailed tuxedo as he took his place near the center aisle.

Brian's parents sat in the first row, next to Dave's parents. One could see such love and pride in their eyes. They were overjoyed that their son found a wonderful woman as his second wife. And, they were impressed at the obvious love that their son's soon-to-be wife's friends had for the couple.

Francine's mother and family were turned, anxiously awaiting the appearance of their daughter in the grand doors. The violinist began playing another song, accompanied by a singer with an aria, when the mahogany doors opened.

Christine Pacque began walking down the aisle in a tea length, light orange, organza dress. She carried a large bouquet of locally grown flowers in bright colors. The doors closed after her, as she proceeded down the aisle and stood at the front of the church.

The doors reopened and a vision in white appeared, with her father at her side. Francine wore a simple white veil on her head which was diminished by her Lazaro gown. The gown had rolls of luxurious fabric, as the designer is known for, but the dress clung to Francine's curves showing her beautiful figure. A long train accompanied the dress.

The congregation rose as Francine and her father began their walk down the aisle. The singer sang the traditional "Here Comes the Bride" as they walked. Brain gleamed as he watched his future bride advance. He had never seen her more beautiful. Tears rolled down her cheek. Jonathan stepped forward watching his new step-mom come down the aisle. He jumped up and down in excitement until his father pulled him back.

Francine's father pulled back the front of her veil and the ceremony began. It was a traditional ceremony, as Brian had insisted, and they exchanged rings with Jonathan watching over the exchange. They gave each other a long kiss and a hug as the pastor exclaimed,

"I pronounce you man and wife."

The congregation applauded and Lilly Lee and Jason stood up while they clapped. Others joined in, giving the wedded couple a standing ovation.

The following reception went off without a hitch, as Noel had planned every detail with precision. As she walked into Vino Antiquty, she noticed a new sign next to the front door. It read, "Noel Noirty and Dominic Pepino - Proprietors". Dominic had surprised Noel with this gift.

"Let's take a picture in front of the sign," Dave suggested to his wife who was in full agreement.

Epilogue

Afte four months of not finding Joe or Pepper Franklin, the Naples Police had to put the case against them in an "Unprosecuted" file. The police had enlisted the FBI in trying to track down the couple. It was determined that the couple disappeared somewhere using one of their vast aliases. They probably had money hidden in off-shore accounts to last them the rest of their lives.

The shock to their son, Dennis, was undeniable. He waited patiently for some word on his parents, hoping that it was some mistake. He hired his parents' attorney to take over financial control of his parents' assets and did exhaustive searches online for his parents.

His only escape was his music. He had numerous guitars but he loved his Martin guitar the most. His Martin was given to him years ago by his father as a birthday present, but sat in an evidence locker at the Naples police station. He wondered if he would ever get it returned.

Money was not a problem, as Dennis had a vast amount of funds unlocked through his attorney that he was previously unaware of having. His parent's accounts were locked, but his father had set up funds in Dennis' name in various US and offshore accounts. He found himself wealthy, but alone, and embarrassed by his parents' folly.

The lawyer recommended putting up the mansion for sale. Dennis contacted Mitzi Vanderlooth to list the property. He was aware that she was one of the women who were doing undercover trying to catch the thieves, but he also knew that Mitzi was fair and well liked by his parents. She suggested that he put his parents' private belongings into storage, including the vast art collection.

That left him with a dilemma of where to live. He decided that he should leave the Naples area and start his dream in Nashville. So, with a heavy heart, but determination to make it as a performer, he moved to Tennessee.

The one year anniversary of Brian and Francine Sherman occurred with the couple moving into their own home in Sherman Park, Illinois. The past year flew by as no other, with Francine continuing to run her business remotely. She occasionally flew to visit customers, but her employees rose to the occasion and service continued with no loss of sales. In fact, several new customers were added to each territory.

Jonathan continued to live with his mother but stayed in his own room every other weekend at Brian and Francine's new place. He was always so excited to come to "his new house". He hugged Francine tightly every time he left with his dad to go home by his mother.

Lilly Lee continued having a long-distance relationship with Jason Breakly until she realized that it was possible for her to transfer to a Naples' psychological treatment center. Their romance was budding, and Lilly was absorbed into the group of Naples women with Noel, Angela, Mitzi and others.

Officer Jason Breakly did pass his detective exam and with the Franklin case evidence, and he was promoted to Detective. Lilly was thrilled that her boyfriend was such a success.

With time, the buzz about the robberies in Naples died. No one had heard from the Franklins in sixteen months. There were several possible sightings of them in Europe or South America, but local agents were sent to check for leads and found nothing. The case remained on "hold".

Dennis Franklin found a new start in Nashville. His skills as a musician quickly landed him gigs at local venues where he gained experience and made friends. He recently started out as a solo and was performing at one of the best stages in Nashville.

He crooned to the music and the audience was transformed into a frenzy when he played his acoustics. His new friends, including a beautiful young woman from Nashville, screamed and applauded as he played. He played a long set before announcing that he was taking a well-deserved break. Several people approached the stage to drop tips into his tip jar. He casually looked at one man who looked strangely familiar. The man dropped a large bill into the jar and returned to the back of the venue.

He looked strangely at the man and the woman, who nodded to him and turned to leave the bar. He sat their transfixed, wondering where he had met the bearded man and Bohemian woman before. Before he left the stage, he picked up the tip jar, not wanting any money to disappear while he took his break.

He looked into the jar and saw a hundred dollar bill sitting on top of the bills. "We will always be close. We love you so much" was scribbled on the bill in familiar scroll. Looking up quickly, the man and woman had disappeared into the night, but he now knew that his parents were ok and still watching over him.

The End

About the Author

Kathleen "Kathy" Balota grew up in the Milwaukee, Wisconsin and lived there until 2014, when she and her husband, Dennis, moved to Fort Myers, Florida. She graduated from the University of Wisconsin-Milwaukee and received a master's degree from General Motors Institute, now Kettering University. Kathy worked for many years in factory management, industrial engineering and lean manufacturing positions. Her hobbies include golfing, biking, and enjoying the beautiful sunshine of Florida.

Kathy's first book, "The Ethical Business Woman", was a sweet contemporary romance with a touch of humor, that was published in 2016. During the past year, Kathy has been working to hone her writing skills and write this sequel, "Hidden Within the Bling". The sequel continues a colorful cast of characters and adds a touch of suspense to the plot.

Kathy belongs to the Romance Writers of America (RWA) and to the Southwest Florida Romance Writers (SWFRW) organizations where she has learned a wealth of knowledge from other talented writers. Although she sees another contemporary romance book in her future, Kathy expects to transition into the mystery and suspense genre.